FINAL SHIFT

SHIFTER LORDS

S.E. BABIN

OHB

CHAPTER
One

Happiness was sunshine on a cool, late summer morning, drinking coffee with someone you love. I tilted my face up to the sky and took a deep breath, content to bask in the warm golden light peeking from the horizon.

Rowan and I were on the back deck watching the sunrise. We'd been married for almost four months, and the bloom still hadn't worn off. Based on the happiness I felt every time I laid my eyes upon him, I thought it never would.

He was everything I never knew I wanted and everything I thought I didn't deserve.

"If you keep looking at me like that, we're going to have to start the morning over."

His low, heated drawl made the hair on the backs of my arms stand up. I leaned closer and pressed a kiss to his cheek. "Would that be so bad?"

Rowan's slow grin made my fingers tighten around the mug I held. How did he make me feel so desired with just a simple smile?

"No, but in about two minutes we're going to have company."

I groaned. "Who?"

"All of your friends. They just left their apartments and are heading this way."

I loved my friends, but they had the timing of food poisoning on an international flight. "Raincheck?"

"Always."

"Let's just sit here until they come."

Rowan turned his head and pressed a kiss to my temple.

Moira was the first to arrive. She grinned when she spotted us. "Tess and Ash are right behind me. You two up for breakfast? There's a new brunch place in town we've been wanting to try."

I glanced at Rowan, who shrugged. "Hungry?" he asked.

When was I not? I nodded. "Let me change. Meet at the vehicles in twenty?"

"Good with me." I sighed and didn't get up.

Moira snorted. "How about we leave, and you two meet up with us when you get moving?" She gave me a meaningful look, which made Rowan laugh.

"Be gone, hag," I pronounced with a dramatic wave of my hand.

Tess and Ash popped into view. Moira turned and pointed at the vehicles. "Come on. Lady Evie and her husband want to have *relations*."

Ash chuckled. Tess let out a warbly sigh. Moira jogged over and ruffled the banshee's hair.

Once they were out of view, Rowan let out a groan. "Should we go to breakfast or back to bed?"

Both sounded equally great.

"If we eat first, we'll have the energy to drag ourselves back home and go back to bed."

Rowan grinned. "I like the way you think, Lady."

His words warmed me. The adjustment from everything I was to Rowan's wife and the Keep's Lady had been somewhat jarring but Hope and Declan had guided me the best they could. Garrett and Simone had also stepped in when they saw me faltering.

Leadership had never come naturally to me. I preferred

leading a quiet life in the background, though life had not complied with my wishes lately. Being thrust into the spotlight made me uncomfortable, but with Rowan's people, things were different. They'd never made me feel less. Not like…

I tried very hard not to think about Caelan these days, though I knew I needed to make a decision about him soon. When he tried to kill Rowan, I'd gone a little crazy and had basically put a fairytale curse on him, one neither he nor his people could break unless I allowed it.

And I hadn't. Caelan blew up my phone the first three weeks of his imprisonment, and Rowan had to get his tech people involved to forward those numbers elsewhere. Whether to him or someone else in the Pack, I didn't ask, but Caelan's calls had abruptly stopped.

But my guilt hadn't.

Rowan rose and held out his hand, gently helping me up. But instead of heading inside, he closed his arms around me and brought me close. "He's fine," he said quietly. "Angry and stir crazy, but fine. I feel your guilt deep within me, Evie, but you had every right to do what you did. If you think he's learned his lesson or feel like you should release his land, then do so, but don't do it out of a misplaced sense of guilt. Caelan was horrific to you and tried to take me away from you. Killing a mate…" His voice trailed off. "The other Lords, no matter how they feel about us together or separately, would have put him to death for his actions. You may not feel this is so, but you saved his life that night."

"I'll go visit in a few days." I tilted my head up to study him, still surprised this handsome, wonderful, powerful man was mine. My husband. My mate.

"I'll come with you." He bent and brushed a kiss over my lips, soft and warm.

We didn't have a courtship. The mating call had been too powerful between us, both the shifter and the fae magic pulling us together so forcefully we were both helpless to deny each other.

While most of my guilt at how quickly everything had happened was fading, I still had moments where I had to sit with my feelings and remember that everything was real and true.

Rowan was mine, and I was his, and we were forever joined by love and magic more powerful than either of us possessed.

He stepped away and intertwined our fingers. "If we don't hurry, we'll never hear the end of it from Moira."

I let him tug me along. "I think we can spare five minutes."

Rowan looked back at me, one dark eyebrow rising, a familiar glitter in his eyes. "Yeah?"

My smile grew. "Yeah." The ever-present link between us warmed and stretched like honey, and I felt his desire and need for me in the spot where that bond lived.

This was real. True. Rowan's love for me bowled me over most days, snatching my breath away even in the most innocent of moments.

He scooped me into his arms and loped into the house. "We only need three."

CHAPTER
Two

Sunday mornings in Emberwood were rarely quiet. Even less so when their Lord and Lady made a surprise appearance. Even so, I couldn't help comparing Rowan's people to Caelan's. I'd never met most of Caelan's people. They preferred staying away or staring from a distance.

Rowan's people, my people now, were the opposite. Everyone here loved him, and by extension, me too. Before we'd made it to the restaurant's door, he'd been stopped no less than half a dozen times by people with well-wishes or those wanting to make small talk. Moira and the others, expecting this exact scenario, had saved us seats, but actually getting inside was proving more difficult than I anticipated.

When Rowan finally broke away and we managed to get inside, the same thing happened with the restaurant staff.

"You're a regular celebrity," I teased.

Rowan snorted. "You actually think they're here for me?"

I blinked and looked up at him. "They're barely speaking to me!"

His lips twitched. "Because you're barely speaking to them."

I stared at him for a moment. "Well shit," I whispered under my breath.

Fortunately, the restaurant was loud, and no one could overhear our conversation or hear the way my heart lurched at Rowan's teasing words. "I never thought of it that way."

Rowan shrugged and led me through a maze of tables, conversation beginning to fall silent when everyone realized who walked among them.

"We'll talk once things settle," Rowan murmured, smiling and nodding at everyone.

I tried to do the same but never possessed the easy charm Rowan could conjure in an instant. I admired that about him. While I was full of awkward smiles and stilted small talk, Rowan commanded any room he walked into by virtue of an easy smile and an offhand comment.

I took a long time to warm up to people, so long that most people walked away before scratching the surface of who I was. Emberwood had proved different for me, especially because not too long ago, Moira and I had gotten sloshed on some magical booze, and I ended up arm-wrestling a veteran shifter.

If I had ever wondered about winning over a bunch of burly shifters, engaging one in a contest of strength was a sure bet. I won the contest, and Moira ended up slung over the back of a Shifter Lord and carried out of the bar to the hoots and hollers of everyone inside. Overall, it was a good night with far-reaching consequences.

I'd ended up married, and Moira was left with a raging crush on an emotionally unavailable man. Fifty percent success rate wasn't bad.

We finally made it to our table. Moira gave me a knowing look. "You'll get used to it," she said quietly. "They love you and it's freaking you out. I can see the panic all over your face."

I frowned. "Panic is a strong word. I don't want to let anyone down."

Rowan's hand settled on my thigh. "You could never," he murmured in my ear.

I shot him a grateful look. "Shifters are so much more open than I could ever be."

Rowan's eyebrows went up. "That's because we can scent many things that others can't. My shifters know there's a mating bond between us, and they know me as their Lord. One of our kind would never—"

He stopped talking and frowned before letting out a self-deprecating laugh. "You know what I was about to say?"

"Yup. A Lord would never pick an ill-suited Lady."

"And Caelan was ready to marry Rachel." He sighed and scrubbed a hand over his face. "He wasn't mated, so he has a small excuse. I retract my earlier thought and replace it with most Lords would ensure the person they chose was well suited to leading a Keep." He leaned over. "And you are. Leadership is not something that comes naturally to many. Right now, they just want to know you." He brushed my hair away from my face. "As difficult as that is for you, they all have your best interests at heart."

Rowan touched his chest. "I feel the knowledge inside."

I swallowed hard. "I'll try my best."

The server interrupted us at that moment. His eyes widened when he spotted me and Rowan, and it took a few seconds before he could speak. "Lord," he breathed. "Lady." He dipped his head. "Welcome to Matty's. Can I get you some coffee?"

Rowan nodded. "Coffee for us both, please." He paused and waited for the server to meet his gaze. "More importantly, we are here merely as your customers and do not expect any special treatment, alright?"

The server nodded as he scribbled. "Of course, sir. Cream and sugar?"

Rowan shook his head. "None for us."

Once the server disappeared, the novelty of our appearance began to wear off, and prior conversations resumed. I snagged Moira's teacup and took a sip of her Earl Grey. Coffee would always hold the number one spot, but caffeine was caffeine.

Ash and Tess sat close together, engrossed in a quiet conversation. They'd resolved their issues and were sharing an apartment on Keep grounds. I still wasn't sure they were end game, but for now, they seemed happy, and the inner workings of their relationship were none of my business.

"Are you ready for the grand opening?" Moira asked.

I groaned. We still hadn't reopened the shop. The plans were in place, and everything fell apart. Then Rowan and I had married, and we put the reopening on hold once more while we adjusted to married life. Repeatedly.

My cheeks colored.

Moira grinned. "Should we delay it for a few more weeks while you and your hubby get it out of your system?"

Rowan leaned over and gave Moira a roguish wink. "We're never getting 'it' out of our systems."

Moira clicked her tongue. "You two are gross."

I nudged her with an elbow. "You're just frustrated."

She sighed and picked up her tea, but not before giving me a dark look.

A strange expression crossed Rowan's face. He opened his mouth and closed it just as fast.

"Spit it out," Moira groused.

Rowan huffed. "I don't want to offend anyone here, but Moira…"

The vampire lifted her brows. "Yes?"

"You're living on Keep grounds. There are several hundred shifters there. You could knock on any single male's door and have a companion for as long as you wanted."

Moira blinked. I blinked. Tess and Ash stopped talking and gawked at Rowan.

"You—" She set her mug down and interlaced her fingers. "You want me to use your shifters as booty calls?"

Rowan snorted. "Obviously you haven't been in close quarters with shifters very much. We possess strong biological drives."

Moira's lips twitched.

"You could have a line out your door, and few of them would blink."

I gasped. "That cannot be true."

Rowan spread his hands out. "I'm afraid it is. The only exception would be if one of them felt the mating tug. In that case, the others would back off as soon as they sense the same."

"I'm a vampire. We don't mate."

Rowan watched her. "You aren't just a vampire, and we all know it. Everyone at the Keep knows you're something more. So don't rule a bond out yet."

Moira's eyes flickered, and I knew Ethan had crossed her mind. The other Shifter Lord spent some time in Rowan's territory not too long ago, and Moira caught feelings, something I never thought I'd see happen.

Ethan was a difficult Lord to read, keeping me firmly on the fence about him as a partner for her. I didn't dislike him as much as I used to, but he wouldn't be the first person I'd choose. Not that such a decision was up to me. Moira deserved happiness, and if Ethan could give that to her, I'd support their courtship all the way to the altar.

But if she could find a mate…

Rowan's hand tightened around my thigh. He was thinking the same thing. Ethan was handsome and powerful, and Moira was cunning and gorgeous. On paper, they worked.

Real life was rarely as cut and dry.

"A mate," Moira mused. "I think the idea is far-fetched, but I'll keep an open mind."

The server came with our coffees and disappeared just as quickly when he saw the look on Moira's face.

"Until then, I'll keep your suggestion in mind." Her brow furrowed. "If such a thing wouldn't cause issues, why haven't any of your shifters knocked on my door?"

Rowan sipped his coffee. "They're being respectful of Evie for now, but it's more than just that. You don't give off welcoming vibes, Moira."

Ash turned his laugh into a cough and turned his face away.

Moira's eyes narrowed. "Should I hang up my shingle and install a light that goes red or green depending on my mood?"

Rowan shrugged. "Men, no matter what species, are generally clueless. If you'd rather handle it like a business than a mutual arrangement, more power to you."

Moira's mouth fell open. "You cannot be for real." She let out a little snort and sat back in her chair, staring at my husband.

Rowan grinned, his eyes warming as he watched my friend. "Your under the sheets activities are none of my business. I'm only telling you shifters are generally up for some tether free extracurriculars if you are."

"And if I like tethers?"

"Moira." I rolled my eyes.

"You do you," Rowan said mildly. "Perhaps I should have said no strings attached extracurriculars."

Moira grunted. "I'll think about it."

From the glimmer of her eyes, I knew she would.

Three

ave you changed your mind?

The voice whispered through my mind, ancient and cunning.

I am not your retirement plan. Danu checked in every single time I communed with the land, to the point where I was thinking about stripping her access to Keep land. Going that far was an escalation I'd rather not deal with, but she wrecked my conversation every time she popped in.

You could be as powerful as you desired, she said, her words a sinuous hiss in my mind.

I can do that already. Once Dad removed the lock on my power, I could sense how far I could go.

The answer frightened me. I didn't need Danu to take the earth if I wanted the world for my own. But that was the difference between us. Danu was of the old pantheon, and I was of none. I continued living life on my terms and wouldn't allow someone like her to sway me.

Danu needed me. I did not need her.

You have my answer. I've been polite to you, but the answer will always be no. If you continue to pop in when I'm refreshing my power, I'll have no choice but to ban you from this property.

Rage brushed over me, Danu's emotions electric sparks against my mind. *You dare?*

I do.

Soil bucked and groaned around me, Danu's temper in physical form.

I stopped the tantrum with a wave of my hand. *Last warning,* I said mildly.

You tempt powers you cannot imagine.

I waited a beat. *And you think you do not?*

A pause, one of surprise, then a derisive snort. *Someone's ego has grown since last we spoke.*

No need for ego. I know what I can do. Leave, Danu. Before I make you.

Her presence slipped from my mind a moment later. I sent tendrils of seeking power to see if Danu hid somewhere close, but there was no trace of her. Maybe I'd given the old bat something to ponder while she slept in her dark hold.

A nudge at my elbow made me smile. Eyes still closed, I lifted my hand and felt the soft slide of fur under my fingers. Rowan settled his enormous head by my thigh and huffed as he adjusted to the most comfortable position.

I pushed his favorite flowers, freesia, up through the ground, encouraging them to open and surround Rowan with their strawberry-like scent. His head moved as he snuffled the flowers. A satisfied bear grunt rumbled from his throat, making me smile.

I sat there for hours, siphoning my power and feeding my Lord's lands—our lands now. I'd never get used to the feeling of being a part of such an amazing stretch of land. I'd claimed Donovan's old lands months ago and was planning to gift them to Rowan before everything happened. With our marriage, Rowan became the most powerful Lord land wise, but he'd also secured the fae crown.

Let's just say we weren't all that popular in the Lord circle at this time. They were staying out of the Caelan issue, but that interpersonal drama had endeared me to them even less.

Not that any of us had ever been friends, Rowan being the only exception.

Ethan didn't seem all that bothered by Rowan's new status or what I'd done to Caelan, which puzzled me. His lack of interest was in direct opposition to how often he had put his nose into our business before. Before Moira, if I had to guess.

Ever since he and Moira became entangled, Ethan's behavior struck me as odd. The Lord had a strong and possibly skewed sense of morality. When he and Rowan found us at the bar, he'd scooped Moira up like she weighed nothing and given her a hard smack on the ass when she'd protested, like he didn't give a shit she was a vampire and could destroy him if she tried hard enough. The Ethan I knew would not have ever made a scene like he did that night.

Didn't hurt that he was a handsome bastard, either. Moira could do worse.

Rowan nudged me with his furry head, almost like he knew what I was thinking about and didn't care for the path my thoughts were on. Our bond was a strange thing, melded with shifter and fae magic, and responsive to our moods and physical emotions. We'd know if the other was hurt or in danger, and we knew when the other was feeling a little randy.

I was neither, but apparently even thinking someone else might be handsome was enough to make Rowan twitchy.

My power trickled to a slow drip, content and lazy. I opened my eyes and ruffled Rowan's fur. "Jealous I might fancy another?"

To that, Rowan shifted in a flash and hauled me underneath him in a swift, graceful move.

He gently bit my collarbone. "Do you?"

I tilted my neck to give him more access. "Never. I merely pondered for a moment how handsome Ethan is."

Rowan stilled for a moment before huffing against my neck. "Oh?" He kissed his way up the column of my throat, the evidence of his desire heavy against my thigh.

"Mmm. He's got this whole mysterious bad boy thing going on."

I felt him grin against my throat. "You like the bad boys?"

I snorted and hauled him up to kiss him. "Nope. Just you."

"Good answer." His clever fingers slid underneath my shirt and unfastened my jeans.

A few seconds later, there were no more words to be said.

WE HEARD him before we saw him. I conjured up a bunch of flowers and vines to cover us seconds before Declan walked into the clearing.

He saw us and rolled his eyes. "Is there ever a time when you two aren't going at it like bunnies?"

Rowan's satisfied grin made me blush. "Remember this conversation when you find your own mate."

Declan scoffed. "Too many choices out there for me to go hunting for one of those."

"I wasn't hunting either," Rowan said mildly.

"Still. Now look at you. Lying in a field of flowers like a regular fairytale princess."

I sent a vine from the ground to smack him on the back of the head. Declan laughed and winked at me.

"Why are you here bothering us?" Rowan asked.

Declan was right. We did look like we'd woken up in the middle of a fantastical tale. Flowers in a riot of colors dotted the landscape in a circle several feet wide. Rowan even had them growing in his hair. I tried brushing them away, but they stubbornly clung to his dark locks.

Declan's expression sobered. "Caelan is asking for an audience."

Rowan sighed. "Tell him I'll call him later."

When Declan didn't nod or walk away, Rowan's eyes narrowed. "He's not on the phone, is he?"

"He sent a representative. As we all know, Caelan cannot leave his lands."

I interrupted. "Who's the rep?"

In a way, I had laid a curse on Caelan's land and his people. Caelan was confined to his lands and would die if he tried to leave. His people were free to come and go, but if any of them tried to further Caelan's agenda or planned to bring harm to anyone, they would die.

The arrogant Lord had sent three people to certain death before he'd given up and believed I was serious about what I'd done.

"A young male shifter, nervous. He said his name was Jensen."

I glanced over at Rowan, who shook his head.

"I don't know him either." I wrapped a blanket of flowers around me and stood.

Declan's brows lifted before he chuckled. "I'll never get used to seeing you do things like that."

"Look away from my wife," Rowan growled.

"Or that," Declan said with a deep laugh. "Your possessiveness has become legendary around town, my friend."

"It's fine," I said with a wave of my hand. "I'm technically dressed." And a lot less concerned about nudity these days after living on Keep land for several months. Rowan was completely unbothered until we mated, and now he got growly whenever someone saw me in the slightest state of undress.

"It is not fine," Rowan rumbled. He wasn't looking at me. A warm gold and silvery pink color outlined his irises. Our bond went tight and warm, rage blooming through the link.

Declan's expression went wary. He held out his hands and took a step back. "Whoa. I'm only here to deliver a message. I'll step out and wait until you are both...decent."

The Second did not turn around and leave his back exposed to Rowan. He carefully walked backward until Rowan finally looked away.

I went to my knees beside him and took his face in my hands. "Rowan." I pressed a kiss to the edge of his lips. "You have to get that under control."

He gripped me by the hips, not quite painful, more possessive than anything. He closed his eyes and took a few deep breaths. "I'm trying," he rumbled. "Normally, those strong emotions fade within a couple of months, but our bond has proven different."

A wry twist to his lips before a short laugh rang out. "Everything about this has proven unique."

"You aren't alone here," I said quietly. The only females I could tolerate looking at Rowan were Moira, Tess, and Hope. Anyone else made me twitchy. Mine wasn't as bad as Rowan, but I had to resist the urge to wrap myself around him like a clingy octopus whenever other women were around.

Embarrassing.

He lifted those beautiful hazel eyes, a leftover shimmer of violence glazing their depths. "You haven't threatened to rip anyone to pieces yet."

I grunted. "Doesn't mean I don't want to." My fingers slid through his silky hair, and I wondered again how I'd gotten so lucky. I never wanted to stop touching him, stop lying with him in fields of fragrant flowers, and letting him worship me.

Rowan smiled and touched his chest. "I feel you right here and know when you're thinking goofy thoughts."

I laughed and shoved his shoulder. "And I feel when you're about to slice someone in two."

His eyes turned serious. "We can send him away. If you want."

I sighed and touched my forehead to his. "He'll send another one. And if we ignore him, another one will come soon after."

Rowan closed his eyes. "I'm not ready for this to be over."

I curled into his lap and lay my head against his chest. His arms wrapped tight around me. "We'll have it again. Consider this a temporary blip."

"Every time he comes back into our lives, he hurts you."

"Arguably, I hurt him worse this time."

Rowan's chest rumbled with a laugh. "Agreed. If we had a bard, he'd sing about your exploits in the pub."

I snickered. "Are you ready to go meet this kid?"

"How do you know he's a child?"

I sighed and slid out of Rowan's arms. "Because Caelan knows my weaknesses. He'll send someone vulnerable."

"Fucking asshole," he snarled.

I bent to gather my clothes. "Agreed. We knew this wouldn't last forever, but it doesn't mean we won't have it again."

I watched Rowan rise, his powerful limbs sleek and graceful as he moved. My mouth went dry as he stalked toward me.

A slow smile curved his lips when he saw where my eyes were. "Maybe we could delay a little while longer."

I laughed and hurriedly dressed. "No, you insatiable beast. Let's get this over with. Then we'll talk about it."

His eyes took on that strange new glow, silver mixed with gold and a touch of watermelon tourmaline—the color of my magic. "Are you sure?"

I took a step back. "Rowan. We can't."

"Says who? We're grown-ups."

I let out an exasperated laugh. "We just did!"

"And?"

I sighed and waited for him to reach me before lifting my fingers and tracing them over his jaw. "We have the rest of our lives. Caelan is a problem, and he's sent that problem to our doorstep. Let's deal with this, and then you can chase me around."

His eyes took on an even deeper glow. "Chasing? We haven't done that yet."

"You're awfully big," I whispered. "Bet you can't catch me."

Rowan's answering grin sent a thrill down my spine. "You forget, little Chimera, I am not just a bear."

"Hmm. I guess we'll find out soon."

Rowan growled and reached for me but missed when I danced out of his arms. "Come on. Let's see what this kid wants."

His sigh was put upon, but he followed me toward the area of the main Keep. We didn't speak as we walked, both of us knowing our days of leisurely peace were over.

At least for a little while.

I hated being right.

While the representative Caelan sent wasn't a child in the strictest definition of the word, he wasn't an adult either.

A shifter of about sixteen stood at the edge of the wards, his hands shoved in his pockets and a wary expression on his face. Several feet back, a female shifter waited, worry etched into the tightness of her jaw.

His mother most likely.

Caelan was a dick.

Rowan stepped up to the edge and stared at the teenager, his eyes flicking once to the woman before coming back to rest on him. "Name?"

"Je-Jensen," the boy stuttered.

"Is that your mother?" Rowan jerked his head in the woman's direction.

"Y-yes."

"She stays outside the wards."

The woman stepped forward, her hand outstretched for her son. Rowan jerked his gaze to her and slowly shook his head. Empathy stretched through my heart. The woman was one of Caelan's people, but she was a mother first, and she had been sent to what her Lord considered enemy territory. She had no idea how this Lord would treat her son once he came onto Keep lands.

Even though I knew Rowan would open a vein before he harmed a child, this woman didn't know him. She only knew the lands she lived on were in stasis, and her Lord was trapped, a trap set by the woman who now stood beside the enemy Lord.

Her hand trembled, but she dropped it, clenching her fists tightly against her thighs.

Jensen turned to look at his mother.

She forced a smile and nodded, dread glimmering in moist eyes. "Go ahead. Your Lord asks this of you."

She looked away and met and held Rowan's gaze. Most Lords would consider eye contact an insult, but Rowan wasn't like other Lords. He inclined his head in acknowledgment to her worry and her son's bravery. Rowan wasn't a full shifter and would never be like the others. What he saw was a mother who loved her child and was forced to send her son into a potentially dangerous situation.

Rowan could have allowed the mother in, but word would get back to Caelan, and he would find a way to use Rowan's empathy against us. He wouldn't promise this woman anything, but he would ensure the child's safety.

I held my hand up and opened a small slice of the wards. "Enter," I said quietly.

Jensen looked at me for the first time, fear and awe written all over his face. From the slight widening of his eyes, I knew he recognized me. I was the woman responsible for their Lord's plight.

But I finally didn't feel the urge to apologize. Caelan had made his bed. I was only making him lie down.

The young shifter hesitated, his throat working as he swallowed. He glanced once more at his mother, who gave him a small smile and a reassuring nod. He straightened his shoulders and walked onto Keep property.

I released my hold on the wards, allowing them to close.

Rowan put a hand on the boy's shoulder. He tensed, but when Rowan merely murmured something and led him toward the main house, Jensen relaxed just a hair.

"I'll follow," I said quietly, knowing he'd hear me.

"He will return shortly," I said to the boy's mother.

"You are Evie."

I nodded. "And you are?"

"Sheila." She made no move to come closer to the wards.

"You've raised a brave young man."

Her eyes flashed. "He should not have to do this."

"I'm aware. Did Caelan tell you why he could not go himself?"

Sheila's lips tightened. "No, but there is a rumor you have confined him to Keep lands."

I nodded. "The rumor is true."

Silence fell between us. Sheila studied me for a long moment before her brow furrowed. "May I ask why?"

"The answer is too long and sordid," I said with a half smile. "A more concise reason is Caelan tried to kill Rowan while on his lands."

"The Lords have been in constant conflict since they began their power games."

"Perhaps," I allowed, "but I'd mated with Rowan before Caelan's attempt. He knew and tried to kill him anyway."

Sheila sucked in a breath.

"We did not allow him onto Keep lands. He worked with someone else to gain access and attacked Rowan when his back was turned."

The shifter paled and shook her head. "He wouldn't."

"He did. Rowan would have died if I hadn't realized what was happening."

I allowed my words to sink in before continuing. "I was well within my rights to kill Caelan. Some think I should have. Instead, I gave him…options. Caelan knows what he must do before the hold on his lands eases."

A dozen emotions crossed Sheila's face before she spoke again. "What must he do?"

"He has two options. Caelan can make amends and broker a peace between us. If he does not wish to do this, he must find his mate."

Anger flashed over Sheila's features. "Finding a mate does not always happen."

I allowed a flash of the Chimera to shine through my eyes. "Then he'd best be rehearsing his apology note then, shouldn't he?"

I turned, but before I left, I couldn't resist adding one more barb. "Rowan is not Caelan. He would never harm anyone's child, even if they belonged to his enemy. Your son will be returned when his message is given."

The wards were all but impenetrable after I'd gotten a hold of them after Dad released the lock on my power, but the space between my shoulders itched as I walked away.

"Wait!" Sheila called.

My footsteps slowed, and I turned.

"Will you spare us?" She wrung her hands together. "If you and Lord Caelan go to war, will you harm his people?"

A shiver of disgust wormed its way through me. How much war and strife had the shifters seen to ask me this question? How low had their enemies sunk?

"Have I ever harmed any of you? At any time? I was willing to marry your Lord, to give him a crown and bear his children. I boosted the health of his lands and gave him all that I was, only for him to throw it all back in my face. Even then, did I harm you?"

The woman stared at me until understanding flickered over her face.

Every woman knew the cost a wrong man could bring to their doorstep. Every woman knew war was only the answer when all else had failed. I never wanted this, but Caelan had brought war to my home, and I was only responding in kind.

Sheila nodded then, her anger washed away with realization. My battle had never been with them. It had always been a battle with myself and my demons until Caelan had involved Rowan.

When he'd done that, I was willing to wipe him and everything he loved off the face of the earth. If Rowan had not been there to bring me back to myself, I would have.

Now I only wanted Caelan to face what he'd done and try to broker some sort of peace between us. Rowan was still a Lord, and working with Caelan was part of the job. Even if I'd made him surrender his Lord title while all this was going on.

I'd made the possibility of Rowan and Caelan working together all but impossible.

I couldn't bring myself to feel bad about doing so.

"Would you like some coffee or tea?" I asked.

Sheila blinked, opened her mouth and closed it before sighing. "Yes. I would. Coffee would be wonderful."

I nodded. "I'll send someone out."

Moira, like Tess and Ash, had a key to the wards. She was the safest and deadliest person to send minus one of Rowan's people, and I thought Sheila might feel more relaxed if someone neutral brought her coffee out.

Not that Moira was in any way, shape, or form neutral. She'd tear someone's throat out if she thought they were looking at me sideways.

But Sheila didn't know that, and Moira could be sophisticated as they came when she wanted to.

Not that she wanted to very often.

"Be nice to her," I whispered. "Her son is alone on enemy land."

Moira snorted. "Have you seen your husband? He and the boy are out on the deck playing checkers."

I blinked. Sounded about right. "Of course he is." With a snicker, I sent Moira out the door with a small tray of coffee with cream and sugar. Was I being too nice?

Psychological warfare meant you had to play with your

enemies' heads just a little. Even the slightest seed of doubt planted in one of Caelan's people's heads, and we might win the day.

Moira grinned and added a few fresh baked chocolate chip cookies from the mysterious shifter pastry chef who kept slipping in and out of our kitchen without getting caught. Even Rowan was mystified because they left behind delicious goods and left no scent behind.

I suspected Moira, but she'd denied being the culprit.

I also suspected she was lying. She stress baked, and Moira had been on a tear over Ethan for a few weeks now.

He'd done or said something to her she didn't care for, and she refused to tell us what it was—only that he was a sonofabitch and she'd tear him apart next time she saw him.

But after that, delicious baked goods started showing up in our kitchen.

"Be careful," I warned.

Moira rolled her eyes and sailed out the door.

I grabbed a handful of cookies and went to find Rowan, spotting him and Jensen hunched over a small table on the patio, both intent on a rowdy game of checkers.

Rowan was losing.

He looked up when he felt my presence and grinned when he saw what I was holding.

I handed over the loot, keeping two for myself and took the spot beside Rowan.

Jensen stiffened at my presence. I squashed my hurt and leaned forward to stare at the board.

"You're losing, husband."

Rowan let out a put upon sigh. "Best of three."

A smile tugged at Jensen's mouth. "Mom will worry if I'm not back soon."

"Raincheck then?" Rowan asked.

"Maybe. If they let me come back."

I doubted Caelan would. "What's your favorite cookie?"

He glanced up. "Snickerdoodle."

"Even in the summer?"

Another tug at his mouth. "Yes. Cinnamon has no season."

Rowan chuckled. "I agree. Cinnamon in all its forms is something to behold. Unless it's one of those fake cinnamon brooms you can taste in your mouth when you walk into the store."

The teen grinned. "Mom hates those, too. They make her sneeze."

I glanced at Rowan. Sadness glimmered in his eyes. He hated this as much as I did. Caelan using this boy to further his agenda was a shitty thing to do. He knew we wouldn't harm Jensen, but he'd put the boy through this to make a point.

"Ha!" Jensen crowed, double jumping to take Rowan's last two pieces on the board.

Rowan snorted. "I'll be damned. I really am terrible at checkers."

He wasn't. Rowan kicked my ass all the time in both checkers and chess. When you looked at my mate, you wouldn't see a scheming, manipulative male. You'd see a handsome and charming rogue who could talk you into just about anything, but you'd underestimate him.

Rowan, like most fae, played the long game. He never wanted to be a Lord and never wanted to hold this much power over people.

But doing so kept the people he loved safe, and so he'd stepped into the mantle of a Lord and had been doing it ever since.

He was good at strategy and mind games and staying two steps ahead of his enemy, but he also trusted too much. Far more than I ever had or would.

Maybe that meant he was a better person than me, but he hadn't expected Caelan to come sailing through the air to put a knife in his back. And I had wondered all along.

Rowan and Jensen put the game away. When they finished,

Rowan tossed Jensen one of the extra cookies. "Let's hear the message, Jensen."

All the tension came back to Jensen's face and posture. He cleared his throat and straightened his posture, the cookies lying forgotten on his thigh.

"Lord Caelan wishes to meet Evangeline Quinn in person. He has a message he will share with no one else and has asked that she come alone and meet with him inside his Keep home."

The bond between us burned with Rowan's fury. I watched his eyes go from the bright hazel I loved into a molten pool of multi-colored swirls.

Jensen swallowed hard and tried to press himself into the couch cushions. I put a hand on Rowan's thigh and sent a pulse of love through the bond.

"Did he say anything else?" I asked.

Jensen licked his lips. "Umm. Just that he has set the meeting date for three days from now. He has granted you safe passage through his territory."

Rowan snorted at that. I controlled Caelan's territory right now. Caelan was merely a figurehead—one who couldn't step one foot off the right path without suffering a grisly fate.

The only one who didn't have full safe passage on his own lands was Caelan.

"Alright," I said quietly. "Was there anything else, Jensen?"

The poor teenager was trembling with fear. "Just—" He licked his lips. "Just that if Evie refused, there would be consequences."

Claws slid from Rowan's fingers—thick, sharp claws that cut through the fabric of his athletic pants. I gave his thigh a gentle squeeze.

"Thank you for relaying his message to us." I rose and reached for Rowan's hand. "We'll walk you back to your mother now."

Jensen stood as well. "Umm. Do you have a message to take back?"

I smiled, though with the way Jensen shrank back, the gesture wasn't as comforting as I thought. "No," I said. "We will reach out to your Lord directly."

Jensen's gaze flicked back and forth between Rowan and me, possibly trying to figure out which one of us was the most dangerous.

Normally, I would have said me, but Rowan's posture was tight, and the glow in his eyes had not faded. He was close to losing control.

I had dealt with enough of Caelan's bullshit to know he was posturing. We both knew who had the upper hand here, and it wasn't him.

"Come," I said. "Let us walk you back to your mother."

Jensen nodded and walked ahead of us, his shoulders tight and his head bowed.

I had a message for Caelan, alright. One I would delight in giving him very soon.

I called Dad to send Sheila and Jensen home. While one day I'd be able to do so without a thought, I was still nervous about my new magic. In my head, I imagined them exploding into a shower of atoms.

Dad told me I was overreacting and that the most that might happen was them winding up in a different place than where I'd sent them.

When I asked if he meant I might put them over the Atlantic Ocean at night, he paused way too long for comfort.

Now he acted as a taxi service until I was 100% confident I'd send people where they needed to go, when I needed them there.

Caelan might shit his pants when those two popped into existence from thin air, and knowing my father's wicked sense of humor, he'd put them right in the most inconvenient and embarrassing place he could find.

Once they were gone and Dad had said his goodbyes, Rowan and I curled up on the couch.

"What's the plan?"

I glanced up at him and smiled. Rowan always had a way about him that made me feel important, even powerful. He rarely questioned my decisions, even when we both knew I was going too far. I almost killed Caelan a few months ago and would have if he had not stepped in. Rowan never told me not to, never questioned my right to vengeance, or even for violence. He merely asked me if I was sure.

His small, quiet question brought me back from the brink of something I could never take back.

I had been well within my rights to kill him, but if I had, I would have broken something inside—something vital.

Rowan realized this and handled the situation with care and love.

Without realizing what was happening, I'd fallen in love with him a little bit at a time. Friendship had come first, kinship second, safety third, attraction next, and then I realized I no longer wanted to live without him.

Caelan was a storm, an ocean squall I couldn't escape, and for a while, I didn't want to. But that storm grew and grew until suddenly, I could no longer keep my balance.

Rowan was a gentle spring rain, a safe harbor I could stand under until I came back to myself.

His brow furrowed. "You're staring."

"Mmm." I touched his face. "Thank you for not giving up on me."

He blinked in surprise. A small smile lifted the edge of his lips. "Bears are stubborn. We don't give up until there's zero chance of winning."

He cupped my chin. "I would have stayed by your side until the bitter end, Evie. Even if you had chosen against me."

Tears welled in my eyes. "Well," I said shakily, "it got real close for a while, didn't it?"

"I knew you'd walk away from him. You're too smart not to. Whether you'd open your heart to me was another matter entirely."

He was right. I kept trying to talk myself out of loving him, convinced we were moving too fast, that I was somehow betraying Caelan.

The truth was love never waited for the right time, but it wouldn't wait around forever. Rowan would have eventually left me if I hadn't given in to my feelings, and he would have been well within his rights to do so.

He was way too much of a catch to wait around for me to get my shit together.

Instead, he'd given me the time I needed, even if the fae bond between us hadn't been so patient.

"How are you feeling?" I asked as I curled into his chest. The bond had made us both feral for each other and showed no signs of stopping. I wasn't worried about that so much as the strange way our bonds had solidified. Rowan knew I was his mate long before I did, but once the shifter bond began to form, the fae one followed soon after. When we decided to be together no matter what may come, those bonds had melded into one and came with some surprising side effects. Nothing major, yet, but Rowan's innate magic had tripled in strength, and he was showing some signs of pulling on my Chimera magic.

I, on the other hand, had an overwhelming urge to eat all the time. Much like the bear I was snuggled against.

He brought his arms around me and rested his chin on top of my head.

"You worry wart," he said affectionately. "I'm fine."

"You'd tell me if you weren't?"

He chuckled. "You'd know. Our bond does not allow us to lie to each other." He paused. "Not well anyway. We will know when something is wrong with the other." He shifted. "Look inside and tell me what you see?"

I sighed and laid my hand on his chest. The moment I closed my eyes and focused, the bond came into view. A few months ago, I could not see our mating bond, but Mom had been giving me lessons. Now I could do things I'd only once dreamed of.

The shifter and fae bonds had melded together in a knot of silver, gold, and watermelon tourmaline. Resting in the center of both our chests, the bond pulsed with life, content and rested. No sign of distress or illness. Rowan's heart beat strong beneath my palm, his breath steady and even.

"Fine," I huffed. "You gotta admit it's weird."

"Everything about us is weird."

I snorted. "And how do you feel about the crown?"

Rowan shrugged. "Same way you do, I suppose. Not something I'm thrilled about, but I wasn't keen on becoming a Lord, either. Duty always sits upon weary shoulders, Evie. You and I will be good rulers when the time comes. We've already proven such."

Mom and Dad were having a tough time ceding power, and Rowan and I didn't give a whit. We'd happily be the figureheads for as long as they wanted.

"I don't know many of the fae, but the ones I've dealt with haven't impressed me much."

"Mmm. Yes. They have tried to kill you on occasion."

"Tough way to start a new job."

Rowan huffed a laugh. "Don't expect a Happy Boss's Day fruit basket any time soon."

A smile tugged at my lips as a confession pushed up from my heart. Rowan wouldn't judge me, but I still felt guilty every time I thought about what I'd done, as if I realized in the deepest recesses of my mind that things were beginning to fall apart. "When everything first started going wrong with Caelan, I seeded his land with the poison plants I made while I was recovering at Hazel's house."

Rowan stilled. "How many?"

I didn't say anything for a long moment. "Do you really want to know?"

His chuckle held a wicked edge. "Actually..." His voice trailed off. "No. Surprise me, wife."

How was it possible to love someone this much? Sometimes my chest hurt because it felt so full. "You're coming with me to Texas."

"You doubted me?"

I shook my head and smiled against his neck. "Never."

Rowan sprawled on the couch behind the office computer reading a Sanderson novel. My finger hovered over the video link and had been for the last thirty seconds.

"You don't have to see his face. Just call him."

"He won't answer. Caelan wants to see my face."

"Yes," Rowan agreed. "Because he luuuuuurves you."

I sent him a dark look over the top of the screen. "I think it's more that he wants to kiiiiillll me."

He winked. "Two things can be true at the same time."

I tossed my pen at him. "Can you be serious for one moment?"

"Mmm." Rowan tilted his head and squinted up at the ceiling. "Not when it makes you this uncomfortable."

All I had to do was click the link. Click it and let it ring. Maybe he won't answer.

"He's definitely going to answer."

"I still think you can read my mind sometimes," I grumbled.

"No, my darling, but I do know the way you think. Hope is written all over your face."

"He doesn't know I'm calling, so not answering is possible."

Rowan laid his book on his chest and looked at me, his eyes filled with understanding. "The moment he sees your name on his phone, he will answer. Keep your answers short. Do not engage with him about personal matters. State the terms of your visit. Get him to agree, then cut the call."

"And if he won't?"

Rowan shrugged. "Cut the call anyway." He smiled at the worried expression I knew I wore. "I love how you can make murderous flytraps and seed your ex-fiancé's land with poison, but the thought of a phone call petrifies you."

I plopped my head in my hands and blew a raspberry. "It's easier when I don't have to see his face."

"You can tell a lot from a man's face when he speaks to the woman he loves."

"He doesn't love me," I said quietly.

Rowan swung his legs off the couch and walked over, bending to press a kiss to my lips. "Untrue. He only realized it when he lost everything." He kissed me again. "Or have you forgotten the whole trying to murder me in cold blood incident?"

I would never forget how I felt when I saw Caelan launch himself at Rowan's unprotected back, and I would never regret what I did next.

Rowan's face softened. "You hold all the power, Evie. Finally, make sure he knows it."

He turned and plopped back onto the couch, scooping his book up. "Now, I'm right at a really good part. No more interruptions, please." He winked and pretended to bury his nose in between the pages.

"You're a pain in the ass," I grumbled.

Rowan laughed. "And handsome and manly and strong and *very* good in bed."

All true. "And arrogant and far too full of himself."

"Mmm. Yes. Well, I can't be perfect every single day. You ask far too much of a man."

I rolled my eyes, squared my shoulders, and clicked the link.

CHAPTER

Six

Rowan was right. Caelan answered on the third ring.

Once, not too long ago, I thought he was the most beautiful thing I'd ever seen. His hair was dark, still tousled, longer on the top than the bottom. I used to think his hair was the only thing messy about him and thought him a storm contained in human form.

His eyes were charcoal grey flecked with gold, the color of the smoke from an out-of-control fire or a storm brewing in the clouds.

He looked the same, but I felt nothing.

For the first time, I felt absolutely nothing when he looked at me. A smile threatened to break over my face, an emotion I couldn't afford to show him. Rowan still lay sprawled across the couch, his eyes moving over the text on the pages. I knew he'd have to re-read those pages later, because his eyes were a little too sharp and interested.

"Evie." Caelan's deep voice rumbled. "I'm surprised to hear from you so soon."

He sat in his office, the books on the shelves behind him as neat as they ever were. One major change he'd made was the absence of any plant life. Caelan liked plants and had made a point to bring in dozens whenever he started pursuing me.

The lack of them now was understandable but still saddened me for reasons I couldn't explain.

"Your messenger came with your demands."

He nodded. "Then I will see you in two days."

A thread of annoyance trilled through me. Just like him to assume I'd do whatever he wanted.

"I do not agree."

A flash of surprise and a slight narrowing of his eyes was his only tell of surprise. "Oh?"

"I will be there in three days. Rowan and two members of my court will accompany me."

A thread of gold ringed his iris. "No."

Rowan's words crept back into my mind. It took everything I had to keep my face mild and uninterested. "Very well," I said. "Call me back when you're ready to meet my terms."

He opened his mouth to speak just as I ended the call.

Rowan's low chuckle sent a thrill down my spine. "Good girl."

He knew I loved it when he said that to me. "You're not allowed to say such things when you know he's going to call right back."

Rowan's slow grin made my stomach tighten.

My computer signaled an incoming call. "Dammit, Rowan," I said through clenched teeth.

His wicked laugh made my lips tug into an answering smile. I hit the answer button.

Caelan's furious face swam into existence.

"Goddammit, Evie. Do not hang up on me again!"

"Rowan and two members of my court will accompany me. They will sweep the room we meet in, and one will remain with me during our meeting. If you do not agree to those terms, we will not meet. We both know you can say whatever you want to say right now. There's no need for these theatrics or for me to travel to you, other than to soothe your wounded ego."

Rowan let out a soft laugh. "Good girl," he whispered for my ears only.

I squirmed in my seat.

Caelan's irises turned full gold now. His teeth pulled back from his lips. "You think now that you're mated to a Lord you can say whatever you wish to me?"

I rolled my eyes. "Let's not pretend I've ever had a filter."

"My original terms stand." He crossed his arms over his powerful chest and waited.

I smiled and disconnected the call once more.

Rowan's laugh was a crack of sound. He put his book down and motioned me over. "Ignore his next call."

I'd barely gotten out of my chair before the video notification went off once more. I stilled but Rowan watched me, his eyes glowing with desire.

"Come, mate. I felt you when Caelan's face came on the screen. You think I'm prettier."

I unbuttoned the top two buttons of my shirt. "Mmm. And if I do?"

His smile widened. "I will just have to ensure you keep thinking so."

He held his arms out.

I launched myself at my husband. Hearing his shout of surprise and the warmth of the bond inside my chest, feeling his hands wrap around my waist as he caught me, I knew every step I'd taken, no matter how awful the journey sometimes, every bit of it had led me here, to Rowan.

CAELAN CALLED BACK four more times, but Rowan and I were a little distracted. The fifth time Rowan's phone beeped.

We lay tangled together on the ground, our clothes haphazardly tossed around the room.

"Hmm. If he video called now, I might answer," Rowan murmured.

I smacked him lightly on the chest. "Cad."

Rowan grinned and held up his cell, peering at it with one eye closed. "The Lord has agreed to your terms but has refused to allow me access to the Keep. You'll have to go in with the other two."

"Of course." Caelan could be such an ass sometimes. "You can wait at the old flower shop." My mother and father had claimed the space for the fae. If Caelan stepped foot on the property, my mom and dad would know, and there would be hell to pay. I'd refused to sell the place, mostly just to piss the Lord off, so the old shop sat vacant, a sore thumb in the middle of a once vibrant town.

Maybe I'd give up the space, but not anytime soon. Caelan could walk past that space every day and think about his mistakes.

"I'm bringing Seymour."

Rowan peered at me. "Out of kindness or extreme passive aggressiveness?"

I tossed my shirt at him. "A little of both. Seymour is adjusting well, but he loves Caelan. I think it'd be good for him to visit."

"And Hannah?"

I shook my head. "Hannah has taken to this place like a duck to water. Her and Moira are getting along like gangbusters."

"Makes sense. Hannah is gentle. Seymour's a thug."

I rose and pulled my pants on. "Seymour was made as an attack flytrap and somehow became a sentient being. He's developed his own personality. I can't help that he has his favorites."

Rowan peered up at me through long lashes. "He's poisoned several shifters since he's been here."

I winced. "Yes, well, Seymour doesn't like surprises. Your people came from behind and startled the poor guy."

At Rowan's lifted eyebrow, I snorted. "He could poison everyone and hasn't done that, so you gotta give him a little credit. Taking him to see Caelan might mellow him out a little."

"Or make him worse," Rowan muttered.

I nudged him with my toe. "I took Seymour away from his best friend. In a million years, I would never have expected him to become what he has. The poor thing bonded with something, showing us all he's capable of strong emotion. Looking back, I should have let him say goodbye."

Rowan's jaw tightened, but he nodded after a moment. "As much as I hate to give the bastard anything, this isn't about Caelan. It's about what's best for your vicious little flytrap."

I went to my knees and kissed Rowan. "I love it when you're grumpy."

Rowan snagged me around the waist and pulled me on top of him. "Tell me what else you love about me."

I pretended like I was going to bite his nose. "I'll recite poetry for you later. Mom and Dad are coming for dinner."

"Do we have to?"

"Considering you invited them, yes." I rolled away and got to my feet, picking up his discarded shirt with my toes. "Put this on and meet me in the kitchen."

"Bossy."

I cracked open the door. "You like it."

I didn't miss the glow in his eyes as I slipped outside.

Yep. He definitely liked it.

DAD AKA CERNUNNOS, aka the former fae king was positively delighted by my current progress in figuring out my magic, but much less impressed by my refusal to try any form of travel farther than a few feet.

We stood in the clearing about twenty feet away from each other. Dad wore his human guise today—joggers, t-shirt, and tennis shoes—but his eyes swirled with magic and annoyance.

"You've used it before."

"Yes, when Rowan was about to die."

The Lord winced at the reminder. He, Mom, Moira, and the

others were on the patio drinking sangria and watching me and my father argue.

"Tap into the same emotion you felt then and move."

I stared at him. "You want me to tap into all-consuming grief every time I want to go somewhere?"

Dad's nostrils flared. "You know what I mean."

"I don't, actually."

He sighed and sat down on the ground, motioning for me to come closer and join him.

When I'd settled across from him, he leaned over and took my hands. "I forget you are not like us, Evie."

I eyed him warily. Amusement made his eyes sparkle.

"You are not human, but you were raised among them and lived like they do for many years. Humans are far more emotional than our kind. As such, you tie emotions to some of your powers."

"Like moving through space and time."

He inclined his head. "You weren't able to use the power until someone you loved was in danger. Now, every time I ask you to try, you think of Rowan, of the possibility of what could have gone wrong had you not reached him in time, yes?"

I glanced over at Rowan, who watched me—a soft ring of watermelon tourmaline magic around his iris. My breath caught. He looked at me as if I were his salvation, and part of me still felt unworthy of his adoration.

"Yes," I said softly.

"Your scenario did not come to pass."

My brow furrowed. "Does it matter?"

"Yes," Dad said simply.

A beat of silence before I took a deep breath so I wouldn't scream. "You are thousands of years old. You've seen entire civilizations fall. I was born this century and married to a man who treated me like shit, then dated someone who hid most of his red flags. Then I met Rowan, and suddenly, he was the most important thing in my world. I will never stop seeing Caelan coming for him, never not think about losing him. The image is forever stamped in my mind." I took a breath, still forcing down the urge to yell at him. "You say things so matter-of-factly as if you have any idea what it feels like to be mated."

I regretted the words as soon as I said them. He and my mom had a complicated history, and if Cliona ever opened the door to the possibility of them being together again, he would happily walk through it and fall to his knees before her.

Dad's eyes flickered.

I opened my mouth to apologize, but Dad stopped me. He reached over and took my hands. "Don't apologize to me. You're right on one part. I may never know what it's like to have the type of bonds you do with your Lord. But that is not my point. You are continuing to see something that never came to pass, and the simple fact is your magic is being affected by your trauma."

I blinked.

Dad's eyes softened. "I may be thousands of years old, but I know complex trauma when I see it. You need to speak to someone. Sooner rather than later." He glanced toward the patio. "Rowan is here, Evie, staring at you like you're the sun. He's alive and breathing and still here to love you for the rest of time. He is not dead. And yet, you relive the possibility every single day."

I swallowed hard, the burn of tears pricking the backs of my eyes. "Why are you so reasonable sometimes?" I choked out.

Dad smiled. I forgot who he was sometimes. Hell, I forgot who I was sometimes. The man sitting before me was an immortal king, and I was his heir.

The side of his mouth lifted in a lopsided smile. "Tonight is the first time someone's ever called me reasonable." He lowered his voice. "You should tell your mother about my reasonability."

"That's not a word," I said with a laugh.

"Should be one." Dad sighed. "Loving one's daughter tends to bring out the kinder, gentler side of a father." He lifted a shoulder in a shrug. "And, since you won't allow me to rip the other Lord into shreds, I suppose this is the next most reasonable step in the process of healing."

"What an altruist you are."

We grinned at each other.

Rowan rose and walked over, lowering himself next to me. "Everything okay?"

"Dad wants me to talk to someone."

Rowan eyed my father for a long moment. They did not have the somewhat easy relationship Caelan and he did. Caelan showed deference to the former fae king. Rowan never bothered. While he respected my father's position, he also recognized how manipulative he could be and suffered no fools, especially when it came to me.

My father, on the other hand, was used to being worshipped and thought Rowan needed to be knocked down a few pegs. But Rowan's mother was a powerful shapeshifting goddess, and Dad was more wary of my mate than the other Lords he'd met. Whether his wariness stemmed from me or from something to do with Rowan's mother, I wasn't sure. I had yet to meet her and had been meaning to try to contact her, but Mom was having trouble finding her. With the absence of the gate, aka me, less powerful fae could no longer travel between the worlds.

People like Mom and Dad and the much older gods like Neit could travel at will, but there were only a handful of those.

Yet one more problem I needed to fix and hadn't gotten around to. In my defense, I had people constantly trying to kill me, so maybe the fae would cut me some slack once I figured out how to be the gate without *being* the actual gate.

"I agree with your father." Rowan looked genuinely pained by the admission.

Dad laid a hand over his heart and gasped dramatically.

Rowan shot him a look. "I expect this will be the only time we agree."

"You never know," Dad said. "This could be the start of a beautiful friendship."

"Doubt it," Rowan said.

Man. He really did not like my father. I glanced up at him, but Rowan shook his head once. "Are you finished training?"

I glanced at Dad, who inclined his head. "She's mastered everything except for traveling. We should convene until after a few sessions with a therapist or whoever the packs use when dealing with PTSD."

Rowan's eyes glimmered. I stifled a smile. "You agree with Dad again but don't want to admit it."

Dad chuckled. "I'll be back in a few weeks." He rose in a graceful motion and held out a hand to help me up. "We'll gauge your progress then."

Dad draped an arm over my shoulder and pressed a kiss to my temple. "Until then—" He looked at Rowan. "Take care of my daughter."

He disappeared in a shower of multi-colored light.

Rowan's jaw tightened.

"What is with you two?" I asked in a low voice.

My mate shook his head once. "He's a puppet master, tugging on everyone's strings."

"Has he ever tugged on yours?"

"Mm." A faint smile tipped his lips up. "He tried. More than once."

My eyebrows lifted. "Oh? I take it that things didn't go well?"

I wondered before. Dad inserted himself *everywhere*. He was the equivalent of an HOA president slow rolling past the neighborhood houses on the weekend, trying to catch someone stepping one inch out of line. Rowan never said anything and always treated my father with respect. Not because he was the king but because he was my father.

"No." Rowan snorted. "I never participated in his schemes. Which is why I think he messed with me less than the others."

"I don't think he's spoken to any of the other Lords."

Rowan eyed me, amusement sparkling in the hazel depths of

his gaze. "Your father has spoken with all of us. I'd wager my entire Keep."

"He's such a nosy Nellie." I looped my arm through Rowan's. "Come on. I made an angel food cake for dessert."

Rowan gasped. "Did you make the cream, too?"

I had no idea he had such a sweet tooth until I moved into the main house. Dude had never met a baked good he didn't like.

"With the vanilla bean," I assured him.

"Gods, I love you," Rowan breathed. He tugged his arm loose and jogged ahead to the kitchen.

Moira watched him go. When I made it to the patio, she rolled her eyes. "Let me guess. You made dessert?"

"Angel food cake," I confirmed. "With the sweetened whipped cream."

"You're spoiling him," Mom observed with a grin. "Good for you."

"He deserves it." I followed Rowan into the kitchen. He'd already pulled the cake and the cream out and held a stack of plates and forks, an eager expression on his face.

I took the cake and whipped cream. "You can have the first slice."

"Yesssss," Rowan hissed under his breath.

With him around, life felt so easy, and I tried to relax.

In two days, I would see Caelan again, the break Rowan and I had taken over for the foreseeable future. I'd be a fool to believe I'd walk away from the other Lord's territory unscathed.

CHAPTER

Seven

I awoke in the circle of Rowan's arms. Pressing a kiss to his chest, I slipped away to pull on a heavy cashmere cardigan and a pair of slip-on sneakers and slipped out of the bedroom.

Moira's apartment was half a mile away, an easy walk for anyone living on Keep grounds. I made a pot of coffee and pulled out a few pastries from the fridge. While the coffee was brewing, I tied my hair into a messy bun and brushed my teeth.

With a thermos of coffee and the pastries balanced in my hands, I headed out to make the short walk.

Moira answered the door, bleary-eyed and wearing a silk nightgown that hit the tops of her thighs. My bestie was stunning, though she never thought so. Moira used her beauty when it benefited her. Otherwise, she was perfectly content to lounge around in joggers, tanks, and bare feet, or nightgown and slippers.

Her dark hair fell loose and wavy around her shoulders. Dark brown, almost black eyes squinted at me. She grunted when she saw what I was holding and stepped back, holding the door open.

The moment I stepped over the threshold, she snatched the thermos of coffee and slammed the door.

"Misty had a wild night?" I ventured.

Moira grunted again while she opened the thermos and poured herself a cup. She took a sip, grimaced, but took another sip. I went straight to the kitchen and put on the kettle.

Moira would always prefer tea to coffee, but she drank coffee when someone offered the beverage. If it were caffeinated, she'd drink whatever someone put into her hands.

I rummaged through her cabinets until I found her London Fog canister and set up her mug with a teaspoon of the fragrant blend. She already had the steamer set up, so I poured a little of the milk she kept in a glass bottle into the metal carafe and turned the machine on, after I added a dash of cinnamon to the liquid.

Moira kept a glass jar of vanilla bean sugar by the kettle. When the tea finished brewing, I added a little sugar and carefully spooned in the steamed milk, gently stirring to combine everything in the exact way I knew she liked it.

I felt her eyes on me, curious and loving. When I turned to hand her the mug, she took it. "You never make me tea. Is everything okay?"

"Everything is fine," I assured her. "I'm here to check on you and hang out. I don't want to be the kind of friend who fades away because one of us gets married."

Her lips twitched. "And you're here to see the baby?"

"And I'm here to see the baby."

We laughed together. Moira was usually up with the sun, but last night was her time to have Misty. The abandoned Chimera baby was flourishing in her new home at the Keep, even as the vast majority of shifters were a little sleep deprived after a night with her. We made a calendar for anyone who volunteered to help, and little Misty was happily keeping those volunteers up all night. At first, we wondered if bouncing her around might harm her development, but shifters always banded together. None of the volunteers abandoned her and visited her wherever she was that day.

Misty had taken to everyone like a fish to water. There wasn't a single shifter in the Keep she didn't like. Gummy smiles and baby laughs were payment enough for a rough night's sleep, and everyone seemed happy to pay.

"When did she fall asleep?"

Moira sighed and took a fortifying sip of her chai latte. "Two. Before that, she was up every hour and a half. But I think she's beginning to see longer stretches of sleep. In a few weeks, the little nightmare might be sleeping through the night."

They'd taken it easy on me through my honeymoon period and had gone as far as to remove our name from the volunteer calendar. I wouldn't let it go on too much longer. Partly to be fair, but also because I wanted baby snuggles just as much as the rest of them.

And soon enough, the Keep would be filled with babies. Several shifters were heavily pregnant after I'd come onto Rowan's land and started working my magic. I had no idea earth magic could work that way, but I'd really let go once I felt safe which resulted in a whole lot of sexy time and a ton of unplanned babies.

Not that anyone was angry about it. The complete opposite, in fact. They borderline worshipped the ground I walked on for a while, which made things uncomfortable for me. Now that everyone was used to me and things had settled down, they treated me as Rowan's lady and not some unapproachable deity.

The arm wrestling incident had solidified me as flesh and blood, and Rick, the Navy vet I'd beaten, still acted as my driver when Rowan wasn't around. He was a good guy who was still begging me for a rematch. I had yet to give him one, but one day I might surprise him.

I still planned to win.

"How are things with Ethan?" She had yet to take Rowan up on his offer of knocking on his shifter's door for some companionship, and I sent up a little prayer every time she refrained. Yes, having some after hours entertainment might knock the edge off, but Moira had never been that kind of person. She had boyfriends in the past, but no one serious and no one long lasting. What she didn't have was a revolving door of men, and I hoped she didn't start.

Moira's eyes darkened. She and the other Lord had a short, but interesting history. I'd never seen her crush on someone the way she was crushing on him, but he wasn't making it easy on her. I wanted to tell her to find another distraction, maybe a hapless human in town who didn't mind being casual.

Shifters and paranormals came with their own troubles. I know I sure as hell did. For a while, I was a walking red flag. Human troubles were a lot less dangerous, and after hanging out with me and all my surrounding drama, Moira could use some down time.

Her eyes narrowed. "You're staring at me like you're about to give an unasked for piece of advice. Please don't."

When I first met Moira, I was taken aback by how freely she spoke. All these years later, I appreciated knowing where I always stood with her. "I only want you to be happy."

"Ethan won't make me happy. He's got more baggage than an international flight." She rolled her eyes. "He's hot in the physical sense, but cold everywhere else."

The temper snapping in his eyes when he hauled her out of that bar months ago begged to differ, but I kept my mouth shut. "Hmm," was all I said.

"I've been eyeing a shifter who lives on the other side of the Keep. Beautiful, mysterious, quiet. He makes these little wood carvings I find all over the place."

I watched her. "Are you thinking about knocking on his door?"

She stretched her long legs out and wiggled her pink toes. "Maybe. I'm not into Rowan's idea of having a revolving door of shifters, but I wouldn't mind having a man around. It's been a while."

My heart ached for her, even as I knew the lack of men was my fault. When your best friend became surrounded by dangerous predators and gods trying to kill her at every turn, having a boyfriend took the back seat to survival.

She rolled her eyes. "Don't you dare, Evie. This is not about you. I could have had a boyfriend if I wanted. Hell, Soren knocked on my door for a straight fourteen days when we were back in Joy Springs." Her lips twisted. "He could have been a hell of a distraction."

Soren was a physical specimen, for sure. Arrogant, like most of the Lords, but also viciously clever. I wasn't sure if I liked Soren or not. He felt impossible to get to know and kept his cards close to the vest. He was witty and funny and occasionally violent.

Most disturbing of all, he seemed a little obsessed with Moira. With Ethan hanging around Rowan's territory far more than he ever had, and Moira obviously pining over him, I fully expected whatever was happening between her and the other two Lords to come to a swift and violent conclusion.

I'd managed to take out two Lords without even trying that hard. Wasn't sure I wanted to know the damage Moira might do if someone pushed her hard enough.

"He did something to you." For a while, Moira seemed interested in Soren, too. Until one day, she wasn't. Since that day, she has refused to talk about it.

Moira sighed. "Soren is a collector. I was not interested in becoming part of his display. He's gone unchecked for too long. Women allow him to play with them and end up crying, discarded like a broken toy."

Moira did not have to say she was no one's toy.

"He wanted a temporary dalliance." Sounded about right.

Moira surprised me by shaking her head. "He wanted to make me his mistress."

My jaw dropped.

A thin smile didn't reach her eyes. "His parents are pushing him to marry and create heirs. Soren has no interest in settling down. He thought I'd be amenable to moving into his territory, living at his Keep, warming his bed, and running his lands."

"With zero commitment on his part," I murmured.

What a stunning display of assholishness. Wow.

"Exactly. He'd pay me a generous stipend like a well-kept whore. His parents would be off his back, and I'd have all the appearances of power and wealth with a handsome Lord on my arm."

"Many women would jump at his offer."

Our eyes met. Moira's lips twitched, and soon we were cackling like old hens at the absurdity of thinking Moira would ever agree to such a one-sided agreement. When Moira met someone worthy, she would die for them. Her loyalty took deep roots. Neither wind, nor hail, nor violent storm could shake her from her cause.

I'd been the ever-lucky recipient of Moira's loyalty, and I tried never to take it for granted.

"I wondered why you were so pissed at him," I said when I finally got myself together.

"He's been backtracking ever since," she said with a sigh. "Regardless, Soren and I wouldn't work out. Especially not after this. Even before…" Moira shook her head. "After seeing everything you went through with Caelan, I'm not sure I'd ever want to be a Lady."

"Even if Ethan was the Lord?" I hedged.

She snorted. "Ethan won't take another Lady. His wall is made of titanium. Nothing gets through it."

She studied her nails. "He has his fair share of women throwing themselves at him. Why would he want me and all the problems I represent when he can have no strings wherever he goes?"

I stared at her. "Problems?"

Moira shrugged. "Like everyone, I carry my fair share of baggage."

I rose and made myself a cup of coffee from her Keurig. Not my preferred type, but Moira didn't drink much coffee and had bought the machine for my visits. "I bagged two Lords," I said lightly. "And look at all my bullshit."

That got a laugh out of her. "True," she said once I resettled. "But Ethan isn't interested. He's made himself remarkably clear about that. I know when I'm not wanted."

Moira scooted closer to me. My bestie wasn't prone to bouts of physical affection, but sometimes she needed the closeness of someone she trusted. I slung my leg over hers and clinked our mugs together. "If Ethan wants me, he's going to have to write out a big sign and show up at my door with a boombox."

"Fat chance in hell of him doing that," I mused.

"Exactly." She nodded. "Ethan fancies himself the strong, silent type, but if the dude wants to tangle, he's going to have to spell it out like I'm illiterate."

I snickered. "I love how we frustrate the men in our life so much they occasionally resort to violence."

"Ethan doesn't have far to go. Caelan seemed prone to bursts of anger, but Ethan is a simmering teapot. One notch up in temperature and he's going to whistle."

Concern rippled through me. As much as I didn't want to say this, Moira was my best friend. I needed to say it. "Have you ever thought about moving?"

Moira's eyes snapped to mine. "Away from you?"

I shrugged. "I don't want you to ever feel like you're trapped, or this is all there is for you. As much as I would miss you, all I want is your happiness. If that means you need to go somewhere else, I want you to do that. But don't think you'll escape forever. I'll track your ass down if you stay away too long."

She scoffed. "I appreciate what you're saying, but I'm happy here. Rowan's Keep is amazing, and he's offered me numerous opportunities to expand."

I blinked in surprise.

"There's a small spot in town and I've hinted around about opening a tea shop."

"That would be perfect for you!" Losing her at the flower shop would mean hiring another helper, but Moira was never meant to work at Little Shop of Florals forever. When we met, we both were at a point in our lives where we needed stability. Once the flower shop was up and running, Moira could have left at any time, but we'd become a family and everyone decided as a unit to stay together.

Being married to Rowan had changed things between us all. My friends followed me here because they loved me, but I never expected things to escalate how they did or for me to make my home here. Ash loved Rowan's lands. He would stay. Tess was firmly attached to Ash, so she would stay as long as he did.

Moira was the wildcard, and I feared she might be falling in love with Ethan, while at the same time being completely oblivious to her feelings.

That was Moira. She pegged me in an instant, but she took a while to come to terms with her own emotions.

"I like it here, Evie. Opening a tea shop sounds amazing, but there's a lot to think about."

"And if Ethan throws himself at your feet and professes his undying love?"

Moira's eyes glittered with amusement. "Then I'd ask him how he feels about a long distance relationship."

"You know part of his territory butts up against Rowan's."

Her jaw tightened. She hadn't.

"And if things worked out for you, I'd be willing to cede a portion of Donovan's old territory—"

"Your territory," she interrupted.

"All the same, if Ethan made you his Lady, I'd cede part of the territory so you could stay close to us."

Her eyes shimmered with tears. "This feels like we're children playing a what if game. If I were a princess, I'd ride a big white Pegasus and make it legal for children to have candy for breakfast."

I looped our arms together. "And I'd bathe in marshmallows and make every night Taco night."

We grinned at each other. "Just saying," I said quietly. "I'd happily give it all away to have you close to us."

She laid her dark head on my shoulder. "I know you would, and I love you for it. We both know Ethan won't do anything of the sort, but knowing you'd do everything in your power to keep us close makes it all worth it."

"You never know," I murmured. "Look at what happened to me. Rowan would have walked away from everything for me."

"And you made him a king because of it." Moira sighed. "Maybe one day I will find someone who'd do those things for me."

"Never maybe," I said solemnly. "You will find him. You know why?"

Moira sighed. "Because I'm amazing?"

"Yup. And gorgeous. And talented. And you can bake like a fiend, and men love bitches who bake."

She let out a bark of laughter.

"And you're super hot and funny and a little wicked."

"Total package," Moira said dryly.

"Total frigging package," I agreed.

Eight

"You ready?"

Rowan tugged on a cashmere pullover and ran his fingers through his messy hair. "Are you?"

"Nope." Today was Caelan's deadline. While I didn't care much about meeting his timeline, I was trying not to be a total asshole. We both knew who held the power here, but I didn't need to rub it in his face.

"We don't have to go," Rowan said as our eyes met in the mirror. "You can tell him to fuck off and tangle him in some thorns or something, and then I can drag you back to my lair and have my way with you."

"Hmm." I pretended to think. "Your idea sounds way better."

He went to grab me around the waist to do just that, but I danced out of his reach, shaking my hairbrush at him in warning. "We need to settle this thing between us. The sooner, the better. "

"While I agree Caelan is an asshole. We shouldn't do anything to make his life easier."

The familiar and rhythmic thump of Seymour's clay pot sounded in the hallway. The Red Dragon flytrap was completely stoked about his visit and was letting us know by impatiently thumping every time he thought we were taking too long. Moira had distracted him somewhat by tossing his favorite crunchy bug treats at him, but Seymour was on a mission and would not be denied.

"I don't plan to," I assured him. "I'm ready to close that chapter of my life."

Rowan came up behind me and slid his arms around my front, resting his chin on top of my head. Our eyes met in the mirror once more. "What's your end game? He won't apologize and there's no fucking way his mate is suddenly going to pop onto his property life an offering from the gods."

I'd made myself clear the moment I'd stabbed him with a poison tipped blade. Either Caelan showed true remorse over his actions or his mate arrived and knocked some sense into him. When one of those two things happened, I'd release the stranglehold I had on his land.

"Crazier things have happened."

"Hmm. True." He kissed the top of my head and gave me a cheerful pat on the bottom. "We're waiting for you on the patio. Don't take too long." His eyes warmed. "There are things I want to do to you the moment we get back."

My cheeks heated. "One day we'll both have to get back to work."

Rowan grinned. "But today is not that day."

He winked and walked away. I allowed myself a small smile even though my stomach was churning with nerves. Rowan and I had married after I'd cursed Caelan. He'd undoubtedly heard by now.

This conversation would not go well. I felt it in my bones.

Regardless, I had to go and see what he wanted. Yes, he was a prick for not telling me over the phone, and yes, there was a strong possibility this was a trap. But, if it wasn't a trap and he genuinely wanted to speak to me in person, Caelan deserved at least that small favor from me.

After a final swipe of lip gloss and a critical look in the mirror, I ran my hands down my hips and straightened my shirt. Inhaling a deep breath, I left the restroom and snagged my purse on the way out. Seymour waited for me by the hall table. I bent and held my hand out for him. In one smooth leap, he landed in my palm.

"Ready, buddy?"

Seymour waved his traps in excitement.

Mom, Dad, Moira, Rowan, Garrett and Declan stood outside waiting for me. Moira and the two shifters had their heads together arguing in hushed voices.

I didn't even try to listen to them. "I've already made my mind up. Moira and Garrett will come with me today."

Declan's lips thinned. "Why wouldn't you take two shifters instead of…" He flicked his fingers at Moira.

Moira's eyes flashed a brilliant electric green. "Instead of a brilliant, beautiful, dangerous vampire?" She snorted. "Unlike shifters, I don't stand around all day flexing my muscles." She tapped her finger against her temple. "I prefer exercising my mind."

Declan rolled his eyes. "This is not brains vs brawn, Moira. What happens today affects us all."

Moira vibrated with anger. "I'm well aware of today's importance, Declan. But I'm also Evie's best friend who's been with her for over a decade. I know her, and I know how this will affect her."

My heart warmed.

"Evie also knows I am formally unaffiliated with the shifters. I pay Rowan rent—"

I glanced at Rowan in surprise. He leaned over. "A very small amount so we can have the paperwork of a business arrangement rather than me showing favorites."

"Ah. Smart," I whispered back.

"Yes, well, thanks to you, I am the most powerful Lord in all the land."

Moira gave us an exasperated look and kept speaking. "And once Evie's shop reopens, I will be employed. I'm also quite reasonable in negotiations." She grinned at Declan, and the sight made me go still. "I have no testosterone, so no one has to worry about me getting too…emotional today."

I chewed on my bottom lip to keep from laughing.

"One day, vampire. You and I are going to tangle."

Moira's crazy grin widened. "I look forward to that day."

"Then it's settled. Moira and Garrett, you're with me. Rowan will also travel with us, but Caelan has requested he stay away from the Keep area."

Garrett's jaw tightened at that one. He'd once been Caelan's enforcer, his third in command, and would have walked through fire to serve him until everything fell apart. When I moved to Rowan's territory, I thought Garrett might have a tough time fitting in, but the opposite proved true.

Both Garrett and Simone were thriving under Rowan's leadership. He'd allowed Simone to act as the Pack's second Omega, a position unheard of in any other packs. Omegas were exceedingly rare, and for a Pack to have two…well, let's just say there were a lot of people pissed off at Rowan's for other reasons besides me.

Not only was Simone the second Omega, she had quite the head for business. Once Rowan discovered her other superpower, he turned her loose on the unsuspecting town of Emberwood. Rowan hadn't said much, but I suspected Simone was the driving force behind Moira's offer to run a tea shop.

Garrett, on the other hand, had found a fast friend in Declan, and they shared duties when it came to Rowan. I initially wondered if it might be an issue to have two obviously powerful shifters doing the same job, but those two were peas in a pod.

And Declan got to screw around more, and he was all about the shenanigans.

So far, everyone was settling into their new positions far better than I expected.

Everyone except Moira.

She claimed to be happy. I knew better. Moira loved Emberwood, I knew that much.

Opening the flower shop back up would help her gain some

stability. But Moira was meant for more. Everyone knew it. I thought the tea shop was a brilliant idea.

Now I just had to convince her.

I walked over and greeted my parents, who were quietly talking close to the outdoor kitchen. They smiled and held out their arms.

My heart warmed. A year ago, I would have laughed in someone's face if they told me this would happen—that my parents would be seated together, on my property, and we would become an odd little semi-functional family.

But here we were—Mom and I not only on speaking terms but growing closer every day, and my dad training me to be the fae queen.

Life was weird.

"Evie?" Rowan waved us over. "Ready?"

I would never be ready. Mom linked our arms together. "You don't have to do this," she murmured.

"Dad has already offered to kill him. Multiple times."

Mom snorted. "I'm sure he has. If I thought you might take him up on the offer, I'd throw my hat in the ring, too. But that's not what I mean." She gently tugged. Dad walked away, leaving only us, out of hearing distance from the others.

"You owe Caelan nothing, Evie." Mom turned me to face her. We shared the same eyes, hers glimmering with empathy. "I don't think your former Lord is a bad person." A sad smile graced her lips. "But I do think he was bad for you."

She touched my heart, the place where my bond with Rowan lay. "Remember who you are when you speak to him. He's angry and hurt and lashing out. Things have not been easy for him, either. Especially now. Remember he is less powerful than you, daughter."

Her eyes took on a hard edge. "And if he tries to make you feel less, you make him remember too."

I nodded. "Part of me wants to pretend none of this ever happened."

"If he never happened, you would not be here, standing on land that vibrates with your power. You would not have that male over there struggling not to look at you, to touch you every time he can."

She took my face in her hands. "You would have missed out on so many beautiful things had your path not led you here, to him. To us."

"I know." I exhaled and pressed a hand to my knotted stomach. "Everything is so good right now. I'm so afraid I'll lose this."

Mom pressed a kiss to my forehead. "You are mated both by shifter magic and ours, tied to Rowan and our court forevermore. Rowan will make mistakes. So will you. Immortality has a way of smoothing even the roughest edges, my darling. Take heart. Your father and I will always be here to guide you."

Tears shimmered in my eyes. "Thanks, Mom," I choked out.

Mom stepped away. "I'm only sorry I was not there to help you through the worst times in your life. I can only try to make up for what I missed by being here now."

I brought her in for a tight hug. "It's enough. I promise."

She ran a hand down my hair and gave me a gentle squeeze. "Go on," she encouraged. "The sooner you do this, the sooner you and Rowan can get back here and practice giving me grandbabies."

I gasped. Mom let out an evil laugh and disappeared in a shimmer of magic.

Mom wanted grandbabies? My feet were rooted to the floor for a moment. The thought of having Rowan's children both elated and terrified me. I glanced at Rowan, who stood there with a curious look on his face.

Our children would be stunning. Rowan would make an incredible father.

"Evie?" Dad called.

I blinked and shook off the shock. "Um. Coming."

Rowan wrapped his arm around my waist. "Everything alright?"

I nodded. "Mom said something weird. We'll talk about it when we get back."

His eyes narrowed, but he didn't push. Rowan never pushed, something I'd be forever grateful for. He simply waited until I processed my thoughts and was ready to tell him what was bothering me.

I intertwined our fingers and reached for Moira, who then reached for Garrett.

"Don't let go," Dad warned.

In an instant, we stood in downtown Joy Springs.

CHAPTER

Nine

Seconds after Dad dropped us off, Moira swore under her breath. "What the hell happened?"

Garrett took a step forward, his face a dark thundercloud.

Rowan's expression tightened, his hazel eyes ringed with color. I tightened my grip on his hand and slowly looked at my surroundings.

Joy Springs, a once flourishing town not too far from Texas wine country, had become a ghost town. Seventy percent of the businesses no longer existed, their cheery facades faded and vacant. No tourists milled the sidewalks or sat on the benches eating gelato.

"Sirena is gone," Moira said.

Things were more than bad if the siren had bailed. Last time I saw her, Sirena was worried about the direction things were going, but she planned to stay as long as she could. Sirens weren't popular and many paranormals didn't trust them. Finding a spot where they were not only tolerated but could also open a business was rare.

Guilt gnawed at me. I let out a heavy exhale.

"This isn't your fault," Rowan said quietly, rightly sensing how I was feeling.

"Isn't it?"

Moira shook her head. "No. We saw this happening last time we were here, and we had nothing to do with that. Caelan brought his own downfall around by his actions."

Things were never quite that simple, were they?

I let go of Rowan and did a slow turn. "Something is wrong."

"In addition to the utter failure of the Lord?" Garrett snarled.

I ignored his anger, knowing his fury wasn't directed at me.

"Can't you sense the otherness in the air?" I whispered. What was it? Magic other than Caelan's tainted the air, its influence seeping into everything around us.

Rowan's brow furrowed. He closed his eyes and inhaled. Garrett did the same.

"What is that?" Rowan whispered.

A deep male voice spoke from behind us. "The gods have come."

I spun. Neit stood a few feet away, hands shoved into the pocket of a pair of blue jeans I could not believe he was wearing.

"Where's your armor?"

Neit winced. "Easier if I blend in. We aren't exactly popular around here."

"What happened?" Rowan demanded.

Neit turned his attention to my mate. "You must be the reason the Joy Springs Lord has fallen." He sucked his teeth and looked at me once more. "I can see why you chose him."

I huffed a frustrated laugh. "Thanks, I think? I'm not looking for your approval. What do you mean the gods have come? Surely you wouldn't have done this?"

Neit snorted. "I'm not in the business of ruining lives, your mother being the one exception."

Yeah. Yeah. He totally wanted to do my mother and was sticking around to play the odds. One of my eyebrows went up.

Neit rolled his eyes. "I don't want to talk about it."

He jerked his head toward the woods. "Let's chat in private. This place is too open."

Dad could have put us into a bubble of silence, but he was gone. When I went to follow after Rowan, he took my arm to stop me. "Going into the woods with a god seems a bit dicey, doesn't it?"

Neit stopped and turned, his eyes flashing that strange violet. "I've never hurt Evie."

Present tense. What about the future? "Do you plan to start?" I asked with a frown.

Neit huffed. "Dammit, Evie. Walk with me, please. I would never harm the daughter of the woman I am desperately trying to woo."

"So you are hot for Mom," I teased.

Neit shook his head and disappeared into the dense forest. Garrett stepped in front of me. "Wait."

Without another word, he followed Neit. I didn't think he'd hurt anyone in my party, but the gods were fickle, and Neit was acting…off. Nervous, even. Odd behavior for a god of war.

Garrett popped his head out a few seconds later. "Come on."

We followed Garrett into the woods.

Neit led us to a densely forested area and sat down on an old stump. "I'm surprised your father isn't here."

I shrugged. "Dad stays out of Lord business."

At Rowan's disbelieving snort, I sighed. "For the most part."

"Lies," Garrett muttered under his breath.

I threw up my hands. "Fine. I have no idea why Dad didn't stay. In fact, he loves drama so much I'm surprised he isn't lurking around somewhere eavesdropping."

Everyone fell silent. Neit squinted up at the trees. "Is he?"

"No." I would know if he was close.

"Very unlike him," Garrett remarked. "Wonder what else caught his attention?"

"Anyway," I drawled. "Why the cloak and dagger act?"

Neit scrubbed a hand over his face and shook his head. "Shit has gotten weird." He rose and started pacing. "I assume you're here to see Caelan. He won't allow anyone on his property, and I don't have the heart to tear his wards down."

Neit said the words without judgment. Guilt flooded me just the same.

Rowan's hand landed gently on my shoulder. "Caelan's actions warranted this retaliation."

He didn't have to say ours, but his claiming of my punishment only reinforced how different relationships can be when you allow yourself to truly trust.

Neit held his hands out. "We all know what Caelan did. You'll find no judgment from us."

A sly look flashed over his face. "Some of us wonder if the punishment fit the crime. We have a betting pool for how soon your father will kill him."

"You will all lose. I don't want him dead." Dad was furious when he realized the extent of Caelan's damage to my psyche and would have delighted in taking Caelan's life if I had allowed him to.

If Caelan had been a bad person, I might have let him. But I wasn't in the business of being in serious relationships with bad people. Even my ex-husband wasn't a bad person in the strictest sense of the word. Yes, he cheated. Yes, he kinda sucked. Was he a murderer or physically abusive? No.

He was just an asshole.

But even assholes could leave lasting damage.

Caelan had been a bit more than just an asshole. He'd come close to destroying me. With trust, patience, and love, Rowan had rebuilt my inner sanctum brick by brick. To Caelan, our mating and marriage must have seemed fast.

Hell, it was. But if he could feel what I feel when I look at Rowan, when I feel him inside that knot deep in my heart, he would realize I was helpless to resist committing the rest of my life to him.

"He's redeemable," I said when the silence had gone on too long. "Or at least I hope he is."

"And if he's not?" Neit asked quietly.

"Then I'll kill him myself."

Rowan's hand tightened. Guess I should have said as long as Rowan doesn't get there first.

"Why are we here?" Garrett asked.

Moira had remained suspiciously quiet since we'd arrived. I glanced over to see her sitting cross-legged on the ground, her face tilted up to the sky. Her eyes were closed, and a faint silver and violet glow surrounded her.

I'd never seen its like before. Rowan and I exchanged a concerned glance.

"I'm fine," Moira drawled. "I can feel your eyeballs on me."

"You're glowing," I observed helpfully. "Is this a new thing?"

She cracked an eye open. "New enough."

Neit's sharp gaze lingered on her. "When were you touched by the gods, vampire?"

Moira's lips thinned. "A couple of times."

I hid my wince. Moira and Ash were both present on Caelan's Keep land when fae and Chimera magic were flying all over the place. While Ash seemed to have escaped unscathed, Moira had suffered some unfortunate side effects.

Several months ago, she was manipulated into pulling a god through worlds—an event that had caused no lack of headaches for us.

Moira refused to talk about what was going on with her and assured me she had it all under control. Dad remained tight-lipped as well. Mom stayed out of everyone's business, for the most part.

I had moderate success, but this was business I wanted to be in because it involved Moira. "Does the glow have a purpose?"

She lifted a thin shoulder. "I sense things."

Moira rose and dusted her hands off. "We're quite alone in

these woods. No trace of shifters or gods." She eyed Neit. "Unusual since we're close to Caelan's lands."

"I cannot give you any information on Keep movements. I've tried my best to give the Lord space." His eyes landed on my face and slid away. "He is not in the right frame of mind to be of assistance right now and could do more harm than good."

"Where are the gods then? This is why you dragged us here, isn't it?"

Neit nodded. "You sealed off Keep property, which might have saved Caelan's life."

I stilled.

"The rest of Joy Springs has fallen to fickle gods."

"Who?" Rowan asked.

"Danu, for one."

At my grimace, Neit nodded. "Yes. After your refusal to take her place, she came here almost immediately and broke Caelan's wards."

A faint smile tipped his lips. "But the old bitch couldn't set foot on his lands because of how you marked them." He chuckled. "No idea how you managed it, but Danu tore up a good portion of the forest close to his property during her tantrum."

I closed my eyes and let out a breath of relief. If Danu had killed him over my refusal to be her retirement plan, I would never forgive myself.

"Who else?" I croaked.

His lips thinned. "I haven't seen anyone else, but I know there's at least one more here. I think it's Titania."

I blinked as dread filled my stomach. Titania had worked with the Lords to stab me in the back when I was away from my lands for a forced meeting with the fae. That bitch was the main reason I'd been trapped in the world tree for months. "She's dead." I'd killed her myself. She'd exploded into ash while I watched.

Neit nodded. "Supposed to be, but gods have a pesky way of surviving the unsurvivable sometimes."

"If she's alive, we'll delight in ensuring she stays dead this time," Garrett growled.

Moira stood by my side. She entwined our fingers together and said nothing, a stalwart and steady presence.

"What do they want with this place?" I couldn't figure it out. Joy Springs wasn't much. The town wasn't close to any major hubs or industry. Wine country was here, but what did the fae care about wine?

Neit shook his head. "It's not Joy Springs. They want it because it belongs to a Lord. Some fae never supported withdrawing from this realm. They believe we have the only rights to the earth and all the other dimensions, and everyone else is an interloper."

"Taking it from a Lord proves the fae are more powerful and sends a message to those who may want to fight back," Garrett said. He swore under his breath. "Caelan long suspected the fae were plotting against him."

"Not just him," Neit said. "Every Lord should be on their guard. The blight on their lands was only Danu's first move. She is ancient and knows how to play the long game.

"So chess, not checkers," Rowan said.

"Exactly," Neit agreed.

"Why exactly are you here?" Moira said. "I don't understand your dog in this fight, or if you have one at all."

His eyes flashed. "When I first came here, I was searching for Cliona."

Neit's lips twitched. "When she proved…elusive, I spent some time getting to know this place." He held out his hands. "There is much charm in this world and many beautiful things to see. While your world is not without its issues—"

Moira and I grimaced at the same time, making Neit laugh.

"I believe it is worth saving. I do not wish to be a usurper, even by association." He pinned me with his strange, violet-flecked dark eyes. "You've proven you can stand against her, Evie.

And I fear we must do so once again. Danu must be driven from this realm."

"And Titania?" I asked.

His teeth flashed in disgust. "Titania is a simpering fool. She is attracted to power and will follow such wherever it pops up. If you banish Danu, Titania will prove no challenge. She has no real use to us."

"Harsh," Moira remarked.

"True," Neit said. "Titania holds power, but hers is nothing compared to yours. She wanted to replace Danu, but Titania could not hold more than one land at a time. Her powers function in a similar way to yours, but she cannot control the earth, only small portions."

I shook my head. "I cannot either. While my power has grown, I am not up to my mother or father's level yet."

Neit's eyes glimmered with amusement. "We both know that's not true. Just ask the Lord when you see him."

He looked at Rowan. "You will have my sword as long as you need to reclaim this place and banish the gods. May I visit your territory when I have need?"

"Guest rights," Rowan said with a nod. "Harm no one and we shall do the same."

Neit touched his chest. "On my honor." With a nod to the rest of us, he disappeared in a shimmer of violet light.

"Well, fuck," I said.

CHAPTER
Ten

"Does anyone have a plan?" Moira asked during the walk to Caelan's.

Garrett cracked a laugh. "I do believe this might be the first time you've ever asked that question."

Rowan snickered. I swatted at him, but I couldn't help laughing either.

Moira snorted. "Assholes, the bunch of you."

"I plan to talk to him. That's all. Caelan has a way of escalating things, so we'll see where it goes."

"I always told him he had a natural talent for starting shit," Garrett said. A tinge of sadness colored his voice.

The separation had been harder on him than Simone. When the Omega realized how Caelan was treating me, she was ready to bolt immediately. Garrett took longer to come around, but he had, and that was the most important thing. He'd tried to help Caelan, and Caelan had refused both the help and Garrett's advice. When I almost died over Caelan's actions, Garrett had walked away with Simone by his side.

"You don't have to go if this is too difficult," I said quietly.

Garrett shot me a look. "I won't back down from a fight if it comes to that. My loyalty is to you and Rowan. Caelan was my friend, but some relationships aren't meant to last. They're meant to be lessons."

Unfortunately, I understood what he meant far more than others might. I'd had a lot of those "lessons" in my life, many by Caelan's hands. I reached over and touched his bicep. "Thank you, Garrett. I mean it."

His eyes softened. "Of course."

We kept walking for a bit before Garrett said, "Simone doesn't want to ask you because she knows things are heating up again, but you made some granola a few weeks ago and she ate the entire batch in less than a day."

Moira cackled. "She'd be mortified if she knew you told us that."

Garrett grinned. "I caught her in the corner of the dorm's kitchen, shoving a palm full in her mouth."

Rowan let out a loud laugh. "What happens in Joy Springs stays in Joy Springs. We'll keep that secret between us."

"I'll make her a huge batch when I get back," I promised. Everyone loved that granola. Two other shifters had come to the back door a few days ago asking if I had any more. I'd planned to make more before Caelan sent one of his people to us. Guess I needed to move up the timeline.

Moira cleared her throat. "If I did anything with the shop, I bet you could sell it there. If you wanted to."

Opening her own tea place had always been on her list, but she felt like she was betraying me. But this wasn't a job. This was ownership. Rowan knew Moira had valuable skills and wouldn't be content with only being an employee. I wouldn't be surprised if he'd made room for her to open up a business and made her think it was all her idea.

I reached for Rowan's hand and entwined our fingers. "You should do it."

Moira blinked. "Do what?"

"Open up the tea shop. You're good at it. You love tea. Your brews are wonderful. I think it will be a hit."

Moira frowned. "What about your shop?"

"That's the thing. It's my shop, but it's never been your dream. You still hold ownership. Keep it, sell it back to me, whatever you want. I can hire someone else to help out. I want you to be happy, and however you make that happen is good with me."

Tears shimmered in her dark eyes. "I—are you sure?"

"Of course." I stopped walking and held out a hand to stop her. "This is what we've worked for."

We stayed together because safety came in numbers, and it worked for a while. Until Caelan blew into my life like a summer storm.

"All those years we spent trying to be safe finally paid off. We're safe now, Moira. Don't hold yourself back because you're worried about me. It's time for you to spread your wings."

She yanked me into a rib-bruising hug. "I love you."

"Ditto," I squeaked.

"I'm still not moving," she said stubbornly.

"I hope you don't." I tugged a strand of her dark hair. "But if you do, I hope it's for a spectacular reason."

She grunted. "Enough sappiness. Someone or something is watching us. Best not poke the bear until we have to."

Moira rubbed her hands over her arms. "This place gives me the creeps now."

I agreed. "We still haven't seen anyone," I whispered.

"I don't smell anyone. The place feels abandoned."

"They're here," Rowan said. "Few would abandon their livelihoods if there was a chance the danger would pass. I can only assume they're hunkering down at home."

"Let's hope," I muttered.

We walked in silence for a while until the Keep came into full view. My heart did a painful stutter, and I stopped in my tracks. Rowan slipped an arm around my waist.

"Steady," he murmured. "He can't hurt you now."

Untrue, but I appreciated the thought. "Do you think I'm here for anything positive?"

Rowan paused and appeared to think about it. "No," he said eventually. "Caelan is a stubborn bastard."

"Yeah," I agreed.

He tugged me to him, sliding a warm hand through my hair to cup the back of my neck. Rowan tilted my chin up and bent to look into my eyes.

His were more green than gold today, a ring of our shared bond outlining his iris. "Remember who you are, Evie, and remember that you are mine, and I am yours. Remember who tried to take that away from you. Know you are far more powerful than he could ever be, but also know Caelan is flawed and part of him is human. He is wounded and hurting, and wounded animals often lash out at the people who can help them."

I swallowed hard. "And if he tries to hurt me?"

His eyes flashed with vivid color. "Then you take that mother-fucker down."

I framed his face in my hands and brought him in for a scorching kiss. "I won't be long."

Rowan nodded and turned to Garrett and Moira. "Evie can take care of herself. You are her last line of defense if something goes awry."

A ring of gold encircled Garrett's irises. He nodded.

Moira's incisors flashed down with a quiet snick. "Ready."

We turned and headed toward the Keep grounds.

Someone I'd never seen before greeted us. He, like many shifters, was tall and lean, but from the way his emotions bristled against my finer senses, his animal rode him harder than most.

His hair was a soft brown, cut into a severe buzz with scalp showing. A hard jaw and ice blue eyes highlighted a harsh face that wasn't quite handsome. This shifter was a killer. His eyes widened slightly when he spotted me, almost like he couldn't believe I was the one who'd done this to their Lord.

His lips tightened with distaste. "Are you Evie?"

I nodded. "This is Moira and Garrett."

The shifter snorted. "I know the traitor."

Words meant to incite, but Garrett had dealt with shifters like this for years now. "Hello, Schute. Nice to see you again."

Schute snorted. "Wish I could say the same."

Garrett grinned, genuine amusement on his face. "How many of Caelan's people did you have to kill to get my position?"

Schute's face turned to granite.

Garrett chuckled. "Just as I thought. Take us to the Lord. Evie has graciously agreed to meet with him, but she does not have much time to spare. The sooner we get this over with, the sooner she can return to her Keep."

Schute let out a disgusted snort. "And whore herself out to her new Lord?"

One moment Schute was standing. The next, he was motionless on the ground, his throat and stomach laid open, and his eyes staring blankly at the sky.

Moira choked.

I swallowed hard and let out an unsteady breath. I hadn't even seen Garrett move.

Gods.

"Um," Moira said shakily. "Holy shit, dude."

"Power is a gift, Evie. He was a waste of space and bad for Caelan's rule. I did that prick a favor." Without a backward glance at Schute's body, Garrett continued forward, his stride relaxed and confident.

Moira and I looked at each other for a long moment. "That was both terrifying and super hot," she whispered. "My lady bits are on fire."

"Did you see him move?"

Moira shook her head. "I should have, but—"

"Ladies," Garrett drawled. "We don't have all day."

Moira fanned herself. "Man. First choice for my upcoming man harem."

I covered my mouth to hide my smile. "Thalia might fight you."

Moira snorted. "I don't think your sister cares much about anything these days."

She wasn't wrong, but Garrett was quite besotted with Thalia, even as my sister wasn't all that besotted with him. For a while, things seemed to be going well between them. Over the last few months, though, Thalia had regressed.

Garrett hadn't said a word, but no one missed the fine tension riding his shoulders these days. My Second or whatever Garrett was to me these days cleared his throat.

We scurried after him. "If you do," I whispered under my breath, "I want to know."

Moira wiggled her eyebrows at me. "Martini and gossip night?"

"As long as we don't get into another arm-wrestling contest."

"Party pooper."

"Stop yapping," Garrett hissed. "At least try to pretend like we have our shit together, okay?"

"We've never been very good liars," Moira drawled.

"For fuck's sake," Garrett said under his breath. "Did you bring her for a reason?" he asked me.

"I have very sharp claws and an even sharper tongue," Moira said with a smile.

Caelan's wards shimmered. A small opening appeared. Garrett walked through without stopping.

"Confidence," he said quietly. "You're the predator here, Evie."

I straightened my shoulders and followed behind, Moira at my heels.

Here goes nothing…

Eleven

He stood in the doorway, a storm in human form. His eyes held the warm molten gold color of alchemy. The Lord wore jeans today, a lighter wash, the waistband frayed with age. He wore a short sleeve t-shirt, powerful biceps bulging against the cotton. Unlike Emberwood, where the mornings were usually chilly and required at least a light sweater, a Joy Springs summer took no prisoners. Even with the cloud cover, the day was scorching hot.

Even with the mate bond warm inside my heart and Rowan waiting half a mile away, I wasn't blind. Caelan was beautiful. He always had been, and even with shadows resting heavy on his face, today was no exception. Grief at what might have been punched me in the solar plexus.

Once upon a time, I imagined a life with him. I thought we would grow old together, have children, and live a life of maybe not complete peace, but enough for us to remain happy, and comfortable. He'd been my everything, and I thought I was his.

But that fickle bitch doubt had crept into Caelan's psyche. And doubt allowed a worm of dark magic to wriggle its way in, and that worm had destroyed us.

Golden warmth crept into my heart, Rowan sensing my

distress. Love swept through my entire body, his presence surrounding me, even from a distance.

I dragged in a breath. Another. One more.

Our gazes locked, Caelan's burnished gold, and mine the multi-colored whirl of my mixed heritage. Light flared in the space between us.

Blood thundered in my ears. Heat roared through my veins. My fists clenched.

I didn't love Caelan. Not anymore. Not like I did. But I still cared for him. I cared about what happened to him.

And I cared that we had torn ourselves apart over pride and power.

My lower lip trembled.

Moira brushed her fingers over my back. "I'll give you a moment."

She jerked her head at Garrett. His jaw tightened, but he gave her a sharp nod. They walked several feet back and waited.

I opened my mouth to speak, but the words wouldn't come. There was so much I wanted to say, and yet, every time I tried before, Caelan would slap me down, shred my self-confidence, and the words would dry up.

He took a step outside the main house, his eyes still glowing.

My feet were rooted to the spot. I swallowed hard and watched him approach.

When he stood less than three feet away, he stopped. "Evie."

"Caelan." My voice cracked.

His gaze dropped to the spot in my chest where the mating bond rested. His eyes flared before he dragged them back to my face. At first, his face went completely blank, but then he sighed and tilted his head to the sky.

A tear welled at the corner of his eye. "Well," he said, his voice a low rumble in the silence, "I've really fucked this up, haven't I?"

I couldn't say anything. He had. He really had. And now it was too late.

Another held my heart.

"I would have loved you forever," I whispered. I'd said this to him before, but he'd always dismissed me, tossed my words aside like they were nothing.

This time, Caelan's jaw tightened. His nostrils flared and he nodded once, a sharp slice through the air. "I know. That's what makes this all feel so much worse."

He exhaled. "I was so angry, Evie. I had all these things I wanted to say—vicious, terrible things. But when I saw you walk through those wards—" He cut himself off and ran a hand through his hair.

"When you walked through, shining and happy, that mating bond a beacon to every shifter within a mile, all those words dried up in my throat, and I felt…" He exhaled. "A horrific sense of loss. Something I'm not sure I'll ever recover from."

We both expected for this meeting to end in a brawl, and part of wondered if we would both walk away at the end of this, but I had not expected this raw honesty from him.

Sometimes, events in your life burned a path right through your soul and nothing you did would make the wound heal. That was Caelan for me. Our relationship had been a meteor streaking through a starless sky—there one moment and burned out the next, only a lump of ash left when it was all over. He would always remain in my heart. I was not the type of woman who stopped caring about someone I'd loved as much as him.

But things were different now. And from the sadness in his eyes and the tightness in his jaw, Caelan realized it as well. There was no going back for us.

"I won't apologize for Rowan." My voice was rough and husky. "I did not plan for him and made no preparations for what happened between us."

Caelan's eyes burned with gold.

"He was my friend first and as much as I resisted what came after, I was as helpless to resist as the moon's call to gravity."

He swallowed hard. "Few resist a mating bond," he gritted out. "But yours isn't just a mating bond, is it, Evie?" His teeth flashed. "Leave it up to you two to forge something never seen before."

The sadness in his words felt like a knife to my heart. Revealing Rowan was my fae mate as well would hint at something other in Rowan's heritage. Not my secret to tell, so I merely smiled. "Perhaps Chimera have their own form of bond, too."

He took my words at face value. "As you can see, no mate has come to save me from myself." Caelan swept his hands out across his property. "We've had no visitors except for the goddess who wanted to tear my heart out. But we have had an exodus of people." His jaw tightened. "And I suppose I should scratch another's name off my list as my new Second hasn't returned and I no longer feel him through the bond."

I winced. "He insulted the wrong person at the wrong time." Not an apology, but an admission. We were well within our rights to answer such an assault with death, though I would have preferred to handle the slight another way. Garrett did not leave me time to process a thought, much less a new punishment.

Caelan sighed. "Unsurprising. Schute was an asshole." His gaze flicked over my shoulder. "Garrett's doing?"

He already knew the answer. "He moves like lightning."

Caelan nodded. "I've never seen anyone faster, not even with the Lords. I am surprised he stays with you when he could be Lord of his own territory."

A scoff from behind. I had to catch myself from rolling my eyes. Of course they could hear us.

"I'd rather wash my balls with a hornet's nest," Garrett drawled.

"Well," Caelan said dryly, "our meetings feel like that sometimes, so the pain level is about the same if you want to think about it and let me know."

That got an amused snort out of Garrett. "You're still an asshole, Caelan."

The Lord sighed. "Yeah. I'm well aware of how everyone views me right now."

Garrett came up behind me so silently, I jerked in surprise. "Dammit, Garrett," I hissed.

He flashed me a grin. "You're down about forty percent?"

Caelan's jaw tightened. "Forty seven. Mass exodus after the land lock."

Garrett let out a low whistle. "Men or women?"

"I shouldn't be telling you any of this, asshole."

Garrett shrugged. "Then don't."

Caelan stared at his former Enforcer for a long moment. "All the female shifters left. Their mates and significant others followed. All the shifters under the age of twenty-five vacated. The rest left once they saw the writing on the wall."

Garrett slowly shook his head. "Fuck man."

"Yeah." Caelan jerked his head toward the Keep. "Come inside. There's lemonade and lunch if you want it."

"Your cook didn't leave?"

"Nah. For some reason, he still likes me."

I looked at Garrett who watched Caelan's back for a beat. He nodded. "Safe enough," he said under his breath when Caelan was far away enough. "I think, Miss Evie, you've beaten him down long and hard enough for him to finally realize what a raging dickhead he's been."

"Umm," I said. "I'm not sure if that's good?"

"It's excellent," Garrett said as he started for the door.

Shaking my head, I glanced back to see Moira walking toward me. "Seems like everything went okay."

I felt nonplussed. "I think so?" Nothing about this meeting was normal. Was Garrett right? Had I beaten Caelan down so much he just gave up and decided to think like a rational adult and realize very little of this had been my fault?

She snorted. "Are you going to remove your grip on his land?"

I slowly shook my head. "Right now, it's the only thing keeping him safe from Danu. But maybe I can allow him to leave his property."

"Baby steps," Moira mused. "I like it."

Garrett turned and waited for us. "You two move like elderly people."

"Piss off," Moira said cheerily, linking our arms together as she smiled at him.

Garrett's eyes narrowed, but his lips twitched too.

The changing dynamic between these two had me a little worried. Both belonged to my "court" or whatever the hell I was supposed to have as the fae queen, and I planned to get rid of neither of them unless they wanted to be let go. Any complications arising between them had the potential to disrupt a good thing.

But...I stifled my sigh. They were two consenting adults, and if the tension beginning to simmer between them had any legs, I'd do well to keep my nose out of it. I'd gotten a mate and a husband out of my own drama.

No need to complicate theirs. They'd figure it out, for good or ill.

That's all I could ask for.

CHAPTER
Twelve

ROWAN

Letting Evie walk into Caelan's territory was one of the most difficult things I'd ever done, but they both needed closure, however it might come. I stood at the edge of the Keep property, the bag over my shoulders slowly starting to twitch.

I opened the bag an inch or two and peered in. Seymour was just beginning to stir, the effects of Caelan's magic wearing off. The flytrap had gotten so worked up when he thought we were going to see Caelan, he became impossible to deal with.

When he bit Cernunnos twenty minutes before the trip, the god had lifted one eyebrow at the plant, and Seymour had shrunk in on himself in terror.

Without a word, Cernunnos flicked a finger at him, and Seymour had stiffened and clunked right over, unconscious to the world.

"Don't tell Evie," he said with a wince.

"I don't think she remembered she wanted to bring him," I'd said. "She's dealing with deep feelings about this trip and is wrapped in her own thoughts."

Evie's dad and I had carefully nestled a bed of soft towels in a canvas bag and laid Seymour down inside.

"How long will he be out?"

"At least two hours," Cernunnos said. "He's lucky I didn't knock him out the rest of the day. The little bastard needs to realize he can't express his feelings by biting."

I'd almost laughed at Cernunnos' complete disbelief at Seymour's behavior. But he was right. Seymour couldn't act like an asshole and get away with it. In some ways, the flytrap was like a teenage shifter, all rage and hormones.

And when Evie had come out of the restroom, she hadn't remembered to take Seymour with us, which was unlike her. She'd remember him by the end of the trip and would regret not having him with her, which was the reason I'd put him in the canvas bag in the first place. At least I could do one good thing here, instead of just waiting for my wife to come back from visiting her ex-fiancé and hope we were still fine.

Disgusted with myself, I shook those thoughts away. Evie and I were mates. But even more than that, she wouldn't rekindle a relationship with a male who'd treated her like less than the dirt under his shoe. My wife was smarter than that.

Even I couldn't argue they both needed closure. Evie needed to realize she was more than the sum of her failures, even if the breakdown between her and Caelan was never her fault, and Caelan needed to realize Evie was no longer on the board of the game he was playing.

This would be their final goodbye, whether they realized so or not. Once we left Caelan's property and dealt with the god threat, I planned to start the long process of retiring. Finding someone to step into my shoes had been difficult, but recently I realized I had a pretty good candidate. I was still watching, though, waiting for the right time to approach.

Once I felt like I could hand the territory over, I would, though the Keep property could prove difficult to figure out as I owned it, not only as a Lord, but personally. The land belonged to me by right of might but also by law.

When everything was said and done, I planned to follow Evie wherever she wanted to go, and if she stayed in Emberwood, I'd happily stay there, too. Eventually, we'd have to take up more duties around the fae crown, but since Cernunnos and Cliona seemed just fine running things, Evie and I had decided to stay out of it. Neither of us wanted a crown.

We only wanted each other.

The bag squeaked, Seymour's displeasure at his predicament toned way down after Cernunnos got a hold of him.

"Bite me and I'll have grandpa knock you out for a week," I said to the bag.

Seymour piped down and went still.

My cell went off, the familiar notes of *Wildflowers* playing. I'd changed the ringtone once Evie had come to the Keep, and I never tired of hearing the song when she texted me.

I forgot Seymour, she'd written, along with an ugh emoji.

I opened the bag, wiggled my finger at Seymour, and snapped a picture of him lying there looking dejected. Once the bag was zipped, I sent the picture to Evie.

IS HE DEAD?

No! Just grumpy.

I paused before sending another message. *How's it going?*

Caelan is serving tea. I'm in the Twilight Zone.

I blinked. Tea? Shaking my head, I sent her one more. *Finishing up soon?*

He asked us to eat lunch. I'll discuss the issue Mom told us about in a minute. Half an hour?

I gritted my teeth. Every second she spent in his presence made me want to scream.

I can feel your irritation from here. This had to be done. It's almost over.

Sometimes I forgot how sensitive the mating bond could be. Come back to me, Evie, I thought, even knowing it was silly.

Love you, she texted before falling silent.

I love you more, I wrote before tucking my phone back into my pocket and sinking to the ground to wait for my mate to finish lunch with her ex-fiancé.

Thirteen

We finished a lunch of chicken salad on buttery croissants and peppery potato chips. The cook had made a wonderful lavender lemonade I begged Caelan to get me the recipe for and topped everything off with a light but airy lemon mousse.

Garrett spoke before I could broach the subject. "Have you sent scouts out lately?"

Caelan nodded. "I'm well aware that Joy Springs is a ghost town."

"Do you know why?" I asked.

Caelan glanced at me. "Rumors are the gods have arrived, though my shifters have seen neither hide nor hair. I've only seen Danu once. She has not returned since her failure to render me to dust."

"Neit is here."

The Lord nodded. "Is he the one responsible?"

"No. He's been here gathering intel, though he's been mostly unsuccessful. Neit suspects Titania and Danu are both here."

"What does Joy Springs have that they cannot find somewhere else?"

"Two things," I said apologetically. "Me. And land held by a Lord."

Caelan locked eyes with Garrett. "My paranoia was not so crazy now, was it?"

Garrett shrugged. "Never said you were crazy, only that Evie was the reason they were here. We were both partially right, so let's call it a draw."

"They want to take Joy Springs and all my land." His brow furrowed, and I saw the second realization dawned in his eyes. "Your land seizure is preventing them from taking what they want."

He slowly shook his head and let out a belly laugh. "I'll be damned. The one thing you ever did to punish me is saving my life. Karma really is a bitch sometimes, isn't it?"

I stayed silent, but Moira grinned. "If Evie drops her hold, Danu and Titania would be on you in an instant."

"They're lying in wait like spiders," Caelan mused. "Can we turn this around on them somehow?"

Garrett's eyes warmed. "There you are," he said with a decisive nod. "Glad to have you back. At least for a moment."

Caelan's eyes glittered, but he didn't spar with Garrett. "Is there a way to get them out of the way permanently?"

"Gods are notoriously hard to kill," I said. "We thought Titania was dead, and here she is popping up again like a bad penny. But I am still the gate. A bad gate, yes, but a gate nonetheless. The more powerful gods can travel without the gates, but maybe there's a way we can rip that power from them."

Caelan's face turned thoughtful. "You think it's possible?"

"No Idea," I said honestly. "I was able to trap Lugh, but it wasn't easy. He's still there as far as I know, unable to return home."

"If we can take the power from them, we can put them somewhere they won't bother anyone else."

"Danu will be more difficult than Titania. She's ancient, probably close to Mom in power level, if not Dad. I'm not sure if I can keep her trapped forever."

"You're more powerful," Moira said matter-of-factly.

I snorted. "Your faith in me is heartwarming, but I'm not sure that's true."

Moira rolled her eyes. "The evening your father ripped that lock off you, Seattle registered a series of small earthquakes."

I stared at her, my mind going blank for a moment. "Seattle has mini earthquakes all the time. Something to do with a fault line or something." Earthquakes and weather never interested me all that much. I was careful to avoid tender spots under the earth's surface when communing with the land, but I rarely paid attention to such things unless they made the news and I happened to be sitting in front of the television. Even then, I never thought too much about them. Sometimes the earth shifted. Balance had to be restored. Nature always took what it needed, so there was no reason for me to investigate natural phenomena unless it turned unnatural.

"Yes," Moira said patiently, "but what are the odds of those earthquakes happening at the same exact time your father was reaching down into the earth to pull you back up? The second he ripped that lock from you, power erupted through the world."

Garrett's brow furrowed. "When were you going to say something?"

Moria studied her nails. "I can't help none of you pay attention to anything but your muscles in your bathroom mirror."

Garrett let out a surprised bark of laughter. "Well, vampire, we were all a little busy at that moment."

Caelan leaned forward, his eyes intent on Moira. "You think Evie would win if she went head to head with Danu?"

Moira's eyes flashed crimson. "Evie always wins," she said simply.

Tears burned the backs of my eyes. Moira's faith in me had always been unshakeable. "That's not quite true," I said hoarsely.

My BFF scoffed. "Please. Even with your power dampened,

you managed to rip your way out of a magical tree that shot you straight into the space/time continuum and then murder said tree horribly, consuming its power. You took down your abuser and his boss, which were freaking Chimeras and almost impossible to kill. You went head to head with almost all of the Shifter Lords and walked out unscathed, and now we're sitting in one of those Lords' dining rooms having delicious lemon mousse. All the while, you have his property held in an iron grip and Caelan trapped like Rapunzel locked in a tower. Except there's no prince to save him. He was supposed to *be* the prince. But you found your own, didn't you? And now you're the fae queen."

Moira shrugged as if all that was in a day's work. "You'll figure it out and kick Danu's ass. As far as Titania, I'm sure Neit would help. Not to mention your Mom and Dad, and whoever else you can bring onto your shiny ship of sidekicks."

I held my breath and waited for Caelan's eruption. But when he didn't get angry at Moira's unflattering description, I started to wonder. Had the Lord truly turned over a new leaf?

That took us to new business. I put down my spoon and shifted. "Releasing my hold on your land will both help and harm you."

Caelan's attention turned to me, those stormy gray eyes lingering on my face. "How so?"

"Danu will have access to Keep property."

His lips thinned with displeasure. "And she'll show up here to kill me."

I made a back and forth gesture with my hand. "She may not have to. My grip on the land has prevented Danu's spell from multiplying. Once I release the Keep, her spell will pick up right where it left off."

Caelan let out a heavy breath and looked up at the ceiling. "And I was infected."

I gave him a sad smile. "There's a solution."

The Lord's jaw tightened. "And here I sat thinking we'd made so much progress today."

"It doesn't have to end," I said softly. "But it does require trust."

"You want to claim my land until the threat is over, just like you've done with the other Lords."

"Until Danu is neutralized, no one's land is safe." I smiled apologetically. "As soon as we figure out a solution, I plan to happily give everything back."

And that was a true statement. Everyone's land held a different signature. Ethan's was surprisingly calm and wild. Rowan's felt like home. Caelan's felt familiar but also sad, like the land mourned what had become of its steward.

I leaned forward. "You don't have to answer now. But I want you to think about all our dealings, all the times you had to trust me and ask yourself two questions. Have I ever betrayed you? And have I ever retaliated when I was not under direct threat?"

Caelan's eyes darkened. "And if my answer to your solution is no?"

I held my hands out. "Then I would say our business is concluded. I will release your land from the hold and let you deal with the fallout."

He leaned forward, too, and slid his palms forward, so close our hands were almost touching. Heat beat from his body. "You won't help me?"

His voice had turned seductive, cajoling. Before Rowan, a tone like that from him would have melted all my misgivings.

Moira let out a light snort. "She's only horny for Rowan, Lord."

Garrett choked. Caelan's eyes flared bright gold. His fists clenched, and he opened his mouth to speak.

Moira didn't pause and continued twisting the knife, as one's BFF did. "You lost your opportunity the moment Rowan carried her away from here, holding her in his arms like the princess she's always been."

My lips twitched. I was far from a princess, but the picture Moira painted must have been quite the sight.

"I've already apologized," Caelan snarled.

Moira grinned. "I know." She lifted a shoulder in a small shrug. "Just thought you should know, in case you had any doubt."

"Moira," I murmured.

Her eyes widened in fake innocence. My lips twitched, and I shook my head. She'd always been an instigator.

I stood. "Think about it. I'll stay close, but out of the city."

Moira and Garrett rose as well. "Let me know what you decide."

Caelan nodded.

I hesitated. "Can you walk me back to the border? I brought something for you."

Caelan's brow furrowed, and he didn't answer right away. He looked over at Garrett, who nodded.

"Fine." Caelan rose in a graceful motion and gestured for us to go first.

As tough as this was, it had gone better than expected. And I planned to keep my word. If Caelan refused my offer, I would drop my hold on his land and let him go it alone.

Even if it ended with his death.

Every step she took brought her closer to me. I took Seymour out of the bag and held the squirming flytrap in a tight grip. He vibrated with energy, sensing Caelan's powerful presence following his maker.

My wife came out of the shadows, Moira and Garrett beside her. Every time I saw her, my heart thundered, love for her roaring to the surface. She had no idea how much her presence had changed since her father had ripped off that lock. Evie walked through the world, and the world responded, tree limbs leaning toward her, grass swaying gently in the breeze. When her feet were bare and she walked the land, flowers bloomed under her skin.

A brilliant smile broke onto her face when she saw me. My heart thundered behind my ribs as I answered that smile. How was it possible to love someone so much it felt like your heart would stop beating without them?

Evie stepped to the right, allowing Caelan to come up beside her. Our eyes met first, a ring of gold circling his iris. Caelan would never forgive me for taking Evie from him.

But his anger was misplaced. I never took anything. A person wasn't something you took. Evie came to me of her own free will.

But I considered her mine now, and that wasn't something Caelan would ever forgive. He played for keeps, but he still couldn't take full responsibility for what he'd done to my wife.

Until he did, he and Evie would couldn't fully repair their relationship. Even if they came to some kind of peace, our friendship was over. We both knew it.

"Rowan," Caelan said, power rumbling through his voice.

"Caelan." I tilted my head.

His eyes flicked to the squirming bundle in my arms. Seymour, the little asshole, sank fangs he shouldn't have, right into my arm, and leaped toward Caelan.

I hissed and slapped a hand over the wound.

"Seymour!" Evie snapped in disapproval. "No biting!"

Caelan caught him in mid-air, laughing as he did. "Hey, little guy!"

Seymour bumped Caelan's chest with his main trap, an odd trilling noise coming from him. Hurt punched me through the bond, and it took a moment for me to realize it was Evie's.

She and I both knew Seymour wasn't coming home with us. Maybe the thought wasn't charitable, but I wondered if Evie could make another slightly less assholish, non-venomous version to replace him.

I liked Seymour, and he liked me, but neither one of us liked each other all the time.

Especially not today.

Evie frowned and came over, brushing her fingers over my wound. Soothing magic bubbled through my veins as the poison evaporated, thankfully before I lost control of all my limbs.

"Sorry," she murmured.

"You're getting better at that." I paused and lowered my voice while Caelan was still distracted. "Though I'd much rather you heal me while we're naked and buried in a hole."

Evie snorted.

Moira clicked her tongue. "Dirty boy," she murmured.

Garrett let out a long-suffering sigh.

"Is he coming home with me, or is this a pity visit?" Caelan asked a moment later.

I felt the spike of grief through the bond. "Up to Seymour," Evie said.

She held out her hand and gestured for Seymour to come. The flytrap hesitated for a split second before he leaped into her arms.

Evie tucked him close and stepped far enough away for no one to be able to hear her, leaving us standing there awkwardly. Caelan and I would never make small talk again.

He watched Evie closely, that ring of gold still surrounding his irises. "She looks good."

I blinked in surprise. My first instinct was to antagonize him because of what he'd done to Evie, but she would want me to let it go. I wouldn't, but I'd pretend to. At least for tonight.

"She does," I said quietly.

"She's happy."

I nodded. There was nothing else to say. Evie was happy. She was blooming away from this cursed place and its brooding leader.

Caelan's heavy sigh almost made me feel bad for him.

But he was a dick, and I'd stopped feeling sympathy for him the second he made Evie feel regret about who she was. I wasn't sad that he'd lost someone so amazing because I'd gained her through trust while Caelan had gained her through stubborn stalking.

"Do you feel good about yourself?" Caelan growled.

Garrett straightened, eyeing Caelan's posture and position. He'd step in if he needed to, but there was no need. I was well equipped to take care of myself.

"Are you fucking kidding?" I said quietly. "I feel amazing."

Garrett snorted. Moira tried unsuccessfully to cover her grin. She reached over and gripped my forearm, squeezing gently. Partly in warning, partly in approval.

"I scored a hot, powerful wife and a mate all in one."

"And the fae crown," Caelan mused. "And more territory than any other Lord has managed to attain during their reign."

"I'd walk away from everything this second if Evie demanded it."

Caelan scoffed. "You always were such a goodie two shoes."

The other Lord was spoiling for a fight. He wouldn't get it from me. "Power doesn't do anything for me except complicate my life. And now that I have Evie, she is far more important to me than anything I can acquire."

Caelan watched me for a long moment. "You truly love her."

"She's my mate."

His nostrils flared. "That doesn't always mean love."

Empathy burned inside me, even as I wanted to squash it down. Caelan had a lot to learn about love, about sacrifice and selflessness. "When you are blessed with a mate, you will feel something unlike anything you've ever known. If what I have with Evie isn't love, then love doesn't exist. What I feel for her is worth all the pain and all the heartache. All I can hope is you experience this feeling one day."

Caelan's eyes dragged back to Evie. "I did."

I shook my head. "No, Caelan. You loved her. In your own way. But a mate…"

There was no way to explain this to him. How could I tell him I'd tear out my own heart and hand it to her if she asked? "One day," I said again. "My only advice to you?" I smiled and let a little of my wife's shared magic out in my eyes. "Don't fuck it up this time."

CHAPTER

Fifteen

We left Seymour with Caelan. I had him in my arms ready to transport home, but his traps started to droop, and he kept looking Caelan's way. I finally gave up and walked him back, depositing him into Caelan's outstretched arms.

"I don't know how long he'll live or how much more he will evolve." The flytrap happily waved his traps at me, as if saying he didn't care even a little.

Caelan nestled Seymour in his arms. "Can I—" His gaze flicked to Rowan.

My mate nodded.

Caelan's jaw tightened. "Can I call if something goes wrong? Or if I have questions?"

This was so weird. A few months ago, Caelan wouldn't have hesitated. Had something happened when I stepped away from them? Had Rowan said something to him?

I cleared my throat. "Yes. Of course. You already know his diet and his preferred snacks. Seymour will let you know when he needs his pot changed."

"He's still venomous?"

Rowan winced. "Definitely. I think his venom is more potent

than before, so make sure to properly introduce him to new people. He's still reactive."

Caelan nodded. "You ready to go, Seymour?"

The flytrap waved his traps in the air and trilled. "Alright. I still have some of those good snacks."

Without a goodbye or a thank you, Caelan turned to go.

"I'll call you tomorrow," the Lord said as he walked away.

"Thank you!" Rowan called.

Caelan held up his middle finger and kept walking.

I sank against Rowan's side.

He wrapped an arm around my waist and turned his face into my hair. "Are you okay?"

"That sucked, but we all walked out alive."

"You would have walked out anyway," Rowan vowed.

All this faith everyone had in me was going to give me a complex. "We need a hotel," I said instead.

"I dunno," Rowan said thoughtfully, staring toward the wooded area. "We can get naked and I can chase you through the forest all night."

A delighted laugh broke from me. "As fun as that sounds, this forest technically belongs to Caelan."

Rowan grunted. "Doesn't have to."

I eyed him. "You little budding despot!"

He laughed. "I know. Our forest is better anyway."

Moira nudged me. "Your mom booked us a few rooms. She'll pick us up in a minute."

"Sounds good. I hope there's a place to eat around there."

Garrett nodded. "Several places."

Mom and Dad appeared in a gust of cool wind. "Everyone good?" she asked.

I nodded. "He'll call tomorrow and let us know what he wants to do."

Dad eyed Caelan's Keep. "Think he'll make the right decision?"

Rowan shrugged. "Considering who I'm standing with right now, I give it fifty-fifty odds."

Dad snorted. "True." He shook his head. "Gather hands so we can get out of here. There's something off about this place."

In an instant we were gone.

MY PHONE RANG a few hours later. Curled in bed with Rowan bingeing mindless tv, I almost didn't answer it until I remembered who might be calling. I snatched my cell from the nightstand.

Caelan's number was on the screen. I waved my phone at Rowan, who sat up and watched me. He'd hear everything we said once I answered.

"Already made your mind up?" I said by way of greeting.

A long pause on the line made my stomach tumble. "Caelan? Everything alright?"

His heavy sigh told me everything. "Don't do this. Please."

"I'm sorry, Evie. My answer is no."

"Caelan. You'll die. The moment I release my hold, Danu will know. The virus already lives in your blood. She won't have to do anything but wait. Don't let it end like this."

"You're already plotting my death, flower girl?" His low chuckle sent a pang of grief barreling through me. At one time, I'd lived for that sound. Even now, I was happy he could still laugh when he spoke to me.

But this was no laughing matter. "No. Never." I swallowed hard.

Rowan reached over and took my free hand, his thumb brushing over the back of my palm.

"You cannot beat her," I said softly. "Please let me heal you."

"And let you claim my land."

"Temporarily. That's all. Only for a little while. You know I'll give it back as soon as this is over."

"And I know you'll relinquish it if I ask you to now. Won't you,

Evie? Will you keep your promise to the man who almost destroyed you?"

I frowned and glanced at Rowan. His brow furrowed, and he shook his head at Caelan's choice of words.

"I—" If I went back on my word, I would break this fragile thread of trust growing between us. "Please, Caelan. I'm begging you."

"Will you keep your promise?" he asked again.

A tear slipped down my cheek. Silence stretched between us. Rowan gave me a sad smile. "Your call," he whispered.

Rowan would support me if I decided not to free Caelan, even if it was for the Lord's own good. But I couldn't live with myself if I did.

"You sonofabitch," I whispered. "You know I will."

"Good. When?"

I bowed my head. "I'll meet you in the morning. Eight good with you?"

"Eight it is," Caelan agreed.

I glanced at the clock. "You have nine hours to change your mind."

Caelan chuckled. "No dice, flower girl."

I squeezed my eyes shut. "We both know a lot of things can happen in a few hours."

We both fell silent for a moment.

"See you tomorrow, Evie."

I hung up before I could beg him again to reconsider. He wouldn't.

Even if it would save his life.

I woke up at six a.m. and checked my phone. No calls. No texts.

Caelan was still on the path of madness. Rowan sat on the edge of the bed watching my frantic pacing. "You can't change his mind."

"I'm aware," I all but growled.

Rowan scrubbed his hand over his jaw. "Are you sure you want to keep your promise?"

"No." I exhaled. "But I have to. The only reason the Lords have trusted me this far is because I've kept my word. I've claimed the least amount of territory possible and healed them all. No encroaching or trespassing. If I don't keep my promise to Caelan, it will destroy my credibility."

Rowan's lips thinned. He knew I was right. Caelan had effectively put me over a barrel. Denying his request would shatter any trust he or the other Lords had in me. Word would spread fast, and I'd find doing any business with them in the future difficult. Not to mention Rowan suffering due to his association with me.

Once again, Caelan was screwing me over. I sighed and sat on the edge of the bed, picking up my shoes as I settled next to Rowan. He put his hand on my thigh. "He's a survivor. All the Lords are."

"He can't fight the gods."

"I didn't say he'd do it alone." When I looked at him, he tugged a strand of my hair. "I can barely stand the guy, but I know you care about him."

At my raised eyebrow, he sighed. "I care, too. But he's still an asshole."

I snorted. "Agree with you there." My shoulders slumped. "I can't let him die, Rowan. Even after everything, he doesn't deserve that."

Rowan's jaw tightened. "I know, Evie." His fists clenched. "But every time I see that bastard, I want to punch him in his smug face. I think about the way he tore you down and how you looked when you woke up at my Keep. I could feel your broken heart even before we were mated."

I scooted closer and lay my head on his shoulder. "All of it brought me to you, Rowan. For that, I could never hate him."

We sat like that for a while until the hour grew late and we had to leave to meet Caelan.

I'd give him back his territory, but I never agreed to allowing him to die.

Sixteen

Caelan was waiting for me at the edge of Keep property. Moira and Garrett had gone back home. There was nothing more they could do, and Caelan couldn't risk killing me until I'd let go of his land.

I didn't think he'd kill me either way, but Rowan wasn't so sure. He stood close behind me.

"Only her," Caelan said, staring at my mate.

"Evie," Rowan warned.

I put my hand on his chest. "Safe passage, Caelan."

The Lord stared at me for a long moment before he snorted. "Once upon a time you never would have said that."

I held his gaze. Gold flickered around the edges of his irises. "Much has changed since then."

"Yes," he agreed, his gaze flicking to Rowan. "Indeed, it has."

Caelan looked back at me. "Are you happy, Evangeline?"

Rowan stepped forward, but I held my hand up. "You know the answer."

His gaze lingered on my face, snagged on my lips for too long of a moment, and dragged back to my eyes. "I do."

Caelan let out a heavy sigh, and he lifted his eyes to the sky. Rowan put his hand on my shoulder and gently squeezed. When

Caelan looked at me again, his expression was different. Less haunted.

In that moment, I thought he might have let me go.

Even though it took everything I had, I realized I had to do the same for him. I looked back at Rowan. Sadness glimmered in his eyes, but all he did was nod.

"I'll be back."

Rowan took a step back. "Take care of her."

Caelan stared Rowan down. "Come, Evie."

He held his hand out. I took it briefly as he opened his wards and let him go as soon as I was on Keep land. "I'm only going to ask you one more time. Are you sure?"

"Where do you need to be?"

I blew out a breath, unsurprised by his refusal. Slipping off my shoes, I buried my toes into the earth, feeling the sickness in the land buried deep below. My magic penetrated his land, concentrated at the center of Keep territory. I closed my eyes against the memories assailing me.

"Where the tree was would be best."

Caelan's eyes met mine. My time in that tree had opened my mind to all the possibilities in my life. My friends and the Lord had called me home, and I thought at that moment, Caelan would be it for me. If someone told me then I'd be here now, I never would have believed them.

I saw in his eyes he was remembering the same. When I'd come out of that tree, I received a second chance, and when Rowan carried me out of Joy Springs, I'd received what felt like a miracle.

He jerked his head. "Do you need anything to eat or drink?"

"We brought snacks."

Caelan tucked his hands into his pockets and nodded. We walked in silence for a while.

"I'm sorry things turned out the way they did."

I glanced at him. Sorry wasn't the right word for me. "Was it worth it?" I asked quietly.

Caelan's soft snort made me smile. "I burned my life down, lost most of my people, and alienated the only woman I've ever loved." His eyes crinkled at the edges, and I saw a flash of the old Caelan.

He looked away, his expression sobering. "No. If I could go back and do everything different—if I could be better, say the right things, I would."

He smiled. "But if I went back and did everything right, I would punish you, wouldn't I? I'd keep you from Rowan."

Back then, I had no idea Rowan was my mate or that he'd be so important to me in such a short amount of time. He was my friend, and that was all. Knowing what I knew now, the thought of being without him made my chest hurt. Caelan was right, but wrong at the same time. If he'd done everything different, we would still be together.

"None of it matters. We're here now, and all we can do is live in the now."

Any answer I gave him would hurt him. And we weren't here for answers.

"It's hard to live in the now when I'm trapped in stasis."

"For now. In a minute, I think your life will get very interesting soon."

Caelan chuckled. "And yet, you won't be here to participate in any shenanigans."

"I'm sure Moira will take up the slack."

We shared a grin, and something eased in my chest. The still empty space where the tree once stood came into view. But this time instead of grief, I felt a new beginning opening up inside me.

Caelan and I might never be friends, but our shared history ensured we understood each other. And even though he had some reasons to hate me, I felt confident Caelan and I would be okay eventually. At least enough for him to successfully work with Rowan again.

"I'll need you to sit beside me," I said as I settled myself into the bare spot where the trunk once stood. Caelan nodded and settled beside me, the deep wildness of his scent teasing my nose.

"I hate to ask this, but I'm going to need you to bare your chest."

Caelan blinked. "Excuse me?"

I snorted. "I need to remove the poison from the spear, and I need to do that at the same time I free your land."

"So you need bare skin."

I rolled my eyes at his suggestive tone. "I need bare skin."

His face creased in a wide grin. "Oh how I wish Rowan were close enough to witness this."

"Don't be an ass," I huffed. "Take off your shirt."

Caelan's eyes twinkled. "Oh the things you say to me, flower girl."

I wiggled my fingers in a come-on motion. "Don't make it weird."

"But you make it so easy." He wore a t-shirt today and slipped it over his head, tossing it to the ground beside him.

I averted my gaze. Caelan, like all the Lords, was a beautiful man, but it didn't feel right to ogle him anymore. I was a red-blooded woman, sort of, and I'd be blind not to appreciate his gods given assets, but the desire I once had for him was gone.

He still cut a stunning figure, though.

"Closer." I reached my hand out.

Caelan obliged, scooting closer until my palm rested against the place where I speared him.

"I didn't think you'd actually do it, you know."

I glanced at him. "Do what?"

"Stab me. Poison me." He snorted and threw his hand out to encompass his land. "Hold me hostage here."

He never knew me at all. I'd do anything to protect those I loved. And I would have done it for him if things had been different. "Mmm," I said noncommittally. "There are no limits to how far I'd go to protect my friends and family."

"And I'm no longer included in that."

Loaded question there. "Caelan."

I could say a million things, drive the knife in a thousand times, hurt him in a million ways, and it would do nothing to bridge this gap between us. At one time, I might have considered saying them. But I'd never been one to hurt someone on purpose. Not the way he'd done to me.

He looked away. "I can see the wheels turning in your brain. After all of this, why are you still kind to me?"

I laughed. "Poisoning and imprisoning you isn't exactly kind."

Caelan shrugged. "But it is deserved. Less than I deserve, actually. Rowan had every right to kill me. So did Ethan. And neither one of them did it because of you."

He wasn't wrong. Caelan had broken one of the Lords' fundamental laws. But death wasn't suffering. And I'd wanted him to suffer the way he made me suffer. I guess sometimes I did believe in an eye for an eye.

"You can still be my friend. Not like we were. Not with Rowan in the picture and this new life I've somehow managed to build. But if you're in trouble and you call, I will come for you. If that's what you want."

Caelan bowed his head for a long moment. When he spoke again, his voice was rough. "I do want that for us. And I will do the same for you."

He reached up and placed his hand over the one I held against his chest. "I will do my best not to betray your trust again." Caelan swallowed and held my gaze. "You've taught me a terrible lesson, Evangeline. One I will not soon forget."

My smile wobbled. "And you've taught me one as well." But unlike his, mine had led to a happiness I never thought possible.

Hot tears spilled from my eyes. "Are you ready?"

Caelan's eyes began to glow. "Yes."

I closed my eyes and sank my power into the earth.

CHAPTER
Seventeen

I'd finally gained enough control over my magic to not end up naked in a hole with my ex-boyfriend. Thank the gods for that.

Caelan's land snapped away from me the second I released my grip and settled with a reverberating sigh that shook the ground. The Lord shivered against my palm, feeling his freedom from the lock I'd put him around him for the last few months.

"Stay still," I warned, my hand still touching his bare skin. Concentrating on that spot where I'd speared him, I sent a tendril of my power through his skin, seeking to pinpoint almost every trace of my magic. True to the promise I'd made myself earlier, I took everything except the most microscopic dot of poison from Caelan's body. He might have made amends with me, but after everything that had happened, I was no longer willing to take everyone at their word.

Only a few people received that much grace from me.

He wouldn't feel it, and even the most adept magic wouldn't know either. My magic was biological in a way—made of life. Even if a mage scanned him, if it managed to pick anything up, the seed wouldn't show up as a foreign body.

Call it an insurance policy against future shenanigans. I'd

remove it eventually, but Caelan would have to prove himself a true friend by his actions. Trusting his word would take much more time.

When I finished, I pulled away and tucked my hands in my lap. Caelan opened his eyes, golden light flowing over the space between us. "How do you feel?" I asked.

"Lighter," he said gruffly.

The ground rumbled beneath us. I smiled sadly and came to my feet. "You're about to have company." Danu must be keeping tabs on Caelan's land and felt the moment I broke my spell.

Dad appeared in a flash of light, his concerned gaze taking in Caelan and me. "We must leave. Now."

Caelan got to his feet and dusted off the seat of his pants. He laid a hand over his heart. "Thank you."

Without giving me time to respond, Dad grabbed my hand. A disorienting lurch later, I stood with Rowan, Moira, Garrett, and Mom on the steps of the main Keep house in Emberwood.

"Dad!" I yanked my hand away. "You didn't let me say goodbye!"

Dad gave me a look that made Moira cover her mouth to hide her smile. "I know you can take care of yourself, but Caelan's foolishness does not concern you. Let him and Danu hash this out."

I gaped at my father. "I could have helped him!"

Dad's derisive snort made me blink. "Just like he helped you a few months ago?"

Rowan looked down at his feet and didn't say a word. *Et tu, Rowan?*

"We made peace with each other."

Rowan glanced at me, one of his eyebrows raised.

My Dad clicked his tongue. "And that seed of poison you left inside him, Evangeline? Doesn't seem very peaceful to me."

Dammit.

Mom's crack of laughter made Moira snicker. Even grumpy Garrett's lips twitched.

I crossed my arms over my chest. "An insurance policy."

Dad waved the words away. "You tried. We all know you did. Caelan is not a child, but this is another lesson he must learn. If he's too prideful to accept your help, then you must let the chips fall as they will."

"And if the gods claim his territory?" I asked.

Dad shrugged a powerful shoulder. "Then the Lord was not strong enough to keep it. Such is the way of kings and queens and gods and Lords. Since the dawn of time, this is how the game is played."

I knew he was right, but it was hard to accept. My feelings about this were all over the map. Caelan's death would devastate me because I would know I was the one who inadvertently caused it.

Rowan straightened and shook his head. "No. I can sense what you're thinking, and the answer is no. You'd be happily working away at your shop if he hadn't come in and upended your life. As much as I hate agreeing with your father—"

Dad rolled his eyes in such an exaggerated way I had to press my lips together to keep from laughing.

"He is right in this regard. Caelan has been a Lord for a long time. We've always had trouble with the fae pressing against our boundaries. Small tests here and there. Repelling them usually worked for a while. This would have happened with or without your involvement, so wipe that guilty expression off your face. Caelan has made his bed. If he seeks our help, I will let you decide what aid, if any, we provide. But until he does, I believe we should stay out of his business."

My lips thinned. Rowan was right too. What were the odds that not one but two men in my life were both right about something at the same time? Astronomically low, and yet here we were. Since when had I gotten myself involved with reasonable men?

Cats and dogs living together and all that...

"Fine," I snapped.

Rowan grinned, his eyes sparkling. He knew how much it was

killing me to defer to them. He snagged me around the waist and pressed a hot kiss into the crook of my shoulder. "You can punish me later," he murmured against my skin.

"On that note," Moira drawled, "I'm out!"

Garrett threw up his hands. "Me too!"

Mom and Dad stepped closer together. "We must be on our way as well. I trust you both are prepared for your visit to court in a week?" Mom asked.

I gave her a halfhearted shrug. "Sort of. Can I borrow a dress?"

Mom sighed. "Evie. Really." She rolled her eyes. "You still haven't touched your bank account?"

"It's not like I can roll into a department store and shop off the rack for a fae princess dress, Mom."

Mom's eyes narrowed, and she opened her mouth to probably yell, but Dad cleared his throat.

"I've hired a new tailor in my court," he said with a meaningful glance at Mom. "I will send her soon. She is also well equipped to defend herself if need be."

I frowned. "Why would a tailor need to defend herself when measuring me for a dress?"

Mom's eyes flashed a strange silver color. "Closure comes soon, Evangeline. Be prepared."

Just when I opened my mouth to ask what the hell she meant by that, Mom winked. "And, for the love of the gods, use that money to buy yourself a new wardrobe. You've been wearing the same things for months and you cannot show up to court in cashmere sweaters and jeans."

Mom and Dad disappeared in a flash of light.

"Since when did my friends and family become bullies?" I grumbled.

Rowan scooped me into his arms. "You get so grumpy when you're wrong about something."

I snorted and smacked him on the chest. "That's because I'm never wrong!"

Mora laughed out loud. "Are we still on for shopping tomorrow?"

I nodded and waved. "Let's go back to that jewelry place."

"Sold!" she called as she walked away.

Garrett gave us a two-fingered salute and headed the other way, leaving me and Rowan alone.

"Hungry?"

"Not for food."

Rowan's slow grin made my heart skip a beat. "Huh. Odd coincidence. I have a large supply of non-food in the bedroom. Would you like to see it?"

I tangled my fingers in his hair. "Always."

Someone was in my house. I froze with my hand two inches from the doorknob and sent a tendril of magic through the crack at the bottom of the door, dropping it as soon as the scent of the intruder hit my nose.

I swore under my breath and unlocked my door.

"Ethan. Godsdammit. What did I tell you about breaking into my house?"

The Lord sat on my couch, looking smug as hell. He held up the paperback I'd been reading, a smuttastic novel about a woman on the run from magical assassins.

One of his eyebrows rose. "Lots of quivering members in this one." He clicked his tongue. "This woman likes variety."

I wanted to choke him. "Yes, well, variety is the spice of life."

Ethan's lips twitched. "You like a lot of choices when it comes to members, Moira?"

I was a vampire hybrid hiding big secrets from everyone. What I liked was peace, quiet, and people minding their own business. I did not have time for any quivering members who wanted to linger.

I shrugged. "Depends on the quivering member."

Ethan chuckled, the sound tightening every muscle in my

body. He rarely laughed, and I felt inordinately pleased I could make him. It seemed like I made him laugh a lot, though the joke was usually at my expense.

"I'll remember that," he said softly, those midnight eyes pinning me in place.

I tossed my keys onto the kitchen island. "Why are you here, Ethan? And how the hell did you get through Rowan's wards?"

"Rowan has given me a temporary pass."

My eyebrows went up. Rowan wasn't the most trusting of Lords, and neither was Ethan. This temporary alliance they had going on surprised me. In fact, a lot about Ethan surprised me these days. When I first met him, I thought he was an asshole. He hadn't done much to change my mind, either, but everything had changed when I snuck into his territory.

I'd made a terrible mistake when I broke into his house all those months ago. The moment I did that, I realized Ethan was much more than he seemed. Every single one of the Lords was brutal and violent when they needed to be. But Ethan had an entire life before, a life where he seemed to be a different person.

A life that held love and laughter.

Time and grief had damaged him. His temples were edged in silver, a color almost unheard of in an immortal, and the edges of his eyes held the faintest of creases, as if the Lord used to laugh all the time and the memory had imprinted onto his skin and never let go—the last stubborn vestiges of the life he had before he became the hard vicious thing to sit before me today.

Except, he wasn't that man. Not all the time. And not right now in the incandescent light of my living room, sprawled on my couch like the room belonged to him.

I could give him no quarter. Ethan barely tolerated me, yet he kept coming around. I wasn't stupid enough to think it was for my cookies. The Lord wanted something from me—something he hadn't yet gotten around to asking me.

"You haven't answered my second question."

I shrugged off my jacket and slung it on the back of my recliner. "Do you want a martini?"

Ethan blinked. "Uh. What kind?"

"Whatever kind you want." I opened one of the upper cabinets and waved my hand around like a bikini girl on a game show. "I collect every liquor known to man."

Ethan frowned. "What kind are you having?"

"I made white chocolate macadamia cookies earlier. I thought I'd make a martini to match it."

I hid my smile when I turned to see Ethan closing his eyes for a moment. The Lord had a serious sweet tooth and tried his best to hide it from me. I looked away before he spotted my attention.

"Sure," he said after a moment. "Thank you."

I turned my back to him and gathered the bottles I needed. "Do you want a couple of cookies, too?"

"Yes," he said too quickly.

I grinned at the cabinet and reached over to turn the air fryer on. The cookies were excellent, if I did say so myself, but they were even better warmed and with crispy edges.

While he didn't move from his spot, Ethan still watched me intently as I made our drinks. When he saw me put on a pot holder and grab the cocktail shaker, he frowned. "What are you doing?"

"The shaker gets really cold and numbs my hand." I confessed. Sensitivity to the cold was a new and odd side effect of the magic exposure I'd received on Caelan's Keep. Most of the time I was fine, but when the temperatures went too low, I had to bundle up or suffer the consequences. Using the steel cocktail shaker with ice sent the temperature plummeting and my hand went numb when I used the thing now.

Ethan rose, his form smooth like water, and came over. He slid his hand over mine and extricated the shaker from my grip. Setting it down, he grasped my wrist and tugged the potholder off.

I stared up at him, entranced by how dark his eyes were and

how godsdamn sexy he was. My heart thumped in my ribcage, and I knew the bastard could hear it, but I didn't care.

Ethan slid his fingers down my wrist, his touch burning a trail of fire down my skin. "I'll do it."

He picked up the shaker and turned away like he hadn't just set my pants on fire.

I tucked my trembling fingers into my pockets. *Asshole.*

Twenty seconds later, Ethan poured the martinis into two chilled glasses and handed me one.

I had to admit. Having a shifter shake your cocktails sent the perfect amount of ice slivers into the drink and made it so damn cold my lips felt frozen after I took the first sip. I should trademark that idea and start a bar with only shifter bartenders. I'd call it The Tipsy Claw.

"How long?" Ethan demanded. He took a sip of the martini, blinked, and took another one. His brow furrowed.

"Good, right?"

Ethan grunted at my magical martinis. "How long have you experienced cold sensitivity?"

I shrugged. "A while now."

Ethan's lips thinned. "Moira."

"Since the night Evie killed Finn."

Ethan swore. "Why haven't you said anything?"

The Lord had brought me cashmere on a cold night not too long ago. He cared in a strange way, or maybe he was just kind. Ethan was a puzzle where none of the pieces fit.

"Why would I?"

The air fryer dinged. Sliding past him, I grabbed the potholder and took out the cookies, tapping them with my finger to make sure they were the perfect consistency.

"Those smell amazing," Ethan said grumpily.

I put four on a plate for him and slid them over.

Ethan looked at the cookies, then looked at my plate. "You only have two."

"I only want two." Sometimes I ate a lot, mostly when I used a lot of magic. I could always eat more than the average person, but I lived alone, and there was something unbearably sad about eating dinner with no one to share it with.

That adorable furrow in his brow wrinkled again. "You should eat more."

"I had some cookies this morning," I admitted.

Ethan hesitated to take one of the cookies.

"Eat. I'll have dinner later. This is a pre-dinner snack."

Ethan gave me a long look but took one of the cookies. His teeth were white and straight, and the way he closed his eyes when that white chocolate hit his taste buds…

I had to look away.

He'd already eaten two by the time I finished one. On his third, I poured the rest of the martini mix into our glasses, making sure it was even.

"You still haven't answered my question."

Ethan took a sip of his martini and watched me. "I want you to come to my territory for a little while."

The cookie piece fell from my hand and clattered to the plate. "Excuse me?"

A small flash of a smile. "You heard me, Moira."

I shook my head. "Why would I do that?"

He took a slow bite of his cookie. "I can think of a few reasons."

Talking to him was like pulling teeth sometimes. "Such as?"

"You make excellent cookies, and I don't have a chef."

My brows drew together. "You want me to bake for you?"

"You're intelligent and beautiful."

I blinked like an owl. "That's not really a reason," I choked.

Ethan shrugged. "It is to me."

"No." I shook my head slowly. "Those are adjectives." Ohmygod ohmygod. He thinks I'm pretty.

Ethan let out a soft laugh. He adjusted and leaned against the island. "Point to you. Alright. You're struggling with your magic and lying to Evie about it."

Every time I started to think the guy was sweet, he dropped a fucking bomb on my head. I stayed silent.

"I have a hybrid mage at my Keep," Ethan said softly. "Someone who might be able to help you manage whatever is happening to you."

My brain snagged on his words. I'd always had magic inside of me. Inherent power given to me by the vampire side, another strange vein of power given to me by what I thought was the fae —though I'd never been sure—and whatever else this was living in my veins that night of exposure.

The fae magic was warm and cozy, and I was convinced my baking and other similar skills were attributed to that power. My vampire powers were all the normal things one of our kind could do. I could run longer and faster than anyone I knew, even a shifter. Super strength and agility came next, followed by the ability to mesmerize, a talent I never used unless my life was in danger. But the other power—the one that allowed me to pull a god through dimensions, that was the one that scared the hell out of me.

I shoved a bite of cookie in my mouth and chewed while I thought of a response. The bastard knew I was tempted by his offer. I could see it in his eyes.

"And I could use your help."

Okay. Hell had officially frozen over. My first instinct was to feel flattered. My second was suspicion. "You're a Shifter Lord. You have access to more assets and information than I could ever dream of. What could I do that you can't do twice as well or four times as fast?"

Ethan's eyes flickered. "People like you."

I tilted my head. "I'm not sure that's true. People like Evie. They're a little frightened of me."

Ethan shook his head. "Disagree. Evie is likable, but most people are afraid of her on a cellular level. People, especially shifters, sense her otherness."

"And they don't sense that about me?"

Ethan's eyes slid over to the tin of cookies. Without asking, I slid the tin over and put three more cookies on his plate. His eyes lit up. "Your scent is mostly vampire. You work with herbs and spices and flowers almost all day, and you have for years. Those things entwine in your scent and hide things." A faint smile. "Though I suspect you know that."

I did. Frigging Ethan. "I like tea. And flowers. Sue me."

"Keep your secrets," he said with a shrug. "As long as they are not harmful to me or Rowan, I will never pry."

"Regardless, you are more familiar to them than Evie. People talk to you. They trust you."

"They don't trust you?"

"Like Evie, I'm afraid most people sense my otherness."

"What otherness?" I sensed something different about him, but I thought it was because of what he'd been through. Much like my herbs and flowers and tea, grief could entangle itself into one's scent for all time.

"If I let you keep your secrets, you will allow me mine."

His tone brooked no argument. "Fine, but I still don't understand how I could help you with anything."

His jaw tightened. "Things are happening in my territory. Unexplainable things. Shifters are coming up missing. I need someone to quietly investigate what's happening so I can fix this."

I shook my head. "What in the world makes you think I'm even a little qualified for investigative work?"

This was madness. A bad feeling crept into my gut. "Ethan. I work in a flower shop."

He polished off his last cookie. "Mmm. Yes, you do. But you haven't always worked in one, have you?"

The past slammed into me like a train—memories I'd long buried rising toward the surface and scarring my heart all over again. No. I wouldn't, couldn't do this again. I set my martini glass down and straightened. "Get out of my house, Ethan Flint."

The Lord ignored me. Ethan crossed his arms and watched me. "You'll receive a handsome salary."

I scoffed. "What the fuck does a vampire need with a salary? Any vamp worth their salt has enough money saved to retire a hundred times over."

His expression didn't change. "True. But you'll also receive protection."

I laughed. "Again, what the fuck does a vampire need with protection? We're made weapons."

"You underestimate my ability to gather intel. Your new magic has garnered interest among some unsavory characters."

A chill ran down my spine.

"They're interested in how that magic of yours morphed." This time, his smile held an edge of sympathy. "And they want to take it from you. By any means necessary."

Inside my head, I was screaming.

CHAPTER
Nineteen

I couldn't sleep. Nestling against Rowan usually put me right out, but tonight my thoughts were filled with worry.

"You want me to text him?"

I sighed against his chest. "Do you mind?"

"Evie. You don't have to ask me. Just text him."

"I don't want to text my ex-boyfriend," I grumbled.

"Well, in a way you do," Rowan said with a chuckle.

"I just need to know he's alive."

He shifted and pressed a kiss against my temple. "Caelan is a stubborn old bastard, and he's a Lord. If he was dead, we would have known earlier."

I reached over for my cell. "Are you sure?"

"You're my mate." He rolled over and pinned me against the mattress. "But more important than that, you're my Evie. You wouldn't be who you are if you weren't worried about him."

He pressed a kiss to my lips. "Text your ex, weirdo."

I laughed. "Fine."

Caelan responded almost immediately.

All good, flower girl. I'm tougher than I look.

I closed my eyes and exhaled. "He's okay."

"Told you," Rowan said smugly. "Pretty sure the only one able to kill the stubborn old goat is you."

I smacked him lightly on the chest. "If he dies, you'll have another Lord vacancy to fill."

"Yeah, those are a real bitch." He snorted. "Though Garrett is the obvious next choice."

"He doesn't want it."

"The best Lords don't."

He gathered me in his arms and pulled me close. "Get some rest. I have a feeling our next few weeks might be more eventful than we're prepared for."

Truer words had never been spoken.

MOIRA SHOWED up for breakfast the next morning bearing fresh-baked muffins and scones. Rowan and I were sitting on the patio when we heard her footsteps coming up the drive. We always made extra coffee for her because we never knew when she was going to show up.

Moira didn't like to eat alone. I discovered this years ago and always tried to include her in dinner and lunch plans, never letting on that I knew. Now, I think she felt a little like a third wheel with Rowan in the picture, but she still sought us out a few times a week for breakfast or dinner.

Ash told me she did the same with them which made me feel better. Moira, despite her occasional grumpiness, needed people. She was thriving on Rowan's land in some ways. Her skin was brighter and she had more time than ever to focus on baking and making new tea blends. But I sensed a bone deep loneliness inside her. She missed us, even though we all lived on the same property.

I didn't know how to help her. Ethan's presence riled her up and made her focus on other things beside herself for a while, but his presence was sporadic. This wasn't his territory, even though Rowan had been extra lenient with Ethan's presence on his land.

Not many Lords would be, especially not if they weren't friends.

But like me, Rowan had recognized something between Moira and Ethan. No one knew how it would play out, but Rowan thought it was worth allowing a little leniency.

Even if it was only for the entertainment value those two brought when they clashed.

"Chocolate chip or blueberry?" Moira asked as she opened the basket.

"Chocolate chip," I said, just as Rowan said, "blueberry."

Moira passed us each a muffin over. "I brought cinnamon scones, too."

"Yes, please!" I made a gimme gesture.

Moira grinned and passed a scone over, too.

"Unlike my wife, I am not greedy." Rowan winked to soften his words. "I'll wait until I finish this first."

"More for me," I proclaimed.

Moira was wearing a pair of buttery brown leggings and a cream colored off-shoulder top. Her hair was down and much longer than I was used to seeing. She'd let it grow since she'd come to Emberwood, and now it fell in a dark silky sheet down her back. Moira never wore much makeup, but today her face was completely bare, showcasing her poreless and perfect skin, but also highlighting the shadows underneath her eyes.

I reached over and nudged her knee. "You can come over any time you want to, you know."

Moira rolled her eyes. "You and your tender heart, Evie Quinn. It's gonna get you one day."

"It already has," Rowan said. "After all, she has me and all this." He waved his hand around to encompass his stunning land. *Our* stunning land, I should say. I'd never get used to this feeling of having so much.

"I've always admired how humble you are, Rowan."

He grinned at Moira. "Yes, well, humbleness is one of my many talents."

The scone she made melted in my mouth. Buttery and flaky with a crunchy sugar crust, I couldn't speak until I finished the entire thing. "You should have a bakery portion in your tea shop. These are phenomenal."

Moira looked uncomfortable. She looked away and sighed.

I sat a little straighter. "Moira?"

"About that." She fidgeted. Moira never fidgeted. "Ethan asked me to come to his territory for a little while."

Rowan's eyes narrowed. "Oh?" His voice was deceptively casual.

"I told him no." But her expression told me her answer wasn't the end of this.

"Then why are you acting weird? And why does he want you to live on his territory? What's wrong with Rowan's?" Ethan wasn't as terrible as I first thought he was, but there was no reason I could think of for Moira to move to his lands.

Moira sighed. "He needs help with something and believes I'd be more successful than he was."

Rowan sat back and slowly chewed on his scone. "Can you share the reason?"

Moira looked pained. "I shouldn't. I'm sorry."

Rowan nodded. "Alright then. I'll call the bastard and ask him myself."

At my warning look, he shook his head. "I get why Moira's not telling me, so I'll go right to the source."

"I don't think he'll tell you anything." I winced at Rowan's stony face. "He's always seemed like the most private of the Lords. If there's a problem and he can't fix it, I don't see why another Lord would be able to." I frowned. "Or would be willing to assist without wanting something in return."

His expression cleared. "What is he offering you?" he asked Moira.

Moira's jaw tightened. "A salary. Magic lessons." She lifted her hands. "That's all."

I knew Moira. She wasn't telling us everything. I let it go for now, but as soon as I could break away from Rowan for some private time, I planned to grill her. Moira was an adult and could make her own decisions, but Ethan rattled her more than I'd ever seen anyone else rattle her.

Soren, another one of the Lords, managed to get under her skin for a brief period of time, but she'd written him off pretty quickly. Ethan seemed to have burrowed under her defenses and squatted there. As much as I didn't want her to go, if that's what she wanted, I wouldn't stand in her way.

"What about your shop?" I asked.

"I told him no," she repeated.

"But you're thinking about changing your mind." One of my eyebrows went up as she opened her mouth to deny the words.

At my look, she sighed and slumped. "I want to open a shop, but I can't deny being curious."

Rowan's expression softened. He knew how Moira felt about Ethan. "Don't set yourself up for heartache." He hesitated, his lips tightening as he parsed out his next words. "I'm not sure Ethan will ever—"

Moira made a slashing motion with her hand. "Don't. I'm well aware of how Ethan feels about me."

That wasn't what Rowan was saying, and I wasn't sure my mate was right about this. I saw the way the other Lord had picked Moira up and hauled her out of that bar. He was enraged when he heard the rumors of Moira taking someone to her bed. And yet, he'd taken care of her when he got her home. Minus giving her a drop of the hangover remedy—a pretty egregious act of passive aggressiveness and maybe even a warning for her not to cross him.

My friend hadn't taken a single man to her bed since that night. She hadn't even given anyone a second look. That annoyed me more than anything. Moira wasn't young, but she was single, and she shouldn't have to diminish herself for someone else who wouldn't give her what she needed.

If Ethan was interested in her, and I thought he might be more than interested, he needed to get his shit together. Maybe inviting her to his territory was a way to get her close without making any commitments.

Kind of a roundabout shitty thing to do, but I put nothing past the Lords.

Except for Rowan.

But I was biased when it came to him.

"You hold all the leverage here. Make a deal with him. Open the tea shop if you want and hire someone to mind it while you're gone. Or split your time. He's the one who asked. Make it worth your while."

Rowan nodded. "Good idea. Remember how much money Evie gouged out of Caelan when he was begging her for crumbs?"

I laughed. The other Lord had fattened up my bank account by quite a lot for a while.

Moira smiled at the memory, her face brightening at our suggestion. "You know what? You're right. I do hold the power here."

"There you go," I said softly. "When Ethan starts doing that Alpha bullshit, remember what I let Caelan do to me."

Rowan gave me a sharp look.

I reached over and patted his knee. "Don't deny it. I allowed Caelan to treat me that way before I had the strength to get myself away."

Rowan's jaw clenched, but he didn't argue.

"Negotiate all the terms. Make him pay you out the ass and guarantee that money if things go sideways. Hell, make him give you the real estate to open a tea shop there, too. The sky's the limit, friend."

And on that note, as I watched a crafty light enter my friend's eyes, I knew she was going to be alright.

CHAPTER

Twenty

Things had been suspiciously quiet for the entire week. Caelan hadn't seen or heard from Danu since I released his land, and I'd heard nothing either. A year ago, this was my dream. Peace and silence.

Now all it did was make me suspicious.

Mom took pity on me and sent over a gown for tonight's visit to the fae court. The dress was stunning, the azure fabric perfectly matching my eyes. But the best thing about it? I could walk in the damn thing. The bodice was a sweetheart style but had enough support to hold the girls up without any extra tape or finagling, and the waist nipped snug around my ribs. I swayed back and forth in the mirror, the skirts swishing around my feet as I moved.

Rowan's eyes lit up when he stepped into the room. He let out a low whistle and motioned his index finger in a turnaround motion. When I finished, he strode over, gripped me by the waist and planted a searing kiss on my lips.

When I came up for air, we were both ready to skip the court and go straight to bed. But alas, duty called. "You clean up nice," I murmured.

Rowan always looked well put together. Though he dressed more casually than the other Lords, he knew when to dress for maximum impact. Tonight he wore a tuxedo, a human style, yes, but one that told the other fae he was one of us because of me, but he was also the Lord of his own territory and not someone to be trifled with.

Not that the fae bothered with warnings like that. Most were curious and fickle beings, and if they thought Rowan might be fun to play with, they wouldn't care about his position. They might hesitate when they realized his connection to me, but even my Dad had to deal with periodic fae bullshit, and he was their king.

Or was. That title belonged to Rowan now.

We were the least royalty-like people I'd ever met, so the thought of us one day officially taking our crowns made me break into a cold sweat.

Rowan did a little twirl for me. "Think I'll fit in?"

I ran my hands up his chest and rested them on his shoulders. "You'd fit in anywhere."

He cupped my face in his palms. "My first introduction to your world. Let's see what happens."

"Your mom is fae. Surely you've been to something like this before?"

Rowan shook his head. "Mom did her best to shelter me from our people." His face sobered. "Your parents did the same, but in a much worse way."

True. I spent my formative years without a mother or a father, and I wouldn't wish it on my worst enemy. "They're making up for it now."

Rowan's eyes softened. "Doesn't make it right." He ran his thumb over my lip. "Your parents will be here in a few minutes. Ready?"

I sighed. "Let me do something about this hair. I'll be right out."

MOM WAS SITTING on the couch when I walked out. Her eyes lit up when she saw me come out of the bathroom.

"You look beautiful." She stood and walked over, reaching out to brush a strand of hair from my face. Just like Rowan, Mom cupped my face in her hands. She stared into my eyes for a long moment until she let out a soft sigh. "Evangeline, you are everything and more I hoped you would be."

I blinked in surprise. "Mom? Is everything okay?"

Her eyes glimmered with silver, a hint to her rule over the banshees. Mom never said so, but I suspected she could sense someone's death just like her banshees could, among other things. "So many things are about to happen, my darling."

I swallowed hard. "Mom? You're scaring me."

Mom's lips trembled. She closed her eyes. "Be brave and strong, my darling. You will need both in the days to come."

My mother popped out of existence in a shimmer of light. Rowan had come to his feet and was at my side in an instance. He gripped my elbow and was about to usher me out of the room when Dad appeared in the spot Mom had just disappeared from.

His face was a blank mask.

"Is Mom okay?"

My father opened his mouth to speak, but the ground rumbled underneath us.

A banshee's scream shattered the night.

"Court's canceled," Dad barked when the scream died off. "Rowan, gather your people. Evie—" Dad squeezed his eyes shut for a brief second. He took my hands and held them. When he opened his eyes, they swirled with ancient magic. "Do whatever you need to do."

The ground rumbled again. "What's happening out there?" I demanded.

Dad dropped my hands. "The gods have shown up."

Rowan turned and streaked outside.

"What the hell is going on?"

Dad shook his head. "The fae are tired of waiting, Evie. I'll do what I can to turn them away. We can't kill our own people. Not this way."

My dad looked stricken, almost surprised this was happening. I wasn't surprised by anything these days, and I'd been expecting this for months now. Maybe not this specifically, but I knew the fae would make their move. I just expected the first move to be against Caelan.

Was this a distraction for something bigger?

"I'll try," I said to Dad as I spun toward the door. "No promises."

"Evie!"

I paused at the door. "If you want me to be queen," I said quietly, "I must do it my way. If our people are willing to move against me and my husband, then they will know why I am your heir and why I was chosen to wear the crown."

Dad and I locked eyes. Pride shimmered in their ancient depths, but I almost thought he might argue with me. Instead, he nodded slowly. "Fair enough, daughter." Dad smiled. "I'll be out in a moment."

I walked out the door and hurried after Rowan.

My husband stood between Declan and Hope, facing the still-standing wards. Several fae stood on the other side. Danu stood in the center and slightly ahead of the others.

She wore her ancient guise today, though we both knew the immortality running through her veins ensured she would be forever young—if she wanted to appear that way. Her hair was long and gray, snarled and tangled with roots and fungi. It fell past her waist and swayed in a phantom wind.

Seeing her outside of the ground was jarring. Danu seemed like the kind of person who belonged inside the heart of the earth and not someone who should be walking on the same earth I was. Her eyes changed color every few seconds, and she stood stooped over, her right hand resting on a polished wooden cane we both knew she didn't need.

Her lips curled in a smile when she saw me. "Ah, *Queen* Evie." She made the word sound distasteful. "So glad you're here this evening."

Danu flicked a dismissive hand toward the wards. "We will both pretend I can't tear through these wards like they're the thinnest tissue paper. In return, you will parley with me and discuss terms."

"Terms for what?" Rowan growled.

A faint smile tipped Danu's lips. "Surrender."

When Rowan froze, Danu chuckled, the sound an ancient breeze in the cool evening air. "The fae have come to reclaim their lands, Lord. We will try to do so peacefully, but if you insist on fighting us, we will respond in kind."

I felt my father's presence behind me. Danu's eyes narrowed when she spotted him. "Ah, Cernunnos. Welcome to the party."

"Leave, Danu. You are not welcome here."

Danu's soft snort angered my father. He went still beside me. As much as I adored my dad, he wasn't used to anyone mocking him. Even my teasing bothered him sometimes, so I was careful to dole out only small doses.

I put my hand on his arm.

"Hiding behind your father, Evie?" She clicked her tongue mockingly. "I'm surprised. With that lock ripped from your magic, I expected you to obliterate me as soon as you saw me. And yet here we stand, all in one piece."

I examined every single person standing beside Danu, taking the time to memorize all of their faces, knowing I'd remember them when I saw them in my court.

I stepped forward. "A queen does not harm her misguided subjects. She shows them a better way."

The bond in my chest warmed with Rowan's pride.

"Every fae standing here with Danu, I give you the opportunity to walk away. If you make the right decision, you will face no consequences from us. If you stand with Danu, I make no promises to your future safety."

Danu laughed in delight. "Your queen's first address is to threaten you! How grand." She clapped her hands together and turned to the others. "You heard her. Leave if you like. Stay if you want to reclaim what was stolen from you."

Nothing happened for a long moment. We waited in silence, and Danu turned toward me. "I think you have your answer."

Forty percent of the fae with her popped out of existence in colorful shimmers of light. One—a smaller woman with multi-colored hair—bowed her head to me before disappearing.

One ally. Maybe.

Only thousands more to go.

Fury flashed in the goddess's eyes. She didn't have to turn around to know what happened.

"Well," I said brightly. "Looks like some of you got a get out of jail free card. Anyone else want to take me up on the offer?"

Several more people disappeared. The odds were looking better and better.

Danu's fists clenched at her sides. "I could take it now if I wanted to."

Rowan's soft snort emboldened me. I came closer to the edge of the wards. "Then take it," I said softly.

"Evie," Dad said in a warning tone.

I held up a hand. "Let her. If Danu wants this land, she will have to go through me." I smiled. "And she isn't ready yet. Now that she's lost almost half her makeshift army, she's not sure she'll be able to overwhelm us. Are you, Danu?"

The goddess' sagging jaw clenched. "I didn't come here to fight."

"Yes, you did," I said softly. "If you saw the opportunity, you would have taken it. But now you aren't sure. You're hesitating."

Danu came within an inch of the wards. "One day," she said softly, so low only I could hear, "Very soon in the future, you will bow to my will. You will take my place, and if you do not, I will take everything you love."

Foreboding walked cold fingers down my spine, but showing fear wasn't an option. "You have no idea what I'm capable of," I said in the same low voice. "I could have killed you that night when we were in the ground, but I stayed my hand. I won't make the same mistake twice."

Danu's eyes flared, the first real flash of fear I'd seen from her. She covered her reaction quickly, and I might have missed it if I hadn't been watching her so closely. "I look forward to the next time we meet, *Queen.*"

The air shimmered around her and she was gone. Seconds later, the rest of the fae followed suit.

I let out a slow, heavy exhale. "Fuck, that was close," I breathed. Everyone else seemed confident I could kill Danu. I wasn't so sure. My magic was new and untried. Danu had millennia to perfect and hone her powers.

I was a magical toddler compared to her, but I also had a different type of power than Danu did. On one hand, our earth powers were similar, though mine seemed less destructive. Mine veered more toward nurturing the world; Danu's toward destruction.

"You did well." Dad stepped up beside me, his swirling gaze lingering on the spot where Danu just stood.

"All bluster," I said dryly.

Rowan came up on my other side. "Bluster is only when you can't back your words up. You don't have that problem."

I entwined our fingers. "She'll definitely be back." But something about this visit was bothering me. "Can you do me a favor and contact the other Lords? Something about her popping up here and doing nothing makes me think she was trying to hide something else."

Rowan's fingers tightened in mine. He nodded. "I'll call them the second we get back inside."

"Why was Mom being so weird earlier?" I asked my father.

His lips compressed into a white line, and for a moment, I thought he might lie to me. Instead, Dad turned to me. "Being a ruler does not mean you are the strongest or the smartest." A slight smile curved his lips. "Though it helps."

He jerked his head toward the main house. As we set off, with

Hope and Declan following close behind, Dad continued speaking. "Your mom isn't a soothsayer or a fortune teller, but just like her banshees, she has flashes of the future. Usually those visions require interpretation. They come to her in confusing flashes or images she can't make sense of."

Rowan held the door open for us.

"Sometimes, her visions are clear enough for her to see exactly what's coming."

Dread tightened my stomach. "She had a vision of what's coming."

"For you, specifically."

I went straight to the fancy espresso machine Rowan bought for me and started making us each a cup. "Is she okay?"

Dad sank onto the recliner and let out a heavy sigh. "Your mother has worried about you the second you became a seed in her womb."

Erm. Okay. Gross, but I understood the sentiment. Amusement trickled through my bond with Rowan.

"There will always be challenges to your rule, but this is a challenge to all of us. If we are to keep peace with the other supernaturals, we can't go around trying to re-take all the land we've agreed to share before."

"We all knew the fae would try something sooner or later. They've been sniffing around for far too long. Caelan's grip on his territory has been weakening for a while now, even before he pursued Evie. His was the obvious place to start." Rowan accepted the espresso I handed him. He brushed a kiss over my cheek. "I'm going to call the others."

But as he walked away, his phone rang. When he brought it up to his ear, and his face went blank, I knew our evening was just beginning.

In total, the United States was supposed to have seven Shifter Lords, their territory divided somewhat equally. With our marriage, Rowan held the most territory as I'd taken Donovan's when he died. The former Lord ruled over the Great Plains area, territory that bumped against Ethan's. Now, with our grip on Donovan's land, Ethan was our closest ally.

It was him on the other line.

Rowan put the phone on speaker and set it on the coffee table. Hope and Declan had come inside and sat on the floor while Ethan briefed us.

"Fae are surrounding all Keep properties," Ethan's crisp, deep voice sounded serious but not too concerned.

"Yours as well?" Rowan asked.

Ethan made an affirmative grunt. "We are unable to leave without getting into a conflict."

Magic versus shifters never ends well. Every Lord retained mages, but a human mage would never be able to perform the same feats of magic a fae could.

The uneasy peace held between shifters and fae was on the brink of collapse, and I didn't understand why. Was this just a small population of fae pissed off they couldn't have it all?

I said as much. Dad cleared his throat and gave me a mild look of disapproval. "Over the years, the Lords have pushed against their set boundaries and expanded their territories without seeking the approval of the fae."

Rowan's brows went up at that. "Recently?"

Dad shook his head. "You are a relatively young Lord and peaceable. Other Lords who've come before you have not been so content with what they've been given."

Declan swore under his breath. "So we're being punished for the mistakes of our fathers."

"In some regards," Dad said. "There are other matters at hand."

He leaned over closer to the phone. I hid my smile. Thousands of years old and still not great with technology. "Tell me, Lord," Dad said. "Have they tried to breach the lines?"

Ethan's low chuckle sent a shiver down my spine. Sometimes I really could see (or in this case hear) why he revved Moira's engine. "They've all tried. If Evie hadn't circled our land with her power, I suspect we'd be having a very different conversation right now. None of them have been able to get through." He paused. "But on the other hand, it's keeping us in as well. All the Lords should have plans for long-term occupation in an emergency, but after a few weeks, this could become a problem."

"This won't stretch into weeks," I assured him. "But Caelan's lands could be a problem."

"Ah yes. We all know you've taken pity on the poor bastard." Amusement colored his tone. "We aren't sure if you did it because you have a tender heart or you decided to throw him to the metaphorical wolves."

Rowan snorted. "Evie warned him multiple times. The stubborn mule decided to take his chances."

Ethan sighed. "I suspect if Caelan doesn't already have a problem, he will very soon."

Danu was playing with him right now, giving Caelan just enough rope to hang himself with. I could take his land. I *had* taken his land. But I knew if I did, we would shatter the tentative peace between us. I couldn't do that to him. Convincing myself not to pop over there and take it anyway felt like an angel on one side and the devil on the other riding on my shoulders and whispering in my ear.

"You've spoken to all the other Lords?" I asked.

"We've either talked or texted. Your Ben is well equipped to hold out for longer than any of us."

Rowan stiffened at Ethan's words.

My dad tried unsuccessfully to hide his smile.

"You know," I drawled. "A single snap of my fingers and I could give your land right back to you, Ethan."

The bastard had the gall to chuckle. "But you wouldn't. I am not as prideful as Caelan. I, unlike some of my brethren, appreciate a strong and powerful woman. Emasculation is a made up term for men who feel women are a lesser species. I *adore* women," Ethan purred. "Especially those whose magic can make the world tremble."

"Quit flirting with my wife," Rowan growled.

"I hope you appreciate what you have," Ethan responded.

"Six months ago you couldn't stand me!" I almost never heard Ethan joking around, and now here he was about to make Rowan teleport through the phone to kick his ass.

Ethan laughed. "What can I say? Being around your crew has lightened me up a little." The teasing note dropped from his voice. "Relax, Rowan. I'm yanking your chain. Regardless, Evie's claim is the only thing keeping us from a full scale invasion. None of us will squander that protection."

I chewed on the edge of my thumb. "Dad? Should I go out there and boost the magic?"

Dad frowned. "Might not be a bad idea. Rowan should be able to help as well."

Rowan blinked. "Excuse me?"

Dad rolled his eyes. "I know you've noticed some odd things happening with your magic. You will never be able to do the same things Evie can, but you can tap into some of her magic—at least enough to boost the claim she's made. Divide and conquer is the best way until we figure out a way to move Danu off the board."

"Ethan?" He was closest. Easier to start with him and move east.

"I'm not going anywhere." He paused. "Bring the vampire. Ask her if she has any more cookies."

I grinned and decided to tweak his nose a little. "I'll ask, but I think she has a date tonight."

Rowan's eyes widened with delight.

"I see," Ethan said. Was his voice a touch rougher? "Then just bring the cookies."

Rowan's cell beeped as Ethan disconnected.

Dad clicked his tongue. "You're poking the bear with that one."

"He started it."

Hope and Declan groaned. "Are you leaving tonight?" Rowan's Omega asked. She was a gorgeous redhead with a mane of wild curly hair and eyes the color of jadeite. We'd struck up a fast friendship during the months I'd been here, and I liked her a lot.

Declan, Rowan's Second, was massive; his arms the size of my waist. He had a good sense of humor and emotional intelligence, and I suspected he had a crush on Hope. The Omega, though, kept Declan at arm's length, though they still shared a warm friendship.

"Want to come?" I asked.

Hope slowly shook her head. "Ethan is too intense for me. Plus, I don't want Moira to claw my face off."

I laughed. "Moira? She wouldn't do that."

Declan snorted. "Yeah. I dunno about that. Have you seen the way she looks at him?"

Moira would be absolutely mortified if she knew everyone noticed her intensity around Ethan. "Never, ever tease her about it," I warned.

Declan blinked. "I wouldn't, but now I'll be extra on guard."

Hope chuckled. "She shouldn't be ashamed about it. Ethan looks at her the exact same way."

Declan nodded. "Dude has it bad."

Rowan grinned. "Alright, you two. The gossip session is over. If you're not coming with us, then get out." He waved a careless hand at them. "Tell the others we'll be back later tonight."

Rowan glanced at Dad. "At least I think so. Boosting the magic shouldn't take too long, should it?"

"No. The first property Evie claimed will take the longest, but even that one shouldn't need more than fifteen to twenty minutes. Pack extra food for you both."

"I'll run and get Moira." I slid my shoes back on and stood.

"No date tonight?" Rowan said with a grin.

I snickered. "I wish I could have seen his face."

"Oh, he's pissed," Rowan said. "Moira will hear it tonight, if she goes."

"She'll go," Hope and Declan said at the same time.

The three of us walked together for a little while. I split from them when they headed toward their dorm, and I took the left toward Moira's apartment. The lights were on when I knocked.

She would have sensed me coming onto her step, and sure enough, her door was already cracked open by the time I reached the first step.

"Come in!" she called. "I'm taking some oatmeal chocolate chip cookies out of the oven."

I slipped my shoes off in her entryway and padded into the kitchen. Her house always smelled like baking. Sometimes it was cinnamon, sometimes it was herbal; today, the kitchen smelled like melted milk chocolate. "I hope you saved me two dozen of those."

Moira grinned and passed over two still warm cookies on a paper towel. "Careful. They're hot."

I didn't listen and promptly popped a bite in my mouth, only to do the "ha hoo ha ha hoo" thing when it burned the hell out of my tongue. She snorted and pointed to the fridge. "Milk is in there."

She snapped a lid on a blue glass bowl and pushed it over a bowl. "Mind sticking this in the fridge? I made too much dough."

I obliged and pulled out a glass bottle of milk. "Where'd you get this?"

"There's a cute little shop downtown that sells to consumers straight from local farms. Their milk is grassfed and tastes way better than the stuff we got in Texas. Plus it's not sold in plastic."

I grinned at her. "What you're saying is I've influenced you. Just a teeny tiny bit."

Moira was also wearing a stunning off-shoulder cashmere sweater, a deep blue color that brought out the pale cream of her skin. She waved her cookie spatula at me. "I'll admit no such thing."

I poured us both a small glass of milk and pushed hers over. "I need to head out to Ethan's."

Her hand froze in the act of scooping a cookie from the pan, but she caught herself. Not in time for me to miss her tell-tale reaction, but I didn't call her out on it. As I explained what was happening, Moira frowned.

"And Caelan's land is still free?"

"Maybe they're saving the best for last."

We both laughed. "When are you leaving?" she asked.

"In a few minutes. Want to come?"

Moira's head snapped up. "Why would I want to go?"

I didn't bother to answer her, just lifted one eyebrow and watched her.

She huffed a laugh. "Fine. He's an insufferable bastard, and yet I want to see him."

I leaned forward. "If it helps, he asked for you. And for your cookies."

Pink touched Moira's cheeks.

"But I told him I wasn't sure you were free because you had a date tonight."

Moira gasped and then let out a wicked chuckle. "You are savage sometimes. How'd he take it?"

I shrugged. "Not sure. I couldn't see his face. Rowan suspected he was furious. Ethan still asked for your cookies, though."

Moira grinned. "I do make excellent cookies," she admitted.

"Yes, yes you do."

We ate in silence for a little while. "Be careful with him, Moira. I know you're an adult and can make your own decisions, but when your heart is broken, mine is too. The Lords are not like regular supernaturals. Caelan was driven by power and status, and it consumed us both in the end. I don't know Ethan well enough to gauge him, but I know there's something brewing between you two."

I reached over and took her hand. "Soren might be the safer choice."

Moira sighed. "He's definitely the safer choice. But Soren is a teenage boy when it comes to matters of the heart."

And Ethan was a man. The unspoken words lay between us. "Rowan wonders if Ethan will ever seriously date someone again after what happened."

Moira nodded. "I know. And maybe whatever this is will burn out." Her nostrils flared. "But when I'm around him, I feel alive, Evie."

My heart ached for her. I knew what that felt like. "Then I assume you're coming with me?"

Moira nodded. "If I'm going to be a fool, I might as well go all in, right?"

I didn't answer her. "It's cold where he is, and I'm not sure Ethan will allow us inside. You might want to bring a heavy coat and put some boots on."

Moira looked down at herself. "The leggings are lined wool, and the top is Cashmere. I have some warm boots. Give me a minute."

She hurried off to the back, so I grabbed another cookie.

When she came back, she was bundled in a heavy jacket and

wore a pair of calf-high waterproof boots. She'd taken her hair down from its ponytail and swiped on some berry colored lip gloss and mascara. "Ready?"

"Dad is at the main house. Rowan is coming with us, but Dad will take him to Ben's territory. You have a few hours to spare?"

Moira looked around her apartment. "I'll have to cancel tonight's cocktail party, but sure."

"Ass," I grumbled. "Just for that I'm taking another cookie."

Moira grinned and reached for a glass storage container. She filled it with at least a dozen cookies and tucked the container into one of the enormous jacket pockets.

"Ready when you are."

Moira always happily tagged along on my trips, but this one made her edgy. As we walked, her eyes kept darting around, and she was fidgeting way more than usual. So much so, I gave her a side glance. "You're twitching like you're an addict needing a fix. Ethan's going to spot your nerves from a mile away."

Moira swore and made her fingers stop tapping against her thigh. "Thanks. I don't know what's gotten into me."

We stopped right before the back door. I dropped my voice into a whisper the others couldn't hear. "Moira. You're intelligent, gorgeous, and bake like Martha Stewart on speed. Anyone would be beyond lucky to have a chance with you. Remember that when you're in front of Ethan."

Moira stared at me for a long moment. "You're a good friend, Evie."

"You too. If he hurts you, I'll kill him with a poisoned rose bush. No one will ever know."

"Thank you," Moira said with a straight face. "I'll take your secret to the grave."

The door opened, and Dad stepped out. He looked between the two of us, one of his eyebrows rising. "Do I want to know what you two are plotting?"

"Murder and mayhem," I said sweetly.

"That's my girl," Dad said. He jerked his thumb over his

shoulder. "Already dropped your mate off at Ben's. I expect boosting the magic will take him a little longer than it will for you."

"Alright. We'll hit Ethan's first, then Thorvin's?"

Dad nodded. He glanced at Moira. "You good with this?"

Moira smiled. "You old softie. Yes, I know where we're headed."

"Alright then. You know the drill."

Moira slid her fingers into mine. Dad touched me on the arm and away we went.

With barely a greeting between Evie and the other Lord, she sank right to the ground and closed her eyes, slender fingers digging into the soil. When magic started flowing around her, Ethan pierced me with his dark gaze.

"It's cold outside. Come into the house."

I hesitated. "You sure?"

His lips twitched. "You've already been inside, haven't you?"

I blinked at him. Oh fuck he knew. How the fuck did he know? "Uhhh," I said eloquently. "No?"

Ethan tapped the side of his nose. "I didn't know who it was at first, you know." He turned and started walking up to the house. "The scent was tantalizingly familiar, but I'd never really spoken to or had many dealings with you before. I didn't put the pieces together until a few months ago."

Shit. Deny. Deny. Deny. "Huh. I have no idea what you're talking about."

"Mmm." He held the door open for me. I hesitated at the entrance.

"Better get inside. I smell those cookies inside your pocket."

Against my better judgment, I stepped into the wolf's den.

"Your scent was all over the house," Ethan remarked as he strode past me. "But I smelled you most in my bedroom."

My cheeks flamed.

"I don't know how much you saw, but I hope you enjoyed the show."

I hoped the floor opened up underneath me and swallowed me whole.

"You tried to hide your scent," Ethan said, "but you were unsuccessful. I have tricks of my own, you know."

He went to the fridge and pulled out an amber bottle. "Would you like some?"

I licked my lips. "I have no idea what that is." My voice was hoarse. Too hoarse. Shit.

"Port. A friend of mine makes it." He pulled two small shot glasses down from a cabinet and poured a thick, tawny colored liquid inside them.

I pulled the cookie container out of my pocket and opened it for him.

Ethan inhaled. "Oatmeal and chocolate." He inhaled once more, a furrow to his brow. "The chocolate smells different."

I looked at my feet. "I made it."

A beat of silence. "From scratch?"

"There's a store that will sometimes have cacao pods."

When I lifted my gaze, Ethan was staring at me. "You are a constant surprise."

I wasn't sure if that was a compliment, so I stayed silent. Ethan's eyes crinkled at the edges, and I shoved my hands in my pockets to help me resist the urge to graze my fingers over those fine lines.

He pulled out a cookie and took a bite. I watched him carefully and noted the moment his expression changed. "Cacao pods," he mused. "Are they hard to find?"

"Very." In fact, I got super lucky to find the one she had. When I asked for more, the shop owner had shaken her head and said,

"I get whatever they send me. Sometimes they come with the shipment; most times they don't."

Ethan stared at the cookie. "You can't buy this stuff in a bag or something?"

"You can. It doesn't taste the same."

"Hmm. These are amazing. I would like it very much if you made them again."

I shrugged. "Depends on if I can find another cacao pod. This was the only one I've ever found."

Ethan nodded and pushed the port over. "Take a bite of your cookie and take a sip of the port."

I watched as he did the same. His eyes fluttered shut as his throat worked, and it took everything I had to clamp down on my visceral reaction. I was already careless when Ethan was around, but he'd shown no urge to do anything else other than tease or taunt me. I wanted more, and if he wasn't willing to give it to me, I'd do my best not to show him how much he affected me.

I focused on my cookie, savoring the sweet milk chocolate flavor exploding on my tongue. When I took a sip of the port and swallowed, I gasped in surprise, an involuntary "mmmm," coming from my throat. The chocolate from the cookie mixed with the sweet taste of the port, a strange but delicious mix of berries and caramel, combined in the most divine taste.

Ethan stilled, his irises ringed in that strange blue and gold glow. Without a word, he took my glass and poured me a little more. "Do it again," he demanded.

My throat went dry. "Ethan."

"Drink, Moira."

Gods. He was so sexy when he was being bossy. I took another sip, unable to keep my eyes from fluttering closer. "What is this?" I whispered. "It's so good."

He went to pour me more, but I refused to give up my glass. "No. That bottle is old, and I bet this is hard to get. Save your stash for another day. I'll bring you more cookies."

Ethan watched me, his eyes still glowing. "What is food and drink if you don't share?"

I felt the same way, but whatever that port was, it felt special. "You did share. More than you should have." I tipped the rest of the port back and sighed when it was finished.

"Whoever your friend is, please send them my compliments. I've never tried my hand at winemaking, but I doubt I could ever duplicate this recipe."

"I'll let them know."

We stood watching each other. Ethan looked away first. "Have you changed your mind?"

He didn't need to clarify. "I don't think staying in your territory is a good idea."

"And why not?" He tilted his head and studied me, his gaze traveling from my face to my neck, to the top of my chest. "Your collarbones are too prominent. Why aren't you eating?"

I stifled my annoyance. "Why are you so obsessed with my eating habits?"

"You're too thin. Beings like us constantly expend magic. Since your magic is altered, I don't think you're fueling your body enough to compensate."

He wasn't wrong. I noticed the changes in the mirror, but I had no idea what to do about it. I was eating, maybe not as much as I used to, but I also hadn't been as active as I used to be. With Evie's shop closed, I had to content myself with baking and puttering around the house. "I eat when I'm hungry," I grumbled.

He came around the counter and walked toward me. I thought he'd stop when he got within a few feet of me, but he kept coming. I took a step back and bumped into the counter. He came so close our chests almost touched. "If you lived on my territory, I would ensure you ate all the time."

I swallowed hard. That sounded like a threat but also like something I very much wanted to see him try.

Ethan lifted a hand and took a piece of my hair in his hands. He rubbed it between his fingers. "Like silk," he murmured.

you were in an inebriated state. I trusted you to watch out for the one woman who might save us all."

He spoke of the night when Evie claimed the Lords' lands to purge the poison seeping in. Ethan had given me cashmere and brought me food while I sat with Evie as she worked, ensuring no one would take advantage of her vulnerability.

"I will do whatever makes you comfortable, Moira. Write out a contract. Put whatever you require in there. More than likely, I will agree to it all." His fists clenched at his sides. "Evie is waking up. We won't have much longer to speak freely."

Ethan turned and studied me. "You remind me of someone. A person I trusted very much. Maybe you won't be successful." He shrugged. "Maybe this won't work out. How will we know until we try?"

He was so serious about this it made me pause. Ethan would break my heart. I knew it. Maybe he knew it, too. But I wanted to help him. I just didn't want to leave everything behind to do so.

Ethan exhaled and turned back to the window. "She's getting up."

"I'll think about it," I said softly. "That's all I can promise."

His shoulders slumped. "Thank you."

Evie knocked on the back door and waved.

CHAPTER

Twenty~Three

"You two looked serious," I remarked.

Cernunnos had just dropped us off on Thorvin's land. The Lord briefly greeted us, thanked me for my help, and hurried back inside. Thorvin was a weird one. He seemed like a decent enough dude, but half the time his head was in the clouds.

I almost felt bad about the time Moira glittered him. Almost.

Moira shrugged. "Ethan is intense."

Yes, he was. I watched her for a moment. "You're going, aren't you?"

"Maybe." She let out a heavy sigh. "But I won't live there. And I guess I need to ask Rowan if it's okay."

My brow furrowed. "Why would you need to ask Rowan?"

Moira leaned against one of the oaks dotting Thorvin's property. "I don't know. I live on Keep property. Will it be weird for me to go between them?"

"No. You're your own person. You're not a shifter, Moira. And you're my best friend."

Relief spread over her face. "I'm not sure why he's pushing me this much, but he backed down tonight and offered to do whatever I was most comfortable with if I would help him."

Interesting. "He's not just asking you to come to try to get you in the sack?"

Moira laughed. "Anything but, I think." Her eyes slid away. "He needs my help with something and claims he trusts me."

"Do you trust him?" Moira was like me in many ways. Earning her trust was a long and arduous path, but once you got to the end, you wouldn't find a more loyal friend.

She sank down onto the ground and sat. I joined her, kicking off my shoes to bury my toes in the dirt.

"He didn't try a single thing when he took me home from the bar that night." She threw up her hands. "He was a perfect gentleman!"

I snickered. Moira would have happily gone along with whatever Ethan wanted that night, even though she was furious at him when he carried her out of the bar.

"Every time I've been around him, he hasn't been a gentleman, exactly, but I've never felt in any danger. I guess my answer is, I trust him more than I do most people, but not as much as you, Ash, or Tess."

"Good answer. You've known us much longer. Ethan is a wild-card, but your instincts are good." I reached over and patted her knee. "If you want to go, go. You don't have to ask for our permission."

"I'll come up with something and see if he signs on." She smiled. "I do want that tea shop."

"And I want to open my store up again." I sighed. "Caelan and Danu threw a wrench into everything."

"You'll get there. This fae thing can't last forever."

My nose wrinkled, and Moira laughed. "Well," she corrected, "everyone involved is immortal, so maybe it can."

"Watch out for me for a little while?"

Moira nodded. Thorvin had already gone back inside and shut the lights off, so we knew we'd receive no hospitality from him. "It's nice and cool tonight, and the skies are clear. I'll enjoy the quiet for a little while."

I smiled at Moira and closed my eyes.

Thorvin's land took a little longer than Ethan's, as Dad thought it might. When I opened my eyes, Moira was in the same place, her pale face tilted up to watch the stars. I stayed perfectly still and watched her, noting the loneliness etched on her face.

I hoped whatever this was between her and Ethan turned into something positive, but part of me dreaded what might come for her. Soren would have been a nice plaything for her if he hadn't been such an idiot, but I suspected if he approached her now, Ethan might rip his throat out.

"Moira."

She jerked and turned. "Sorry. I was lost in my thoughts."

I smiled sadly. "If things don't work out, you always have a place to come back to. And, if you only go to his property for a few days a week, you can still eat dinner with us whenever you want to."

Moira stood and dusted off the seat of her pants. She held out her hand and helped me up. "Anyone else to take care of, or can we go home?"

I grimaced. "Gotta hit up Soren."

Moira winced.

"Dad will take you home if you want to go."

She nodded. "I'll probably take him up on that."

Dad, as if saying his name summoned him, appeared out of thin air. "Finished?"

I nodded and jerked my head in Moira's direction. "Mind dropping her off first?"

Dad gave her an odd look. "You don't like Soren?"

"Soren is fine," Moira insisted, rolling her eyes at my knowing look. "I'm just tired. That's all."

Dad held out his hand to Moira. "Back in a moment."

In a flash, they were gone.

I stuck my hands in my pockets and walked some of the

perimeter of Thorvin's land. The last time I'd been here, the bastard had shot Garrett. I still hadn't forgiven him for it, even as I couldn't say a word to him about it. If I did, I'd have to admit to trespassing on his land, something that could get me and Caelan in big hot water.

So I kept my grudge at a distance.

Dad reappeared, making me jerk in surprise. "You know you can do this on your own," he drawled. "Instead of using your old man as a taxi service."

"I don't want to get lost in an infinite stretch of space and time."

Dad rolled his eyes. "Hand, please."

A few seconds later, we stood on Soren's land.

The Lord was already outside waiting for us. I'd been to his property only once before, when the weather was much cooler.

Tonight, I grimaced as humidity smacked me in the face. I didn't miss Joy Springs as much as I thought I would, but the one thing I would never miss again was 100% humidity. We were far enough up in the state to avoid the worst of it, but Soren's territory was located in the deep south. Some of his states were Louisiana, Mississippi, and Alabama.

Tonight we stood in Louisiana, in a small city close to New Orleans. This house wasn't Soren's main Keep home, but it's where the Lord preferred to spend his time. He liked being where all the action was.

I suspected that was because he had a revolving bedroom door and showed no signs of slowing down anytime soon.

He rose from his seat on the wrap-around porch and walked over to us.

Soren was gorgeous, an absolute specimen of male in peak physical condition. He was tall, around six foot five, and had the build of a quarterback. His skin was tanned, either from a lot of sun or some undeclared heritage he never spoke about. But the most stunning thing about him was his eyes.

Where mine was an azure color, sometimes becoming more

green or bluer depending on my mood or what I wore, Soren's stayed a bright, startling blue, the color of a sunny sky. His hair was wavy and the color of a roasted chestnut, and his jaw was sharp and clean shaven.

Like Ethan, Soren had grown on me a little, but I hated one thing about him. He knew he was stunning, and he used it to manipulate people sometimes. Or maybe all the time. Hell, I don't know. Moira and I were probably the only ones who hadn't fainted right into his bed, so he wasn't sure how to take us.

He also used his physical beauty to mask his true self. So much so, he'd made Moira give up, which she almost never did if she liked someone.

"Hello, Soren," I said politely.

His lips twitched. "No Lord Soren anymore?"

"I'm a Lady now, so I can call you whatever I want to. I'd suggest being careful."

Soren grinned, his teeth white and straight, and damn it, did that guy have a small dimple on the edge of his mouth? The world was not fair. How had I not noticed that before?

"Do you want me to stay?" Dad asked in a low voice.

"Your daughter is safe with me," Soren said, dipping his head to my father.

Dad stared at him for a long moment before he nodded. "I'll be back in half an hour."

"Forty-five minutes," Soren said quickly. "If you don't mind. I wish to speak to Evie before she starts."

Shit. I hoped this wasn't about Moira.

Dad looked at me. I shrugged. "Forty-five is fine."

"Very well." He disappeared in a shower of light, leaving me and the other Lord alone.

I'd never spent alone time with Soren. He had never done anything untoward or tried to harm me, but he also didn't come around too much. He and Rowan were not friends, only acquaintances and their territories weren't close to each other.

"Would you like a drink?" Soren asked.

"Not before magic but thank you."

Soren dipped his head. "Come, sit for a few minutes. I made a small charcuterie board."

I blinked in surprise. Rowan had accidentally taken the bag of snacks, and I was starving. Thorvin hadn't even come out to say goodbye, much less offered me a bite.

"Alright then."

Soren laughed as he led me up the porch steps. "Let me guess. Thorvin was the prior visit?"

I sat in the chair next to the one he was sitting in when I arrived. To my great delight, the *small* charcuterie board was enormous. I suppose to a shifter, this would be considered small.

"Help yourself." Soren poured himself a glass of wine and me a glass of water.

I gave up all pretense of being cool and piled my plate high with cheese, meat, olives, and nuts. "Thank you."

Soren was buttering me up for something, but only a fool passed on free food.

"My Keep hosts many mages. Our grocery bill gets astronomical when they're training." Soren added a few things to his plate and watched me while I ate. Not in a creepy way. More in a curious way.

"I know you want something," I said through a mouthful of salami. "Spit it out."

Soren snorted. "Through everything, you've been kind to us."

At my startled look, he pressed on. "We did not deserve your kindness, Evie. Not even a little bit. And at the end, neither did Caelan."

I swallowed and watched him warily. Where was he going with this?

"None of us are surprised you ended up with Rowan. He is the only one of us who has managed to stay in power and build a vibrant community at the same time. Plus, the bastard is like you. Far too empathetic to be a Lord."

"Careful how you speak of Rowan," I said softly.

Soren held his hands up and laughed. "Peace, Evie. That is not an insult. The opposite, in fact. Caelan is a caged beast on his lands, though rumor is you've brought down his prison walls." He cocked an eyebrow.

I nodded. "True."

"Thorvin's cage is his mind. Ben shuns all of us. Rowan would kill us all if he could manage it without you finding out."

I went still at his words. Could they be true?

"And Ethan rarely ventures from his lands. The most we ever saw was when you kept kicking the hornet's nest."

He didn't know Ethan was coming around Rowan's Keep. Interesting. "And you?" I asked.

Soren spread his hands out. "I'm the Lord of a territory where people don't give a shit about me. These people don't need a Lord, Evie. If they spotted me wandering their lands, they'd shoot first and ask questions later."

"Then you shouldn't have chosen Louisiana," I said with a laugh. "Though Texas might have you beat on that front."

He shook his head. "Caelan's people love him. I'm not quite sure how he managed it, since he treated you so poorly, but..." His voice trailed off. "Well, I suppose, *loved* is the right word, since most of his people abandoned him."

Soren clicked his tongue. "Crossing you leads to dire consequences, sometimes."

I shoved a piece of cheese in my mouth and glared at him.

"Regardless, I'm more curious than anything. Why have you dealt with us so fairly when you deserved to raze us to the ground?"

I studied him for a moment. "I'm not sure I understand the reason why you're asking me. Is kindness so foreign to you that you can't figure out the motivations behind it?"

"Something like that, I suppose."

Soren was serious. My heart hurt for him in that moment. What must it be like to grow up without experiencing kindness in your life?

"I'm afraid you won't like this answer. My kindness wasn't for any of you. I had no motivation to show you kindness, because doing so is my first instinct. I could have tried to kill you all, but why? None of you like me. All of you thought I was a threat. I repeatedly tried to show you who I was, and yet, here I am, sitting with you, Soren, explaining my kindness wasn't an act. It's who I am."

"I like you," he said after a long silence.

If he'd said those words to me a few months ago, there would have been a flirty twist or maybe a lusty wink added at the end. But tonight, we were alone. I was mated, and Soren knew he had zero chance with me. The poor Lord, for all his beauty and success, looked tired.

"Are you shitting me?"

Soren let out a small laugh. "You are quite likable, Evie. Even when you're dangling one of our kind by his ankle."

We grinned at each other. Ethan had been a real shit that day, and I'd repaid his shitheadness by throwing him around with some vines. To be honest, it was kind of awesome.

"You didn't ask me to sit to tell me I was likable. What's really on your mind?"

Soren looked out over his land. "I'm wondering if I've made too many mistakes. How do I know when it's time to cut my losses and do something else?"

I tossed my water off the porch and reached for the wine bottle. Soren's soft laugh made me chuckle. "You're wading in deep, philosophical waters now, and I'm not qualified to give you a good answer."

"I'm not looking for a good answer. What would you do?"

"Starting over isn't so bad," I admitted. "Gotta say, it worked out pretty well for me."

"Indeed," Soren said. "You found yourself a mate and a new territory."

"Can you quit being a Lord? Is that what you want? Do you have to give Ethan two weeks' notice?"

At his smile, I threw my hands up. "No idea how any of this works. I can't just stop being a Chimera. It's in my blood."

"The Lord power will never leave me," he admitted. "I don't like where I am and would like to have the chance to rule over another territory. Or at least experience once. Our kind are not so welcoming to each other sometimes." He snorted. "Rowan and Caelan being the exceptions, though Caelan preferred using his lands to ensure he stayed close to you."

Of course he did.

"Where would you want to go?"

"Somewhere cooler," Soren said dryly. "I'm not from these lands."

"Oh? Inquiring minds want to know."

Soren sipped his wine. "I'm from Alaska, actually."

"Oh my gosh. Really?" I frowned. "Wait. Who's the Lord over there?"

He glanced at me in surprise. "You always were bad at asking questions. Rowan rules over Alaska."

I frowned. "Right. I'd forgotten." Our territory stretched over Washington, Oregon, some parts of Idaho, and even into Canada, but Alaska was included in there. Donovan's old territory was the Great Plains, so we ruled over that, too.

"You have so much land you've forgotten what you control?" Soren teased.

I waved a hand at him. "If you were to go somewhere else, who would take this portion?"

Soren's derisive snort made me wince. "Anyone besides Ben and Rowan, I think. They'd all jump at the chance to take another's territory."

"What about Garrett?"

Soren slowly turned and eyed me. "You notice it too?"

I nodded. Soren scratched his chin, a thoughtful look on his face. "You've given me a lot to think about tonight."

"How do you feel about the Great Plains?" I blurted, surprising both of us.

"Around Montana?" A pale band of gold glowed around his iris.

"Ethan's territory bumps up against Donovan's old lands, but yes. Part of Montana, North and South Dakota, a little bit of Wyoming, and Colorado."

"Wild lands." Soren's voice went a couple octaves higher.

"Definitely."

He grunted. "Your kindness is showing again, Evie Quinn."

"I haven't made any promises. I'm not even sure it's doable." I slid a look his way. "But if it is, would you be interested?"

A slow smile broke over Soren's handsome face. "This is unheard of, but if it's possible, and there is someone willing to take my place, I would welcome a change into the wild lands. They may not be where I was born, but those places have mountains and trees and cool streams." He closed his eyes for a moment. "I do not know how you work such magic on us Lords, Evie, but I welcome the change you bring into our immortal lives."

I reached over and patted his arms. "No promises," I said again, "but I will see what can be done. We're immortal, Soren, but we are also living, breathing people who need beauty, hope, and challenge in our lives. How long have you been unhappy?"

He put his hand over mine and held it there for a moment. His palms were rough and calloused, and his hands were several degrees warmer than normal. Typical shifter heat. "I didn't realize I was so unhappy until you barreled into Caelan's life with the force of a 747."

I winced.

"Do not feel shame. You and Moira were the best things that could have happened to us. Some might disagree, but you mated with one of us and changed all of us." He smiled. "And I expect Moira will continue to do so in your stead when you fully settle into your role as Lady."

Soren winked. "And queen."

I grimaced at the reminder. "Speaking of, Dad will be here soon. I'll refresh the magic and get out of your hair."

"Call me if the fae become too much, and I will fight at your side."

Warmth bloomed in my chest. "You have your own troubles." I hadn't seen any sign of the fae here, but Rowan said they were close, and I believed him.

"They're outside of the main Keep house. I plan to head there as soon as you finish."

At my flash of alarm, he chuckled. "I keep more mages than the others. We will be fine."

Soren removed his hand and stood. "Polish off the rest of that board. I will leave you to your communing or whatever it is you do." He bowed at the waist and touched his hand to his heart.

"Thank you, Evie. Your assistance will be remembered."

I raised my wine glass to the Lord. "Thanks for the food."

"You are welcome." With a wink more reminiscent of the old Soren, he stepped inside his house and shut the door.

"Huh," I whispered. Tonight was shaping up to be one weird night.

After I refreshed the spell, Dad showed up, but instead of going home, I asked him to take me to where the fae were. A terrible suspicion was beginning to build inside me.

Mom and Dad believed the fae wanted their lands back. Maybe that was true. It probably was. The dispute between the Lords and the fae had been building for years now, but it had only escalated recently.

And I suspected I might be the reason why.

Dad got that crinkle in his brow—the one that said he'd do as I asked but wasn't happy about it. "What are you up to?"

"Got a hunch."

From the odd look he gave me, Dad had no idea what a hunch was. I gave him what I hoped was an innocent smile. "I promise I'll only be a minute."

"Don't step across the boundary, Evangeline."

He knew I was up to something. I made the sign of the scout. "I promise."

Dad sighed and shook his head. "Come on, then."

I put my hand in his and we were gone.

Just like at our Keep, the fae had gathered in large numbers at Soren's main house. I hadn't told the Lord I was coming here, so hopefully we could get in and out before his people sounded the alarm.

A tall woman with multicolored hair stood at the front. She jerked when she saw me come into existence. Her eyes lingered on Dad first before sliding to me.

"Queen," the woman said in a deep voice. She dipped her head, which seemed a little insulting, my father confirming it with his rigid posture.

Too bad for them I'd never cared about all that nonsense. I'd rather hold the respect of my people than enforce all the bowing and scraping that sometimes came with a position. "Who are you?" I asked.

"My name is Nyria."

She looked like a Nyria, if that made sense. The woman was tall and slender as a reed. Her skin was the pale porcelain of someone who saw little to no sun. Her eyes were a crystalline violet, and if you passed her on the street, you'd know right away she wasn't human.

"To what do I owe the pleasure, Nyria?"

"Did you take this land, too?"

I blinked in surprise. "No. Why would I do that?"

Synchronized howls rang in the distance. Shit. Someone had sounded the alarm. I'd have less than a minute before they reached us.

"You seem to be taking a lot of land these days," Nyria said, those strange eyes taking my measure.

"Your source of info is flawed. Danu poisoned these lands in order to force me to take her place."

Nyria blinked. "You lie."

Dad stepped forward. "Your queen does not lie to you. Danu has threatened her multiple times and poisoned fae and human lands to force her hand."

I glanced at Dad. Danu had poisoned the fae, too?

Nyria's lips thinned. "You'd keep us from claiming our birthright?"

Dad snorted. "Human lands do not belong to us. Not completely, and not anymore after our bargain."

"Then we have nothing," Nyria said. "No property. No claim. No home."

Dad frowned.

"Why do you say this?" I asked, that suspicion growing even deeper.

"We've been stuck in this place for months." The surrounding fae murmured their assent. "Unable to return to our lands, and unable to purchase or claim property here, we've been close to being homeless! And our queen—" the word was a sneer, "has yet to answer any of our concerns!"

I had no idea anyone had concerns. "Who did you speak to about this?"

"Danu! Titania! We even tried to beseech one of the Lords, and he refused to speak to us."

"Which Lord?" Dad demanded.

"The studious one," Nyria said. "Not close to this place. He wouldn't even come outside!"

I rubbed a hand over my face. This was not good. And I wasn't surprised Thorvin had blown him off. He would have blown me off, too, if I hadn't insisted.

Dad turned his attention to me. He stepped closer and bent to whisper in my ear. "They're speaking of the tree."

I nodded. "I've been remiss."

"So have we all, it seems." Dad paused. "Do you have a solution?"

I turned my head and covered the side of my mouth. "If I reveal myself to be the bridge, all hell could break loose."

"Then we send them home together. They won't question our magic."

I nodded.

From behind, the howls grew closer. "I'll field off the wolves. Give me a moment."

Dad disappeared.

"I'm sorry your pleas went unanswered. Do you wish to return home?"

Nyria blinked in surprise. "What?"

The other fae shifted on their feet and looked around. "Do you want to go home?"

"Yes!" one of the fae shouted. The others murmured their assent.

Nyria's brow furrowed. "You can do this?"

"With my father, yes, we can. In the future, if you have any grievances, I suggest you reach out directly to me, Cernunnos, or Cliona. Or, if you are on these lands and can't reach me, please request an audience with my husband, Rowan."

My father came over the rise with three silver wolves flanking him, one of them with glowing golden eyes. Hmm. I wonder why Soren wouldn't ask whoever this was to take over his territory if I could get the transfer approved.

A flash of light and golden eyes stood before me. No matter how long I lived among shifters, I didn't think I'd get used to one second seeing a wolf and the next seeing a giant buff nude guy.

Soren was gorgeous. This man was dangerous. Like his Lord, this male was tall, maybe an inch or two shorter, and built like a swimmer. His eyes were dark and his hair was a strange mix of ash blonde and light brown. A scar bisected one of his eyes, cutting through the top of his brow to the bottom of his eyelid. Whatever caused the injury must have been severe for his innate magic not to heal him. He was lucky he still had use of his eye.

"You must be Evie," the wolf drawled in a slow southern accent reminiscent of thick honey. He walked over to me, completely uncaring of his nudity.

I inclined my head. "And you are?"

"Seth." His dark gaze flicked to the fae. "I'm Soren's Second."

"Pleasure. I'll be out of your hair in just a minute."

"Does Soren know you're here?"

I winced. "Not quite. I was just with him a few minutes ago, but decided a detour was in order. These are my people after all."

Seth grunted. "They're unable to cross, thanks to you. Does it matter?"

"I think I can get them to vacate." My gaze went to Nyria, who was watching us with interest. "But it's not safe to drop my magic until everything is resolved. Not just this matter."

"Are you planning on taking our land?"

I sighed. "Why does everyone keep asking me that? Have you ever seen me snooping around here?"

A slow smile curved Seth's lips, turning him from dangerous to holy shit handsome. I blinked and looked away. Goodness. Maybe Moira should come here and do some hunting and pecking.

"I'd remember you," Seth said, still holding onto that smile. "Maybe you should come around more often."

"Wolf," Dad snapped. "Tone down the wattage."

Seth's chest rumbled with a laugh.

"Anyway," I drawled, sending Seth a dark look, "I think I have a solution."

Seth cocked his head. "Will Soren be upset with you?"

"Uh. I don't think so?"

"Mm. Pity. He's a sight when he's pissed off."

I sighed. "You seem like a lot to handle."

Seth grinned again. "Would you like to try?"

A bark of laughter escaped me. "I see Soren has taught his Pack well. And thank you, but no. You already know who my mate is. He would not take kindly to this nonsense."

Seth swept his hand out like he was a game show host. "If you ever find yourself interested in a little nonsense, you know where to find me. In the meantime, please do carry on."

"Nyria?" I asked.

The fae turned and looked at her companions. Not a single one said no. When she faced me once more, her eyes were suspiciously moist. "We would very much appreciate going home."

I reached out for Dad's hand. "Then let's make it so." Once our hands were clasped, I spoke. "Hold the image of your home in your mind and don't let go."

Dad didn't do much at all, much of the magic he expended was just to make it look fancy. I was the bridge and the only one who could send everyone home.

Starting with the fae closest to the back, I concentrated, plucking the image from their mind. The bridge power wasn't something I could explain exactly. I trapped Lugh in another realm and locked him in, but I could also travel back and forth to wherever I wanted—provided the realm existed in the tree's purview.

A shimmering image appeared in my mind. I focused on it, opened up the bridge power living inside me and flicked my fingers. Several of the fae gasped, but I didn't stop. I sent each and every fae to the place I plucked from their mind. When Nyria was the only one left standing, I opened my eyes.

"How do I know you haven't sent them to their deaths?"

Dad snorted. "If you knew my daughter, you'd know she would never break her word.

Seth glanced at me, one eyebrow raised.

"Guess you'll just have to trust us."

Nyria didn't like my answer, but if she wanted to go home, she had no other choice than to trust me. "Ready?" I asked.

She closed her eyes. A second later, she nodded.

When she was gone, I dropped Dad's hand.

Seth was watching me a little too closely. "Your father had nothing to do with that show. Why are you hiding what you can do?"

My shoulders stiffened. How in the world could he know that? "No idea what you're talking about."

Seth tapped the side of his nose. "Shifters have sensitive noses. Some of us can sniff magic out like a bloodhound. Your dad barely used any power." He took a step closer, intruding into my personal space. Dad flicked out a hand.

A shimmering barrier of light appeared between us. "Keep your distance," Dad growled.

Seth's eyes narrowed, not with anger. A more dangerous emotion. Curiosity. I was itching to leave this place. Soren, I could handle. We understood each other in a way. This curious wolf made me nervous.

Seth sensed my wariness and smiled. "Little fairy, you're more interesting than you seem on the surface, aren't you?"

I scoffed. "Hardly."

Dad took a step closer. We joined hands once more.

"Please offer my apologies to your Lord. You should be able to leave your Keep now with no protests from the fae."

Seth continued watching me even as I raised a hand in farewell and disappeared.

Twenty~Four

Our home was full when I finally made it back. Hope, Declan, and Moira shared a couch. Garrett and Simone shared a loveseat. My mother sat on the floor, and Rowan sprawled in my favorite chair and a half, bought for me last month when he saw how much I loved the smaller chair.

He was a bear and wanted to be next to me any time he could, even if all I was doing was reading a book.

His eyes lit up when we shimmered in, and he patted the space next to him. I went straight over, kicking off my shoes to the gods know where, and curled up beside him, burying my nose in his chest for a moment.

I loved the way he smelled, like pine and woods and a little bit of magic.

Moira grinned and winked. Rowan pulled me in closer and held me.

Things would go faster if I just spit everything out while we were all here. "I know why the fae are so angry."

Rowan stilled.

"It's my fault," I admitted.

"It's not," Dad interjected.

I gave him a quelling look. "It is. When I destroyed the tree and became the bridge, I thought it would be better to keep the power a secret. Maybe it was for a while, but all I did was foster anger and resentment. I trapped every single lower fae where they were."

Rowan's hand slid down and gripped my own.

"I separated people from their loved ones and didn't once think about the impact it might have." I swallowed hard, guilt flooding me. "I am so sorry, Rowan."

"Evie. You take the world's burdens upon yourself. No one could have predicted what might happen, and you were right to keep the power a secret. You've been hunted your entire life. Becoming the bridge and being responsible for every single fae who wants to cross is an unfathomable burden."

"One we need to figure out how to fix," Dad said. "And soon. Nyria will tell others what happened tonight, and when she does, our kind will seek you out."

My phone signaled an incoming text. I ignored it. All the important people were here, and Ash and Tess were safe on Keep grounds as far as I knew. I'd look at it in the morning after a good night's rest.

"There's something else," I said to Rowan.

He chuckled. "Isn't there always?"

His phone beeped next.

One more text and there might be an issue. I pressed on. "Soren wishes to move territories."

Rowan blinked. "Seriously? He's tired of his den of iniquity?"

Declan snorted. "That bastard's harem is infamous."

Moira winced, her relief at not taking that final step with Soren written all over her face.

"Seems that way. He wants to return to a place with nature."

Rowan sat a little straighter. "He told you all this?"

"People confide in me," I said with a shrug. "He's tired, and he wants to leave the south."

"Does he have a succession plan?"

I glanced at Garrett. "Not quite."

The shifter's eyes narrowed. "Louisiana?" He shuddered. "Absolutely not."

I laughed. "What? Why not? I hear the food is amazing there."

"I wouldn't know and don't plan to find out," he grumbled. "I'm not opposed to moving Soren to a new territory, but I don't want to take his place."

Rowan shifted to where he could cradle me against his chest. He toyed with my hair as he spoke. "Are you at all interested in becoming a Lord?"

Garrett didn't need a moment to think about it. "In the past, I might have said yes. Working for Evie is a dream. I get a good paycheck, and I've only been shot once."

Everyone besides me laughed. When I thought of that night, the trauma of watching him almost die hit me all over again. But I had to admit, Garrett and I started forming a bond afterward when we'd woken up naked in a hole together. Odd how we'd gone from him threatening to murder me to him being equivalent to a Lord's Second.

"Just once?" Moira asked. "Those are rookie numbers."

Garrett flashed a grin. "I'm surprised it hasn't been worse, actually."

"Stop," I begged with a groan. "I want no one I care about in danger. Not even you, Garrett. I care about you the least."

We grinned at each other. "Are you sure you don't want your own territory?"

Garrett shook his sandy colored head. "I'm getting the best of both worlds, Evie. I protect your interests while not getting caught up in politics. You give me the freedom I need, and I get the autonomy I want."

"Simone?" I asked.

My friend and Omega shrugged a slender shoulder. "I'm with Garrett. I'll be with you for as long as you want or need. Going back to Pack politics and a strict hierarchy—" she shuddered.

Rowan stared at them incredulously. "Damn. I guess I'm chopped liver."

"Not at all," Garrett said. "You're the fairest Lord I've ever known. But Evie—" he slid a sly glance my way, "keeps things interesting."

My mate's knowing chuckle made my lips twitch. "It's going to get worse," I said with a sweet smile.

"Dad canceled court, but pretty soon you two will have to start traveling with me."

Simone perked up. "We get to go to the fae lands and see a real castle?"

Dad nodded. "Many real castles. Evie and Rowan will have numerous social events to attend once things settle down."

Garrett's expression turned thoughtful. "And Thalia?"

"She's safe on my lands," Rowan said. "Though I think you know this by now. She's shown a great interest in the mages."

Garrett frowned. Caelan had placed Garrett in charge of Thalia when my father twisted the Lord's arm into taking her on as a charge. When Garrett came with me, Thalia had to come with him. She was my sister, though we weren't very close, and her magic was wildly different than my own.

Thalia was a Seer and could not be left alone for very long lest she be thrust into a vision and injure herself. She didn't remember most of her visions and needed someone there with her to write everything down for interpretation later. While my sister was doing the best she could with the hand she'd been dealt, Thalia would never be able to work or drive or do any of the things normal people could, and finally coming to terms with those limitations was difficult for her.

I rarely saw her anymore, and she made it clear she didn't want me coming around for a while. While this wasn't my fault, and I refused to accept blame, I respected her wishes and had let her be. She'd find me when, if ever, she wanted to talk.

Complicating things was Garrett's crush, though I think he was on his way to being over that, especially with how snarly Thalia was these days.

"She's surrounded by powerful shifters, Garrett. And no one knows she's here."

"Caelan does." Garrett and the other Lords had once been close friends. After everything, Garrett's trust in him was shattered.

"Caelan has his own shit to deal with," Rowan assured him. "And if he did decide to harass Thalia, he's down half his people, and we have a full house. He won't get very far."

Garrett closed his eyes and let out a heavy breath. "You're right. Thalia isn't helpless, either."

I'd seen them out sparring a few times over the last month or so, and let's just say Thalia really got into trying to beat the tar out of Garrett. And she was surprisingly light on her feet. A few of the other shifters were now taking turns training her. She'd be fine if Garrett decided to take a trip or even an extended absence.

That left one more person in my court. "Moira? You interested in taking a trip to the fae court once this is all over?"

Moira yawned. "I am, but I'll need to balance that with the potential tea shop and other things."

Meaning other people.

My phone went off again. I dug it out of my pocket and looked at the screen.

Rowan did the same.

Dread and fear filled me. "Titania made her move."

I scrambled out of Rowan's arms. "She's decimating Caelan's land."

Dad rose. "If you're coming, join hands and don't let go."

Rowan stood, followed by Garrett, Moira, Declan, and Hope. Simone wasn't much of a fighter and stayed behind unless she was absolutely needed.

Just as Hope's fingers touched mine, a knock on the door sounded.

"Who knocks?" Declan said with a snort. "This place is usually Grand Central Station."

Rowan got a weird look on his face. "Moira, did you give Ethan any travel potions."

Moira turned bright red.

I coughed to cover a laugh. Rowan dropped my fingers and went to the door. "I'm assuming you got a text, too?" he growled.

"When Caelan couldn't reach you two lovebirds, he messaged me." Moira's eyes snapped to the sound of Ethan's voice.

Oh yeah. She had it bad.

"Come on, then. We're about to leave."

Rowan came back into the room with Ethan on his heels. He didn't bother greeting anyone, and his eyes went straight to Moira.

Hope nudged Declan just as he opened his mouth to probably say something dumb. Garrett's eyebrows went high, but he was smarter than most. He kept his mouth shut. Simone openly gawked at them and then looked at me and pointed while mouthing, *"what the fuck."*

Dad rolled his eyes. "Grab hands with your neighbors. We don't know what we're walking into." He paused. "And also, once this is all over, no more free rides. Evie either learns how to do this herself or you guys hire an Uber."

"Dad!"

"I'm serious," he growled. "I'm the fae king, not a taxi service."

"Technically, you're supposed to be retired," I grumbled.

"Can you all stop arguing so we can go save the life of a Lord?" Ethan asked blandly.

I slapped his hand in mine. Ethan took Moira's, and my friend was still bright red. Once we were situated, we disappeared in a shimmer of light straight into holy mortal hell.

Twenty-Five

CAELAN

I was going to die tonight. The thought hit me for the first time with such a wave of knowing, I almost sent the white flag up right then. Strange that I'd die on the coolest summer night I'd ever seen in this place. The stars were bright in the sky, and a gentle breeze rustled through the leaves of the trees standing high around us. Only a shifter could hear that noise.

A human would have only heard the screaming.

My land rumbled and bucked around me, roots flinging themselves from the ground, spearing the dredges of my people. I couldn't fight an enemy I couldn't see. None of us could. We weren't mages. We were shifters. Most of us had no inherent magic other than the shifting ability we were born with. Being resistant to magic would help none of us if we got speared through the eye by a tree root.

I never thought Evie's type of magic would be so dangerous, but here Danu and the blonde bitch with her were showing me how very wrong I was. I'd seen Evie fight with her earth power, but there was a grace to hers, a thoughtfulness in her actions.

This was straight terror.

Titania floated above us, her hair streaming like pale tentacles waving through quiet waters. I'd seen this bitch once before—

right before she sentenced Evie to certain death in that damned tree. Moments before Evie destroyed her.

Or so we'd thought.

The goddess laughed as she swept through my people, the sound like a chorus of bells. I clenched my fists, lowered myself into a position, gathered my magic, and prepared to let go.

Every Lord had one devastating power they kept close to the vest and never revealed unless it was a life or death matter. Even then, some Lords chose to take their secrets to the grave.

I'd never seen Rowan's, and we agreed to let him keep his secret until he was forced to use his. I hoped we'd never see that day.

We popped onto Caelan's land straight into chaos. Shifters lay scattered on the ground, most injured, some unmoving. Roots slashed and punctured anything in its path. The earth rumbled under my feet. I went to my knees and punched power through the ground, before one of those roots hit us.

Moira swore under her breath. "What the hell."

Rowan put his arm out. "Stay where you are." His voice was low and urgent. "Do. Not. Move."

Magic shattered the air, veins of golden power snaking through the ground, touching each and every shifter. At its nexus stood Caelan, a glowing specter of power. He was down on one knee, his arms stretched out like he was taking a benediction. Every vein in his body glowed with power, but as I watched, his skin broke and split, every bruise and cut and broken bone from his people disappearing, only to reappear on the Lord.

Ethan let out a low whistle. "The Blood Dominion," he whispered.

"Don't move," Rowan said again.

I was still on the ground, my fingers sunk a few inches into the earth. Danu lurked somewhere beneath us, the oily feeling of her magic seeping into my skin. But something else was happening.

I sucked in a breath. Caelan's magic overwhelmed my body, Pack magic searing my veins. I'd made a huge mistake. That tiny kernel of magic I'd left inside him had linked us. I could feel the immense power roaring through his blood because the same flowed through mine.

"Evie?"

Rowan's voice sounded like it was underwater.

Caelan threw his head back, an unearthly howl tearing from his throat. A second later, he leapt for Titania's throat.

"Move," Rowan growled. Garrett peeled away from the group. My feet felt like they were nailed to the ground.

"Nnnngghhh," I said.

Moira went to her knees beside me. "Evie."

Her eyes widened when she saw me. "Oh shit. Rowan. Her irises. Look at her eyes."

Rowan spun. He sank to the ground and gripped my chin. "Evie. Your eyes are gold. What the hell?"

His attention snapped to Caelan and back to me. "Shit. You're linked to him. How do I fix it?" When I didn't answer, Rowan let out a string of invectives. "Evie!"

"Nnnnggghh," I said again. My breath came in heaving rasps, my heart pounding against my rib cage. I had to release him. If I didn't, I would overload myself. I sprawled out on the ground, my cheek touching the cold earth, and I sent a small tendril of vine toward Caelan.

I had to touch him to release him, and moving was out of the realm of possibility right now. The vine lifted from the earth and shot upward, slapping Caelan on the back of his calf.

I took back that piece of me as soon as my power touched him, sweet relief pouring through my veins.

"Fuuuuuuuck," I wheezed.

"Thank the gods," Rowan swore.

Ethan chuckled. "Seems like your little insurance policy came back to bite you in the ass."

"Fuck off," I wheezed.

"Asshole," Rowan snarled. "Go help, Caelan."

With a savage grin, Ethan leapt into the fray. Rowan returned his attention to me.

"I'm fine. I promise. Go help Caelan."

"I'll stay with her," Moira said.

Rowan frowned. I pushed at his thigh. "I'll be up in just a minute. Promise."

With a short nod, Rowan rose and ran after Caelan.

Moira helped me up. "You sure you're alright?"

"I am. Just taken by surprise."

"You got hammered," Moira said with a short laugh.

I swayed on my feet. "Magic overload." A laugh bubbled from me. "Won't do that again."

Moira slapped me on the shoulder. "Yeah, I don't believe you. Plus, this is a once in a lifetime event. Caelan will probably never let himself loose like this again."

At that moment, Titania made a mistake. She moved a hair too slow to miss the lethal edge of Caelan's claws.

He was a thing of violent glory, unleashed and unholy power fueled upon the backs of his people. Magic snapped and cracked around him, strikes of golden lighting casting a glow across his land.

Blood sprayed from Titania's throat, cutting off her scream of alarm. Her power failed, sending her slight body crashing to the ground. Caelan followed her down, ripping and tearing through her golden skin.

Rowan and Ethan stood in a half circle around him, neither interfering in his vengeance. Caelan methodically tore her apart; Titania's body so damaged she could no longer fend him off.

"Holy shit," Moira whispered.

Caelan looked like an avenging god, intent on destroying any and all threat to his rule. When Titania lay in pieces at his feet, Caelan rose, his skin etched in rivers of molten gold. His gaze found Rowan first.

My husband stayed perfectly still and dropped his eyes, something I had never seen him do. When Caelan turned his attention to Ethan, the other Lord did the same.

Caelan was a threat to anyone or anything who threatened his territory right now, and from the magic blazing through his veins, neither Lord would be able to stand against him. He slowly turned, his unholy gaze finding me. Our eyes locked for a long moment before Caelan cracked his neck, a terrifying motion that made him look like a puppet on a string and stalked toward me.

"Oh fuck," I whispered.

"Man," Moira murmured. "He is the hottest he's *ever* been right now."

"Shut up," I hissed.

"Mmmm. So dangerous and lethal. Look at him prowling toward you like an animal. He wants to do things to you. Duuu-urty things."

My lips twitched. "I hate you so much."

She leaned closer and whispered in my ear. "Filthy things."

"I am married, you asshole."

"But neither of us are blind."

"Moira!"

Her wicked chuckle made me snort.

Caelan stopped inches away from me. Cuts and bruises marred his perfect skin, some of the wounds close to mortal. How was he still standing, let alone walking?

His head moved slowly toward Moira. "*Leave.*"

The voice that came from him was low, rough, and gritty. Moira stiffened.

"Evie..." Moira swallowed hard. For the first time in a long time, she looked truly afraid. Not for herself, but for me.

Caelan looked like he wanted to eat Moira and not in a fun way.

I gave her what I hoped was a reassuring smile. "It's okay. I can defend myself if need be."

Moira's nostrils flared, and I could see her about to argue.

Lightning still cracked in the sky and through the ground; Caelan's people still lay prone on the ground. But everyone was still alive. For now.

"Do as he asks," I said quietly.

Her lips compressed, but she took a few careful steps backward.

"Out of earshot," Caelan growled. Blood dripped from a deep cut at his temple, snaking down his jaw to drip onto his chest. My power rose, the need to heal him almost overwhelming. I shoved it down. He was still connected to everyone, and I wasn't sure what my power would do.

Didn't stop my magic from reaching out to him.

Caelan, damn him, felt it and closed his eyes, tilting his neck up as if he were a cat instead of a dangerous god. Were we still connected?

Shit. Not good.

Rowan and Ethan were walking up behind him, but Caelan's attention snapped to them. "*Leave.*"

My husband's eyes began to glow.

I didn't want anything to escalate. With Caelan in this state, I didn't think Rowan would win. "Please," I beseeched him. "It's okay. I don't think he'll hurt me."

"I would *never* hurt you," Caelan growled.

Well. Not quite true and far too late for such a declaration.

The bond between Rowan and I tugged, his concern flooding

our link. I sent love and reassurance to him. "Trust me," I mouthed.

Caelan saw what I mouthed but his intense stare never wavered. Whatever he wanted, he was willing to take everyone out to get it. This could either be what he needed for closure or something that might backfire spectacularly. Since I didn't see a way out of it without violence, I'd grant him this one time grace.

Rowan didn't like it, but when I nodded, Rowan took a few steps back. Ethan kept his distance, but he wouldn't care if Caelan gutted me either way.

"Alright, Caelan. You got me."

His soft snort told me what he thought of that. "Walk with me."

"Alright." I schooled my emotions and did my best to slow my wild heart rate down.

He held out his arm, just like he used to, and tears welled in my eyes. How things had changed.

I slid my fingers over the crook of his arm. Caelan's eyes shut for a moment, and when he opened them, his stare rocked me back on my heels. My mouth tasted of copper and fear.

"Tell them to keep their distance," he growled.

"They heard you."

At his nod, we were off, my bond with Rowan tugging painfully the farther we walked. If the roles were reversed, Caelan would have burned the world down because he wouldn't have trusted me or Rowan. And that was ultimately the reason why I married Rowan. He trusted me in matters like this, even when we were all in danger.

"Are you alright?" His skin against my fingers was so hot it had to be uncomfortable for him.

"As long as I hold the power, my people will live."

I glanced at him. "I don't understand."

We walked for a little while longer, turning a corner in the path, obscuring us from Rowan and the others. Caelan spoke once more.

"Every Lord has a power they rarely reveal. Mine calls on the entire Pack. I take their strength, but I also take their wounds. For now, they are in stasis, not healed, but not dying either. This power makes me almost invulnerable, but when I release it, I will become almost human in strength and magic for several hours until my own power replenishes. As a downside to becoming almost godlike, If too many of my people succumb to their wounds, I will die as well."

I stopped in my tracks. "*Caelan*. Why?"

He looked away. "Because I did not think you would come." A harsh breath escaped him. "I did not think anyone would come."

Even after I promised him I would always be there when he asked, Caelan still wondered whether I would leave him high and dry.

I couldn't help myself. Tugging him closer, I brought him in for a hug. His arms slid around my waist and crushed me to his chest. Caelan buried his face in my neck and inhaled a shaky breath. I said nothing when I felt hot tears fall against my skin, but I held on to him.

I knew what it felt like to be abandoned, the hopelessness that came with knowing no one was going to come and save you. I'd felt it on that cool night lying broken in the field of heather thousands of miles away from home and many times before then, and I felt it when Caelan abandoned me due to his own prejudices.

How could I do the same to him? I would never be the kind of person who would confront him with his own cruelty when he was breaking down in front of me. I rubbed my hand down his back and through his hair, murmuring soft, nonsensical words.

He shuddered and brought me to the ground, still holding onto me tightly. There was nothing sexual in this, only a raw and heavy grief and a need to share it with someone. I sent a small spiral of power into the ground and brought up a cage of vines and flowers to give us some privacy, ensuring I gave the cage a little extra padding to muffle the noise.

Dad's magical training helped, but some things did not come

as naturally to me as they did with him. He suspected part of that had to do with my Chimera heritage. I was a lot stronger with illusion and earth power than with his form of wild magic.

But what I made would do for now.

I kept the top open to the sky above, the golden lightning a show unlike anything I'd ever seen before. The scent of blooms rose through the air.

"I am sorry," he gritted out, his face still buried in my shoulder.

"You've already apologized and made amends."

"I'm sorry for being a stubborn ass."

"Ah. Yes. You haven't apologized for that, but I suspect I don't need to tell you the cost." It was written in his skin, in the blood and cuts and broken bones I couldn't see.

He sighed against my skin. "I've been such a fool."

"You're still alive, Caelan. You have a second chance to get things right."

He pulled away then but didn't let go of me. Our faces were so close, our noses almost touched. There was an intimacy between us, but no longer a spark. Those belonged to Rowan.

"Thank you for coming."

I touched his face. "I'm sad you didn't believe me."

He looked away, shame flickering over his features. "I'm not sure I would have done the same for you."

"I know," I whispered.

He closed his eyes and let out a heavy sigh. "You were right to leave me."

I smiled. "I know that, too."

The golden light in his eyes faded just a touch. His chuckle was genuine this time. "Your mate and Ethan know my secret. We live in unprecedented times."

"You can trust Rowan. Ethan is a sonofabitch, but he seems to operate by his own fucked up code of honor. Plus, I think he has a crush on Moira, so your secret might be safe with him since we're all linked together."

His eyebrows flicked up. "Moira. Huh. No shit?"

"We'll see where it goes." I pulled back a little more. "I'm not sure if I can, but I'd like to heal you. If you allow me to."

He snorted. "After all this, I'll allow you to do whatever the hell you want, Evie."

"Danu still lurks below. If you want me to put a barrier up, I will. Doing so will shove her out of your lands."

"Why hasn't she attacked?"

"She knows I'm here. Titania is—" I paused. "Titania *was* a lot more impulsive than Danu. Though you did a hell of a good job making sure she won't rise again." We shared a savage grin. "If I claim the outskirts of your lands, Danu won't be able to claim any of the Lord's territories. We can talk details later." When I was sure that old bitch wasn't listening.

He nodded. "Then yes and thank you. I won't be able to use this power again for a while. My lands and people are the most vulnerable they've ever been."

I touched his cheek. "With this, I can fully purge the poison from Danu. You and your lands will be completely healed. I'll also try to heal your people if I can, but I've never tried such a thing before. Some of them have lost a lot of blood."

When I first arrived, I could feel it seeping into the earth.

Caelan's eyes met mine, both of understanding what I meant. I wasn't sure I could save everyone. With his life force linked directly to his people's, I had to try. He put his hand over mine. "I can never thank you for what you've done."

"We didn't do much of anything tonight. You had it well under control. But I hope I can do something now. Ready?"

"I am."

I squirmed out of his grip and sat beside him, keeping a hand on his arm. "Try not to move."

My other hand went straight into the cool dirt, the familiar magic of Caelan's land rising to welcome me. I sent everything I had down into the earth, following the golden veins of magic from Caelan to his shifters and went to work.

CHAPTER
Twenty-Seven

I gasped. Two of his shifters were near death. The only thing holding them to the world was Caelan. I had to heal the Lord before I could heal his people.

"Evie?"

"Mmm?"

He rarely interrupted me when I was in the middle of using my power.

"There's one more thing."

I cracked an eye open.

Caelan wouldn't look at me. "I've only used this power once before. There was a consequence I wasn't prepared for."

I stayed silent, even as dread crept down my spine.

"The last time, some of the survivors..." Caelan blew out a long breath. "They lost their autonomy. A cruel punishment for anyone, but a death sentence for a shifter."

His meaning struck me like an ice pick to the heart. "You made them your slaves?"

"I didn't mean to." He bowed his head. "Once I cut the power, I thought everything was fine, but afterward, I felt a few of them tied tighter to me than ever before. They couldn't leave the pack or do anything without my say so."

"Oh Caelan." What a terrible burden to bear.

"All of them decided to go out on their own terms." He swallowed hard. "There was nothing I could do. The mages couldn't reverse it. No one could help me. I—I don't blame them."

"If I see those bonds, what do you want me to do?"

Caelan said nothing for a long moment. "If they are close to death, let them go."

"Do you want me to try to save them if I can?"

Hope flared bright in his eyes. "I—yes. If you think you can. If they won't be bound to me, do everything you can. I will be in your debt."

"There are no debts between friends."

The guilt on his face broke my heart. Caelan would have a lot of soul searching to do when this was over, but we were finally walking on the right path.

"Anything else?"

He shook his head. I closed my eyes once more and dove back into the web of golden threads.

Danu lurked close, so I decided to claim the land and cast her out first. Easy enough to do. I circled Caelan's massive territory with a thin band of my power, claiming only the first few feet of his property.

Danu barely had time to shriek her fury before she was sucked out of the place like I'd put the top of a vacuum right over her head. I chuckled under my breath and kept working. The wards shuddered seconds later, Danu trying to take them down.

She might succeed with the wards, but Caelan's land was officially off limits. Ha. Interpersonal skills and communication for the win!

I never thought Caelan and I would be sitting here together healing our issues, and yet, here we were, trapped in a cage once again.

Every strand of gold led back to Caelan, a shining thread of magic leading to a corresponding wound on his body. His insides looked worse than his outside.

I sucked in a sympathetic gasp and reached out blindly. My hand pressed against his lower abdomen where the worst of the internal bleeding was.

"Don't move," I whispered.

Caelan chuckled. "A few inches lower and it's going to be a party."

"Ass." I had to laugh. "If you have any around that area, you're going to have to ask Rowan to kiss it and make it better."

Caelan let out a bark of laughter. "I've missed you, Evie."

"Shh. I'm working here."

I focused on mending the internal bleeding first. Caelan's sigh of relief and the gold vein disappearing told me I was on the right path. The creak of growing vines and the heavy scent of blooms was the only outward sign of how much magic I was using.

I moved next to a deep cut on his chest, and so on and so forth until every vein but the thicker ones were gone. If Caelan hadn't said anything, I might not have noticed. A few had that slightly thicker, brighter thread linking them to their Lord.

"I'm not sure what you might feel, but don't break our contact."

"Understood," Caelan rumbled. "How many?"

I counted the threads. "Eight."

Caelan let out a string of curse words. "Can you unentangle them?"

"I'm not sure. I'll try. Just make sure we're in contact no matter what happens."

"The chance to keep touching you for the last time?" Caelan rumbled. "Count me in."

"Caelan. Be serious."

He grunted. "Do your worst, Evangeline."

I dove back in and examined the threads more thoroughly than the others. They were all tied to shallower wounds, which was unusual. I followed the threads back to the shifters. Six females, two males. The males felt younger to me. I pulled their bodies down from the surface deep underground and held them there, ensuring they had a pocket of air.

I examined Caelan closely, looking for something to sever their threads and couldn't find anything. Another scan of his body revealed no other wounds, nothing else I could heal. Frustrated, I chewed on the side of my lip. Could I somehow transfer this bond away from Caelan?

I racked my brain. I'd need something extremely long lived, something I could fortify with magic. Shifters were immortal, so I couldn't tie their bond to something that would have a short natural life cycle.

I'd need something natural to suit my magic, yet also *unnatural.*

There were a few trees with unusually long life spans. Not native to Texas but Joy Springs didn't have the typical Texas climate. I could tweak Caelan's land a little in one spot—adjust the soil and nutrients, maybe cap his land in sort of a bubble that would keep the tree thriving.

"How do you feel about a new tree?" I murmured.

Caelan stiffened. "As long as you aren't trapped inside, I'm amenable."

"If everything goes well, I won't be. Titania is dead, so the odds are looking good."

"Don't even joke about that," Caelan growled.

"I don't know if this will be painful. This is all theoretical."

"Comforting words."

I sent my power soaring through the world, searching far and wide for a specific seed.

Caelan gasped. "Evie. What are you doing? I feel…"

"Looking for something."

He sucked in a breath. "Gods. Is this what you feel like all the time? Like you can touch the inner heart of the world?"

"It's a recent thing, no thanks to that hooker Danu."

I stopped at something familiar, paused, and examined. Close but not exact. Discarding it, I kept searching.

There. A teeny tiny, dormant seed. I pulled it to me, yanking it from its habitat toward me. "Where do you want it?"

"Back of the property," Caelan said. "There's a dense canopy of trees and no structures. Few go back there."

I searched until I found the spot, carefully cradling the seed in my magic. "Alright. Here goes nothing. Hang on tight."

Caelan gripped my thigh.

I changed the soil, adding more limestone and rock, and built up the space as closely as I could to its natural environment. "Your land in this spot will be colder. Can't be helped."

Caelan gently squeezed my thigh in the affirmative.

I nudged the seed to grow, smiling when I saw the seedling break through, encouraging it to grow, grow, *grow*. The seedling poked through the dirt, growing and spreading, its trunk twisting like a braided vine. Ten feet, twenty, thirty, it climbed until it slowed at forty-five, fifty, then sixty feet. Mature, but still young.

"I'm going to try to transfer the bond."

Caelan went still. "To what? That tree?"

"Yes. I'll know if it worked in a moment. Stay quiet."

I gently plucked those golden threads, double checking to ensure all the wounds were healed. Once I was satisfied, I gently unwound the threads from Caelan's psyche, holding them tightly in my mind.

Caelan let out a sharp breath and sagged.

"Easy," I whispered. Slow, ever so slowly, I moved those threads across Caelan's land, stretching the golden threads across the earth. A thought occurred to me.

"Shit," I cursed under my breath.

"Evie?"

"Hold on."

Holding onto those threads with one part of my mind, I searched again for one, two, three, four more seeds, planting them at various corners of the United States, hoping against all odds this would work. I set one on my property, one on our joint property, one right at the edge of Thorvin's, Ethan's, Soren's, and

Ben's. I'd ask them later if I could move the trees onto their properties, but if I left only one, Caelan's shifters would never be able to leave.

If they wanted to move Packs, they couldn't, and I wouldn't do the same thing to them that Caelan had all those years ago.

I shifted the nutrients in the soil once more and changed the atmosphere, encasing the tree in a small, self-cycling bubble. Once that was done, I carefully transferred all eight of those threads to the home tree on Caelan's land.

They resisted at first, but magic like this only needed a life source, one rife with magic, and it had one in these trees. When it realized I'd offered a good substitute, those threads settled and entwined with the tree. Once I was confident they'd stay, I let go.

But I wasn't done yet. Carefully weaving a strand of each thread together, I created one extra thread and attached to each one of the other trees, creating a nexus of a sort.

The shifters would be able to travel to each of the other Lord's territories and their surrounding areas. I'd need to check the magic periodically, but as fixes went, this one wasn't bad.

I waited a while, ensuring nothing would come loose, and when I was sure, I carefully let go and returned to Caelan's land, once again plunging down into his land to find the source of Danu's poison. My influence had scattered her magic and finding everything felt like gathering lost marbles.

After several sweeps, I was confident I had it all. The last step was Caelan. I shifted, briefly opening my eyes to face him, startled to see his eyes wide open staring at me with molten gold burning in his irises. I swallowed hard and looked down.

"You've become quite skilled since I last saw you."

"Training with Dad."

"This power suits you. I wish I would have seen how great you could become and how lucky I would be to bask in your light sooner."

"We're almost finished," I said quietly. "One more thing."

I reached up to touch his face and closed my eyes. Danu's poison still lived inside him, a sentient, evil thing. Focusing on that darkness, I encapsulated it and slowly pulled it from his skin. Caelan grunted when I freed him, his hand tightening on my leg.

I crushed that power in my hand, dark glittering ash falling from my palm when I opened it.

"There." I let my magic go and removed my hand from Caelan's face. When I opened my eyes, he was still staring at me.

I dropped the cage, sending the roots of the flowers out onto his land. A riot of blooms covered the ground, a carpet of color brightening the night. "I need to get back to Rowan."

Caelan smiled sadly. "Thank you, flower girl. I'm not sure I would have survived this night without you."

I wasn't so sure he would have either, but I shook my head in denial. "Your shifters might sleep for a while. When they wake up, I want you to call me. I'll need to explain what I've done."

Caelan unfolded himself and rose, holding out a hand to help me up. I swayed, the amount of magic I used catching up to me. He steadied me with a firm grip on my waist.

"Need help walking?"

I shook my head. "No. Just give me a moment."

He waited until I took a few baby deer-like steps, firmly taking my elbow to escort me back.

"What exactly did you do?" he asked. "I feel the new tree. Lots of magic pouring off that thing."

I knew what he was asking, but explaining my process was too much for me right now. "I took the links from you and put them in a long-lived tree."

Caelan's eyebrows flew up. "It worked?"

I nodded. "With some caveats."

"Alright," he said slowly. "Anything I need to worry about?"

"Not really. I'll need to—"

Caelan's phone buzzed several times in rapid succession. He let out a low laugh. "What are the odds this is about you?"

"Pretty high."

I offered him a sheepish smile. Caelan let out a loud laugh and sighed. "Come on, flower girl. Let's get you back to your mate."

When we turned the corner, Rowan took off running. He was at my side in an instant, his arms reaching out to scoop me up in a fierce hug. The bond tugged between us, bright and warm. His hand tangled in my hair, a shudder of relief shaking his shoulder.

"Evie. Thank the gods. Are you alright?"

Caelan huffed. "I'd never harm Evie."

Rowan spun with me in his arms, his eyes glowing with fury. "You hurt her all the godsdamn time when she lived here."

Ethan put a warning hand on Rowan's shoulder.

Caelan sighed. "I'm well aware of what I've done, and I know my actions are unforgivable."

"Caelan—"

His gaze flicked to me. "Unforgivable to your mate, I should say. Your tender heart has once again given me more than I deserve."

Ethan frowned. "And your silver tongue doesn't hurt."

Caelan grinned. "I'm afraid Evie has planted a permanent structure on my property. Mind sticking around for a little while? I've summoned the Keep mages to tend to the wounded. Though I'm not sure anyone is wounded anymore, thanks to Evie."

"They're all unconscious," Ethan said, giving me an odd look. "We saw the moment Evie started working."

"Like magic," Rowan said dryly.

"Let me check on them. Please stay. We need to look at the tree Evie summoned."

Rowan blinked. "Another tree?"

"Mmm. Yes. It was the only thing I could think of that had room to put everyone."

Rowan and Ethan both stared at me confused.

"I'll explain when we get there."

Caelan was back in less than a minute, relief all over his expression. "The healers said they expect everyone to wake up in a few days. They've asked me to extend my thanks."

"Where were your mages when Titania and Danu came onto your lands?" Ethan asked.

"I have very few left and couldn't afford to risk them. They were instructed to stay put until I called for them." His expression darkened. "Or until they felt me die."

Ethan looked around Caelan's Keep. "Things are that dire then."

Caelan nodded. "I made my bed."

"You sure did," Rowan muttered.

I tightened my grip on his waist. "Just for tonight can we try to be at peace?"

Rowan glanced down at me. "Like Caelan, I appreciate your tender heart. Unlike you, I will never forgive him for what he did to you."

I reached up and touched his face. "You don't have to. But civility would be nice."

Rowan's lips thinned before he nodded. "Fine. You have ten minutes, Caelan."

Ethan chuckled. "Show us this tree, Evie. I'm all atwitter with curiosity."

• • •

THE TREE WAS massive and gnarled and had strange leaves resembling a toilet brush. It loomed above us and sparkled with a mix of crimson, gold, and watermelon tourmaline magic—Caelan and my power combined.

"That thing is quite ugly," Rowan observed.

I smacked him gently on the chest. "What did the tree ever do to you?"

"I'm with Rowan." Ethan shook his head. "You'll be glad it's at the back of the property. The thing is an eyesore."

"Rude," I huffed.

Caelan's look held mild amusement, and I could tell he was thinking along the same lines as the other two. "Alright, assholes," I growled. "The bristlecone pine is one of the longest-lived trees on the planet. Records hold some of them at almost 5,000 years old. I had to find something old and strong enough to hold those bonds, and this was the one and only thing I thought might stand a chance."

I gestured at the admittedly hideous tree. "And I was right."

I crossed my arms and glared at all of them.

Caelan laughed. "I'm grateful, Evie. But you have to admit, it is pretty ugly."

"Yes, well. You are welcome."

I turned and placed my hand on the gnarled trunk. All the bonds were there and content. "There are other trees on the boundaries of the other Lords' properties. I plan to ask permission to move them inside their borders when I have extra time."

Rowan's expression cleared. "Oh shit. Evie. You have to maintain these, don't you?"

His brows drew together, and he shot Caelan a dark look.

I hurried to explain. "Not often. The atmosphere is the most delicate part. This tree prefers high elevation and limestone-rich soil. I'll need to ensure the right mix of nutrients and atmosphere, but I think I'll be able to maintain the rest at a distance. Since this one is the anchor tree, it may require an in-person visit, maybe once or twice a year."

Rowan looked furious. "You just can't let go, can you?"

"It was my decision," I said. "If Caelan held onto those bonds…" My voice trailed off. "Let's just say, this was necessary."

Ethan had a thoughtful look on his face. "Your gift enslaves people," he murmured.

Caelan looked away, his jaw tightening. "A small percentage, which is why I almost never use the power."

"Evie won't always be around to fix things for you." Rowan's eyes were glowing again.

Caelan held up his hands. "I'm well aware. Can we not fight anymore, please? I'm exhausted, and I'm sure Evie is, too."

He looked at me and placed his hand over his heart. "I'll call you when they wake up. Thank you again. You've given me a gift I can never repay."

I dipped my head. "You're welcome."

Caelan turned to go. "See yourselves off. I'm going to bed."

"Someone needs to take care of Titania, ASAP. Do not leave her lying on the ground for long. Danu is gone, but I wouldn't put anything past her. Behead her, then burn her to ash."

Ethan's stoic face widened into a wicked grin. "Sometimes I think you're more bloodthirsty than we are."

"Titania has risen from the dead once," I grumbled. "No reason to risk fate again."

Caelan nodded and walked away, leaving us standing next to the ugly tree.

Ethan waited until he was out of earshot. "Why'd you do it?"

He didn't sound angry or annoyed, only curious.

"The thought of enslaving his people devastated him. I did the only thing I could."

Ethan crossed his arms over his chest. "Moira and everyone else are with the healers. I'll text them and let them know you're back."

He looked at Rowan. "Mind if I crash at the Keep tonight?"

"Of course. We have a few empty apartments. Hope will show you when we get back."

Rowan wrapped his arm around my waist and buried his nose in my hair. "I'm sorry."

"Don't be." How could I be mad at him? My ex-boyfriend had all but commandeered me to speak to him while under the influence of an unholy power that might have gotten us all killed.

"Are we good?" he murmured.

"One hundred percent," I promised.

Dad returned with everyone in tow, got a gander at the tree, snorted and barked, "Let's get the hell out of here."

Seconds later, we were home.

Twenty-Nine

Moira yanked me inside her apartment and shut the door. "Are you okay? Rowan is furious!"

I rubbed the space between my brows. A rare headache was beginning to form. "I'm fine. He has every right to be mad, but neither of us could help what happened."

Moira's eyebrows rose damn near to her hairline. "And what exactly happened?"

"Nothing. He had to come down from his power, and I had to claim the land to keep Danu from trying again once I was gone."

Moira's jaw dropped. "He let you?"

"Caelan has seen the error of his ways. This time, he was properly chastised. I think going forward, things will be better." I frowned. "Though I don't expect us to spend much time together. If I can't maintain the main tree at a distance, I may have to visit his Keep a couple times a year."

"Rowan will be ecstatic."

"Rowan will come with me." I waved a hand at her. "Enough about me. What's going on with Ethan?"

Her lips tightened. "Nothing. There was far too much action tonight for us to even speak."

I turned the doorknob to leave. The only thing I wanted right now was to faceplant onto my bed. "He's staying the night tonight," I said with a grin. "Plenty of time to chat now."

"Begone with you, hussy."

I laughed and slipped out the door, hurrying back to the main house.

Rowan was waiting for me on the couch. He closed his eyes when I walked in and exhaled.

I kicked off my shoes and went straight to him, curling in his lap and tangling my hands through his hair. He wrapped his arms around me and kissed me fiercely.

When we finally came up for air, I took his face in my hands. "I know how hard that was for you, and I'm sorry. Caelan was…" I exhaled. "Dangerous. The power you Lords hold is terrifying."

"He really would have enslaved his people?"

I nodded. Rowan sighed. "I want so badly to hate that bastard."

A laugh bubbled from my lips. "Me too."

"You did the right thing, Evie. Even if he didn't deserve it."

"His people are blameless."

Rowan snorted. "Garrett and Simone are blameless. The rest of them watched him treat you like shit and did nothing about it." He paused, then begrudgingly said, "Though no one deserves to be enslaved."

"Right," I agreed. "I did it for both. Caelan, because of how desperate he was, and his people, because no one deserved a consequence like that."

"And those trees?"

"I'm hopeful everything can be done at a distance."

"Good." He rose in a fluid motion, taking me with him. I wrapped my legs around his waist.

"I plan to keep you busy for the next twenty-four hours. Text Moira and tell her to eat breakfast with Ethan."

I cackled. "Careful. She's the kind to kill you in your sleep."

"As long as I was beside you, I'd die a happy man."

The things he said to me…

True to his word, the world was quiet while Rowan kept me happily trapped in the bedroom, coming up for air only for food and bathroom breaks.

Two mornings later, someone banged on the front door.

A deep male voice shouted, "None of us are going into your den of sin. Evie's father is here! Get your ass out of bed and let her train."

"Fucking Declan," Rowan growled.

I snickered and rolled over. A proprietary grip on my hip kept me from sliding out of bed. "One more round?"

"Rowan! I'm tapping out. I need a shower, food, and fresh air."

"How you wound me, woman." His chestnut hair was mussed, and his hazel eyes were twinkling as he watched me. He lay on his stomach, his face turned to watch me.

I reached over and ran my fingers through his hair. "I will always be yours. No one, no matter our history, will ever tear us apart. The moment that bond solidified between us, there would never be another. You are mine, and I am yours."

Rowan's eyes turned that strange mix of colors. Silver, gold, and watermelon tourmaline. "Mine," he growled.

"Yours," I promised.

I slid away to his groan of protest. "Now get up and shower."

His eyes lit up. "With you?"

I laughed and took off running. "If you can catch me!"

"Any word on Danu?" I asked Dad half an hour later.

"No. She's lurking close. I feel her oily presence."

"I can't keep ignoring her. The longer I do, the more time she has to plan something else."

Dad frowned at the magic in my hands. "Too much Chimera," he lectured. "Focus only on your fae half."

Easier said than done. "My magic mixed a while ago. I can't separate it on a whim."

Dad rolled his eyes. "You can do whatever you want. Once

you get used to tapping into different parts of yourself, this will all seem so much easier."

"Says you."

Dad snorted. "Mom and I have decided enough is enough."

The magic I held fizzled and died. "Excuse me?"

Dad smirked. "If we are to unite our people, we can no longer be neutral."

His words were a drastic turnaround from the last year or so when he and Mom flat out refused to get involved in anything involving the gods. "What changed your mind?"

Dad gently smacked my hands once more. "Try again."

I rolled my eyes and started to gather magic once more.

"You had zero compunctions about killing our people if they stood with Danu."

I dropped the sputtering magic once more. "Danu is wrong."

"We're ancient, daughter. Right and wrong are never concrete in our eyes. But we've realized as rulers, we have the right to dictate the state of things. All we can do is try to be fair and just. The world doesn't belong to one people. It belongs to all of us."

"Glad my murderous intentions opened your eyes," I said dryly.

"No. Your words didn't change our minds. Your intent did. If they hadn't left, you would have taken them all out. I felt the intent behind your words."

Dad paused and watched the small ball of power grow between my palms. "Killing them would have devastated you, and I know you still would have made the choice."

Rowan listened intently from the sidelines, his gaze resting on me. Our bond warmed. He, of all people, knew how much I struggled to make the right choices and how so many times, those choices had awful endings—even if they were the right ones.

"I rarely see you hesitate in taking anyone out. What made you and Mom wait so long?"

Dad inhaled a slow breath and sighed. "There are not as many of us as there used to be. Infighting and skirmishes with other supernaturals have dwindled our numbers. We always tried to err on the side of preservation. Perhaps we should have been more focused on the future."

"Danu still gathers our people to her side. Apparently sharing is caring wasn't taught in school during her formative years."

Dad chuckled. "Fae aren't so great at sharing. We like to hold onto things, no matter if doing so hurts us in the end."

He took my hands and shaped them, sending a small pulse of power through my fingers. "Like this."

Pure fae power sifted through my fingers, no trace of the Chimera to be seen. "Whoa."

"Don't drop it," he warned. "Look inside and see what's different."

I closed my eyes and dipped into my vast reservoir of power, far deeper than it was a few months ago. The Chimera magic swam with the fae power, but a small siphon of it rose from that well, up through my body and into my palms. "Huh."

"Drop it and try again without my guidance."

I did as he asked, my mind half focused on other things. I'd been mulling a proposal for a while and didn't see the harm in bringing the idea up now. "What if we made some of the fae Lords or something similar?"

Dad frowned. "You want to give the fae official territory like your Rowan has?"

I lifted my shoulder in a shrug. "Why not? The Lords have territories. As long as we don't encroach on the humans, it shouldn't be an issue. There's plenty of property for sale all over the country, and it's better for the fae to own it than a developer."

Dad's lips twitched. "True. Though the fae believe sharing to be such a human concept. I'll run it by your mother. Could work, provided we can convince them they don't need to take the Lords' property when they can have their own, and sharing would benefit everyone."

I managed to make a lopsided ball of pure fae power. "Hot damn! Look at me! I'm a wizard, Dad!"

Rowan burst out laughing.

As expected, Dad didn't get the reference, but he beamed with pride, nonetheless. "There! Now practice until you can conjure it in your sleep."

I groaned.

"Every little bit helps, Evangeline," he said in a no-nonsense tone. "Until you can master the basics without thinking they're silly—" he did a perfect imitation of my whiny voice "—you won't be able to master the deeper parts of your power."

I opened my mouth to argue that I was doing just fine, thank you very much, but Dad shook his head and speared me with a look. "There's no argument about how powerful you are, daughter, but you haven't tapped even twenty percent of your power."

Shock made me blink at him owlishly. "What."

Rowan sucked in a breath. "Holy shit," he murmured to himself.

"I know you feel that vast well of power living inside you. The lock made you rely on what you had, not your potential."

"Danu is such a bitch," I muttered.

"I suspect Titania also had a hand in the suppression."

At my sour look, Dad sighed. "They must have gotten to you when you were away from your human parent's observation. Perhaps even Lugh helped. He's a talented illusionist, as you no doubt learned. Regardless, the lock is gone, and you'll never be taken unaware again. Now is the time to hone your power to the best of your ability. Soon, once you learn how to mold your will to your magic, you will be unstoppable."

"Kinda thought I was already."

Dad gave me a savage smile. "Imagine how people will tremble when you come into your true potential."

My true potential sounded scary as hell, if I were being honest because sometimes, I even scared myself. Twenty percent of my power. Jaysus, Mary, and that other guy. That lock on my power must have happened in childhood because I couldn't imagine for a single moment having that kind of magic during puberty. I might have opened a wormhole into another dimension or something.

Rowan sent a pulse of love through the bond. When I glanced at him, his eyes were warm with empathy. Meanwhile, all I wanted to do was put my head between my knees and have a panic attack.

"Dad. I don't think having that much power is a good thing."

My father's first reaction was a thunderous frown, but he paused and slowly nodded. "Absolute power corrupts absolutely. Is that what the humans say?"

"The quote is attributed to Lord Acton," I said. This quote had played on repeat inside my head after my attack and I was wrestling with the unholy power burning through my veins.

"Unchecked power will ultimately lead to corruption and moral decay," Dad added. "He is not wrong. But you have never been the norm, Evie. You are the queen our people needed. Your mother and I have always struggled to solve problems without using force or manipulation."

"Have you forgotten the threatening that went down a few days ago?" I asked dryly.

Dad chuckled. "No, but you gave them the choice, and that's the important thing."

I wasn't so sure. "The choice was my way or the highway. Not much of a choice, is it?"

"You always want the best for everyone. Danu's side wants to take and give nothing in return. You want to distribute and live in harmony. Big difference between the two, yes?"

"Well. Yes." I doubted I'd ever be completely comfortable with being a queen because I didn't like telling people what to do. When I was younger, I used to believe most people were ulti-mately good. I wasn't sure I believed that anymore. Not after dealing with the fae and the Lords, not to mention the Chimera who'd repeatedly tried to kill me.

Ruling people felt like a power no one should have. But one could argue a good ruler is better than allowing a bad one to come to power. I could, and had, argued with myself over this many a night since taking the crown, but Dad was right.

I had a burning desire to do what was right. People should be free, but there should also be someone powerful and good to ensure they stayed that way. Swaying people to my way of thinking made me feel squicky, but the Lords didn't deserve to lose everything they'd worked for. Neither did the fae deserve to lose their homes because they didn't have land.

My destroying their tree had worsened everything, and few people knew what I had done. After visiting Caelan, I had an idea on how to fix the bridge and remove the cursed power. No idea if my idea would work, so I planned to experiment before I said anything to anyone.

If it worked, I could solve most of our problems quickly. If I told people and it failed, I might not have to worry about becoming queen officially because I'd have hordes of angry fae after me.

"We lost her," Rowan said, his words penetrating my whirling thoughts.

I blinked. "Sorry. I was off on a philosophical roller coaster."

Dad brought my palms together and extinguished the still burning magic. "Get out of your head, daughter. You are a natural leader."

He looked at Rowan. "Make sure she gets to bed early tonight. She's exhausted."

Heat colored my cheek. A slow smile worked its way onto Rowan's lips. "You got it, Dad."

I let out a surprised laugh. My father rolled his eyes. "Cheeky bastard. I like you less than the other one."

"The difference between me and the other one is I don't care." Rowan's smile took on an edge.

Dad huffed. "Three days from now, we'll train again."

Without waiting for my response, he disappeared in a shower of light.

"Do you think you'll ever get along with him?" I asked.

Rowan rose and pounced, scooping me into his arms. He buried his nose into the crook of my neck and loped toward the house. "I didn't marry him."

"Rowan! I'm starving. Food first!"

"Dirty girl. What thoughts are running wild in your head? I was merely carrying you to the kitchen to make you a sandwich."

"Liar," I said with a laugh. "But I really do want a sandwich."

His drawn out groan made me grin. "Five minutes. That's all you get."

He kicked the front door in, shattering the door jam. "I'll do it in three."

Rowan loped through the house and tossed me onto the bed, kicking the door shut. This time, it held, the result of reinforcement after the last time he broke it.

Having a bear shifter for a mate was hard on indoor structures, but I wouldn't have it any other way.

CHAPTER

Thirty

MOIRA

Ethan stood in my kitchen. I shrieked and dropped my tea cup, brown liquid spraying the side of my cabinets. One moment the cup was in the air, the next, Ethan held it in his hand, the rest of the liquid still inside.

I blinked. No one, not even me, could move like that. He straightened, holding the cup out.

I took it and stared at him in silence.

"Your door was unlocked."

My eyebrows lifted and I sipped my tea. We both knew that was a lie.

Ethan sniffed. "Do you have any more tea?"

I pointed to the small ceramic pot. "Earl Grey. I added lavender, vanilla, and cream."

He tried not to look eager as he rummaged through my cabinets for another mug.

"Ethan?"

"Hmm?"

"How'd you really get in?"

"Does it matter?"

"Considering I am a woman and I live alone, yes, it matters."

Ethan went still. When he turned, his eyes held a touch of

glow. "No one would harm you here. If they tried, you would gut them."

His confidence in my gutting skills warmed the cockles of my cold, dead heart, but even I wasn't invulnerable. I tugged my sweater closer and shivered.

His eyes snapped to the belt of my sweater. "You're cold. Do you have a heavier cardigan?"

"*Ethan.* How did you get inside my apartment?"

"You need better locks," was all he said before he stormed past me, heading toward my bedroom.

I scrambled after him. "What the hell? Ethan!"

He barreled through my bedroom door and went straight to my closet to flip through my clothing.

"You cannot be in here!"

"Why don't you have more sweaters?"

I shoved against his side. "Get out of my bedroom!"

A lacy nightgown lay carelessly tossed across my recliner and the bed was still unmade. I'd tossed my slippers in a haphazard pile by the nightstand, and a racy dark romance novel lay face down by the lamp. Heat rose to my cheeks.

"You're cold all the time, Moira. Why haven't you bought anything?"

"Because I'm busy!" Lies. I kept forgetting, only remembering when I was back home and shivering in the few cardigans I had.

I wore the cashmere he bought me all the time, but what I really needed were a few heavy wrap sweaters to wear around the house.

His lips thinned. "If you lived in my territory, I would remedy this."

I huffed. "Rowan is not my dad, nor is he my Lord. I am not a shifter, lest you forget!"

"You are one of his people."

I crossed my arms over my chest. "I'm Evie's people."

"Then why hasn't she bought any for you?"

"Because I'm a grown woman!" I shoved him one more time, but he was a brick wall.

Ethan reached out and gripped the cardigan I wore, rubbing the fabric between his fingers. "Cashmere but too thin. Two ply." He clicked his tongue. "Cheap, Moira. You're a vampire. I know you've got a hoard of cash stashed away for a rainy day."

"Oh my gods. I'm going to murder you." Also, how did this guy know the ply of cashmere fabric?

This time he let me push him out of the closet and back into the kitchen. The bastard hadn't spilled a drop of his tea. "Have you decided?"

"If I had, my answer would change after this stunt," I muttered.

His stunning eyes narrowed. "How often do you wear that nightie you threw on your chair?"

I choked on my tea, making him laugh. "Gods. You are such an asshole."

Ethan grinned. The sight made my stomach tumble. He really was a gorgeous bastard. "Come, Moira. Stay with me for a little while. Help me while I help you."

His eyes had warmed into the color of a starless winter night. He leaned forward, balancing the teacup on his knee. "You'll have all the warm sweaters you could ever want."

"I haven't decided yet."

He set his mug on the counter and reached for my hand. "Whatever you want, Moira. Write it up and send it. Just say yes."

His palm was warm and calloused. When he touched me, I wanted to agree to everything, and I suspected the bastard knew it. I tugged my hand back. "You might regret those words."

One side of his lips tugged into a half smile. "I won't regret anything if you say yes."

He picked his mug back up, went to the teapot and poured another cup. With a jaunty salute, he opened the door and left.

It took me another minute to realize he'd stolen my mug along with the rest of my damn tea.

Thirty-One

Ben waited for me at the edge of his property, opening the wards long enough to allow me entrance. Rowan had grumbled about me going by myself, but I'd felt Danu creeping around the edge of the wards, so I called in Dad.

Rowan had done his best to shore up the magic around Ben's Keep, but Ben's magic was different from other shifters, and Rowan's tweaks didn't take as well as they should have.

Ben and I had sort of dated once upon a time. I could have lost my heart to him, had he allowed it, but like Caelan, he couldn't accept me as I was until it was too late.

His eyebrows rose when he saw I was alone. "I'm surprised not to see Rowan at your heels."

The words were teasing, but there was a deeper meaning behind them. "Don't get any ideas. Rowan and I are just fine."

Ben's smile was a flash of teeth. "You look good, Evie."

"Thanks. No one has tried to kill me for a few days."

The Lord laughed. "Come. I'll take you to the fae. They've set up a barrier that's become quite annoying." He rolled his eyes. "Fortunately for us, their numbers are too low to block all our entrances and exits."

I stopped him with a hand on his arm. "If you don't mind, I'd like to refresh the spell first."

Ben inclined his head. "Everything alright?"

"Danu is testing borders again. I don't feel any danger here, but your call concerned me."

"We haven't had anyone powerful enough to break through the wards yet, but they're testing them. Every time they do, they weaken just a little. I don't want to keep summoning the mages. If anything happens, I want them at full power."

"Fair enough. I'll shore everything up first, then escort your unwelcome guests away."

"Will anywhere do?"

"Do you have any patches of flowers?" I always preferred working within blooming flora, but no one had ever asked me before.

The edges of his eyes crinkled in a stunning smile. Ben was a beautiful man. Tall, built like a lumberjack and powerful, not just as a shifter, but as a healer. I met him at Caelan's Keep when he worked for the Pack. He never wanted to be a Lord, but when Finn, the male who turned me into a Chimera, killed Halvar and took his place for months, there was a vacancy only Ben was powerful enough to fill. Plus, Caelan saw the relationship building between me and Ben and had ushered him out with little fanfare.

A shitty thing to do, but all the Lords played for Keeps, and Ben hadn't pursued me once he left. Not until later, but by then it was too late.

Ben's lips tugged up. "I do, actually. One of our more senti-mental shifters planted them after your assistance all those months ago."

I grinned from ear to ear. "Pax?"

He rolled his eyes. "Yes. He's still hoping the mating bond between you and Rowan is fake."

"I like him." Pax and I had worked together to save Ben a long time ago. He'd made his intentions toward me known, but I was involved with Caelan at the time. Shifters liked Floromancers. More than liked them.

We were good for their land, and strong land meant an even stronger Lord.

"Don't tell him that," Ben rumbled. "He might kidnap you and take you to his lair."

"I'm sure I can take care of myself."

Ben gave me an appraising glance. "Far more than before, I'd imagine." He jerked his head toward the main house. "Pax planted behind the house, and I don't know how the asshole managed it, but the patch blooms all damn year."

I glanced up at him in surprise. "Oh? Different flowers?"

He nodded.

"Ah. He's just good at gardening. No magic involved. Though I am surprised he comes out in the middle of winter to tend the garden."

"Pax is an odd duck," Ben said. "Hell of a warrior, but a little touched in the head."

"Ben! That's not very nice."

He shrugged. "I'm serious. There's something not quite right in his shifting, and he gets oddly fixated on things. Like you." Ben frowned. "And flowers."

We walked around the back of the house. I sucked in a shocked breath and took a numb step forward. "Holy gods."

One of my bucket list items was Butchart Gardens in British Columbia. I'd only seen pictures online, but the gardens blew my mind. From everything I read, a human was responsible for all its glory. I hadn't yet approached Rowan with my ideas, but one day I wanted something to parallel those gardens.

Pax had somewhat done this in the small space Ben had given him. An explosion of color greeted me. Pinks, blues, purples, whites, and brilliant yellows bloomed in an array of different flowers. I closed my eyes and let the scent of a thousand blossoms gently filter past me. A blooming Dogwood stood in the middle, heavy white and pink blossoms hanging on heavy boughs.

"He did all this?"

"Yes." Ben sounded disgruntled about it. "If I gave him more land, he'd turn the godsdamn thing into a fairy wonderland."

I clicked my tongue. "Pax has a gift, Ben. One you should not squander. If I could, I'd take him back to Washington with me."

The shifter in question stepped out from behind the Dogwood, a pair of clippers in his tanned, scarred hands. "If my Lord approved it, I would come with you."

I froze. Would he? How would Rowan feel about me bringing home yet another shifter with the promise of Lordhood in his veins?

I turned to Ben. "He heard everything you said," I murmured.

Ben sighed and squeezed the bridge of his nose. "Would you want to leave?"

Pax flicked his pale gaze to Ben. "To go with a beautiful, powerful woman who creates beauty with only a touch of her hands? I would be honored to serve such a creature."

The Lord snorted softly. "A godsdamn plant loving Shakespeare over here."

Pax grinned widely. "Do not shun what you do not understand, Lord Ben."

I held up a hand. "Remember, Pax, I am mated. If, and this is a big if, Rowan says I can bring you home, you'd have to..." My voice trailed off as a thought occurred to me. "How do you feel about the fae?"

Pax returned his attention to me, a soft golden glow warming his iris. Not as powerful as any of the Lord's yet, more a promise of his potential. "I am quite fond of you, and you are fae, are you not?"

"Gods," Ben groaned.

I held up a finger. "Hold that thought."

Keeping both of them in my peripheral, I pulled out my cell and fired off a text to Rowan.

Not only did he say yes, he thought it was a good idea. I tucked my phone into my pocket and walked back over.

"How would you feel about serving in a queen's court?"

Ben stiffened. "Evie. You cannot be serious."

"I assure you, I am completely serious. Will you let him go if he wishes?"

He sighed and nodded. "Godsdammit. Yes. I will. This is going to make my entire Pack jealous as hell. Why is it that with every visit, you throw everything into upheaval?"

I grinned. "Guess I just have a way about me."

"Yes," Pax said immediately. "As long as you are the queen I will serve."

"I do not require service. Not in the way you are thinking. I only hold my court members to one oath. Protect each other and protect the court. We are family, and we always stick together. Can you agree to such?"

Pax's eyes widened. "Truly?"

I nodded. "That's all, Pax. I promise. You will be bound to me, and as such, to Rowan by virtue of our relationship, and the rest of my court."

He dropped to one knee, the clippers discarded at his feet. "Yes. I swear it."

Ben shook his head. "Are you sure, Evie?"

I liked Pax. He gardened like a damn fairy. He was pretty to look at. And Ben didn't appreciate him. What the hell was there to think about?

"Come here, Pax."

The shifter rose and walked toward me. Even knowing he was a wolf, Pax reminded me of a panther. Once again, he went down on one knee.

"Give me your hand." I made a small cut in his palm and did the same to mine. Now that I was a Lord's Lady, I used blood in addition to the binding oath. Everyone, including Moira, had undergone a second binding once I mated with Rowan.

Magic sizzled in the air between us as I clasped our palms

together and said the words of binding. Pax's eyes swirled with gold and...

Hmmm.

"What's going on with his eyes?" Ben demanded.

Watermelon tourmaline swirled alongside the gold. Had something gone wrong? Power sizzled between us, sealing Pax into our court.

My phone started buzzing less than thirty seconds later.

"Rise," I said hoarsely.

Pax rose, swaying slightly, his eyes wide and glowing. He bowed his head. "I—is it supposed to feel that way?"

I smiled, a little unnerved. Our binding felt fine, but something had happened. "Like champagne fizzling in your veins?"

He nodded.

"It will fade."

Pax took his place beside me. "Thank you, Lord Ben."

Ben looked a little put out, but he was still gracious. "You're welcome."

"Mind if I use your plot of flowers?" I asked Pax.

"It is yours, my lady." He bowed deeply, making Ben let out an incredulous laugh.

"Thanks." I headed over to the stunning display, pleased to find small stepping stones allowing me to traverse the garden without stepping on any of the flowers.

With no further ado, I settled myself into the garden and got to work.

WHEN I RETURNED HOME with Pax in tow, everyone was sitting outside on our patio. Declan was the first to rise, followed by Hope, whose eyebrows went up. Pax was a gorgeous male, and she'd have to be blind not to notice. And none of the women on Rowan's lands were blind.

I made introductions and left Pax to get acquainted. Rowan followed me inside the house and watched me carefully.

"How'd he win you over?"

"He planted the most incredible garden I'd ever seen because he had a crush on me."

Rowan stared at me for a beat before he burst out laughing. "To think, if I would have known that I would have planted the finest garden in creation years ago."

He sighed and opened his arms. I stepped into the circle and laid my head against his chest.

"Danu is still here," I murmured.

"I know."

"I have one more thing to do tonight before I get some rest. Tomorrow, I plan to go out and settle this once and for all."

Rowan exhaled a deep sigh. "Figured as much."

"I don't think she will have many allies. And if she does, if things go well tonight, she won't have them for long."

"Dare I ask?"

I had hope and a plan. Nothing concrete. "Mum's the word, just in case it doesn't work."

He sighed against my hair. "Evie, international woman of mystery."

I pulled away and went straight to the fridge. A tray of sandwiches made by Rowan's cook was calling my name. Rowan grabbed the lemonade and we headed back outside to help Pax get acclimated to his new home.

A couple of hours later, I retreated back to the old cottage I stayed in when I first arrived. I kept a lot of plants in here and occasionally used it as a workspace, but tonight, I had something very specific I was working on.

Mom shimmered in half an hour into my experiment. I asked her to come to see if what I was thinking might be viable. I'd spent the last few hours hunched over the coffee table, carefully creating something I'd never done before.

When I made Seymour, I was pissed off. When I made Hannah, I was in a softer mood and wanted to give a plant lover a special gift. Both had turned out unique but not quite right.

Mom got onto her knees beside me. She tied her hair in a knot and fastened in on top of her head.

The sound of soft pecking alerted me to a new presence. I turned and smiled as I saw who awaited me at the window.

"Mind if I let him in?"

Mom glanced over her shoulder to see Poe. "Oh!" She smiled. "Not at all."

I got up to open the back door. Just as I was reaching for the handle, Mom spoke again. "You can invite the phoenix you stole from me in, too."

I winced. "How long have you known?"

Mom's soft snort of laughter made guilt churn in my stomach. "How long did you think it would take before someone noticed a multi-colored glowing bird flying through the air over a Shifter Lord's Keep?" She rolled her eyes. "Honestly, Evie. And not only that, the Lord you were dating at the time."

"In my defense, you were the wicked stepmother back then."

"I'm well aware," Mom said primly. "But I would like to meet Poe's companion if you'll allow it."

I opened the back door. "Fetch Fee," I said.

Poe paused, tilted his feathery head and eyed my mother. Mom stayed still and let him examine her.

He made a quorking sound. "Evie mom good?"

Mom gave Poe a sad smile. "I had to pretend for a long time, but you can see my heart, Poe."

Poe studied her for a long moment, dipped his head, and flew away. I waited by the back door for a few moments until Fee streaked through the sky. Mom sucked in a gasp and came to her feet.

"Oh, Evie. She's stunning."

And she was. Fee was fully grown now, her tail feathers several feet long and her wingspan even wider. Her feathers were a bright mix of vivid orange and royal purple, and her eyes had turned into a shimmering crystalline shade that constantly changed.

We didn't see much of the birds anymore, not with the expansion of our territory. They'd taken to exploring far and wide but were never far from each other's sides.

"Hi Fee," I said, holding out my hand. She shifted in a flash of light to a smaller size and landed on my hand. I brought her inside, Poe following close behind, and shut the door.

Mom stared at the bird with wide eyes. Fee didn't go to her, merely watched her with those strange eyes.

I stroked a finger down her back. "This is Cliona, Fee. My mother."

Fee tilted her head back and forth.

Mom bowed her head and laid her hand over her heart. "You are magnificent."

Fee gave a little trill.

"Hold your hand out," I said.

Mom raised her head and blinked, suddenly unsure.

"It's okay. She won't go if she doesn't want to."

Mom slowly held out her hand. Fee trilled once more and hopped onto Mom's arm.

"Oh my goodness." Mom let out a delighted laugh. "You know, I've had birds my entire life, but none that looked like Fee. And never a phoenix. Do you realize how lucky you are to have such a close relationship with her?"

I guess I never really thought about it. She needed help, so I helped her. "She's fast friends with Poe. And I can't take all the credit. Caelan had her for quite a while."

"The Lord was good to her?"

"Poe and Fee explored every inch of his territory. He never caged them."

Mom tentatively stroked the back of her head. "Do you know the legend of the phoenix?"

I researched enough to know what they needed to survive and some of their powers but never did a deep dive. "Not really. I know they are powerful healers, and they're rumored to be able to resurrect the dead."

Mom's lips quirked into a smile. "That and more. This little girl can grant immortality if she so chooses. But you can't force her. She has to choose you."

"Fee!" I gawked at the bird. "Raising the dead and throwing out immortality to the worthy? You're going to be a busy girl when you're all grown up."

Mom chuckled. "She is all grown up. But Fee hasn't chosen anyone yet. Not that she could in a place like this. Everyone here is immortal, are they not?"

"I think so."

"Hmm. Well, phoenixes go where they are needed. Maybe she's not ready to answer a call yet."

Someone knocked on the front door. For crying out loud. I left Mom with Fee and answered the door. Tess, Ash, and Moira stood there holding wine and something that smelled amazing in a takeout bag.

"You up for a visit?" Ash said. "We haven't seen you in a while."

I was always up for a visit with the dryad and his companion banshee. "Come on in. As long as you share whatever's in that bag."

Ash grinned. He brushed a kiss over my cheek and walked in. Tess, looking pale and lovely in a lavender sweater and jeans, gave me a quick hug. She paused when she saw my mother, swallowed hard, and came inside.

"Hello, Tess," Mom said.

Tess dipped her head. "Hello, Cliona."

They'd never have the kind of relationship Moira and Mom did. Not with Mom being her queen and the experiences Tess had growing up. When Mom pretended, she did it hard core. She had a lot to make up with everyone, not just me.

Ash stopped abruptly when he spotted what I was working on. He handed the bag to Tess and crouched down to peer at the small seedling. When his eyes met mine, he let out a surprised chuckle. "You figured it out. Hot damn, Evie. I knew you would."

I blinked. "This will work?"

Mom lowered herself to the floor gently, Fee still perched on her hand. "The dryad is correct. I'm glad he came. He is more adept with natural magic than I am. I can help you with the fae side, and Ash can help guide you as I assume he's a little better with trees than you are."

I shrugged. "Most of the time, I use vines and flora. Trees are an afterthought. Though I did just create those bristlecones."

Ash blinked. "A bristlecone pine? When you went to Caelan's. You're keeping it alive in *Texas*?"

I nodded and briefly explained what I'd done. When I finished, Ash sat back and gawked. "You created a network of ancient pine trees to hold enslavement bonds and threaded them to each other so they could travel wherever they pleased, both freeing them and ensuring they didn't die."

I squinted at him. "Um. Yes? I think?"

Ash let out a bark of laughter. "We have dedicated scientists who spend their entire lives trying to understand physics and quantum mechanics, and mages who do the same with magical theory, and here you are busting out complicated magic using logic and trees."

Tess let out a warbly giggle. "As much of a disservice as it was not to train Evie in all her magic when she was younger, it did force her to use her magic intuitively. She bypassed all the rules no one ever told her about and created her own. That's the way magic should be, isn't it? Intuition driven by will and formed with one's innate power?"

Man. Sometimes Tess dropped serious knowledge. We all stared at her for a long moment, before Ash smiled. "Yeah. Tess. That's exactly right. I couldn't have said it better."

"I never thought of it like that, but I guess you're right." A thought occurred to me. "Is this why I'm having so much trouble with Dad's magic lessons?"

Mom's brow furrowed. "I—I want to say no, but this would make so much sense." She let out a disturbed chuckle. "I feel befuddled. I never feel befuddled. Have we done a disservice to all our children by being so formal with their education?"

"I don't mind being a science experiment as long as it helps other people," I said dryly. I had some training, but I never knew who I truly was, so the education I received was lopsided at best. Add in the Chimera attack and well, here we were.

I stared down at the seedling. "Mom. Can you take us somewhere this evening?"

"After dessert," Ash said. "We'll go with you."

"Did you bring enough for Moira?"

He rolled his eyes. "Of course I did."

"I'm texting her right now," Tess said.

Forty-five minutes later, we were full of pie and hope. We stood on the edge of Donovan's old territory and Rowan's. I held the small seedling in the palm of my hands. We'd worked on it a little more at the cottage, but to test it, we needed to plant it first, then encourage it to grow.

Dad and Moira had popped in, and Rowan and Ethan tagged along when they saw us all piling out of the cottage. Ethan had sworn up a blue streak when he spotted Fee.

He slapped his hand over his chest like a senior citizen having a heart attack and screeched, "Is that a godsdamn *phoenix*?"

Rowan nodded, a sober expression on his face, though his eyes twinkled with mirth. "Yes, yes it is."

"Fucking hell," Ethan said under his breath. "And you signed up for this?"

I didn't hear what Rowan said, but Ethan shot him a dark look.

My friends stood in a semi-circle watching quietly as I crouched to plant the seedling. "No idea if this is going to work," I whispered.

Ash put his hand on my back and bent beside me. "Have faith.

You've done amazing things, Evie. Consider this one more thing to add to the list."

I smiled up at him. "I'm glad you're here."

Ash's eyes grew suspiciously moist. "I'm glad for many things, and you are at the top of the list."

I reached back with a dirty hand and squeezed his fingers. Ash went to his knees and started digging out a small hole.

I gently placed the seedling inside.

"Start with the roots," Ash encouraged. "They're the most important part."

I held out my hand. "Want to do it together?"

Ash smiled. "Truly?"

I nodded. "Ready?"

"Ready."

We closed our eyes, and together we worked as one, deep into the night. When the work was finally done, we marveled at our handiwork.

A tree double the size of a redwood loomed above us, sparkling with emerald and watermelon tourmaline colored magic. Ash and I hadn't created a specific kind of tree. We formed it to suit our wishes and our purpose, Ash's magic adding a touch of dryad power to keep the hybrid healthy and hale. As an added touch, Ash could now transport to the tree any time he wished because a piece of his magic lived inside.

Branches swept down from the trunk, some lying heavy on the ground. The leaves were soft and a bit fuzzy, pink and white blooms on the tips of the branches.

"Whoa," Ethan breathed.

Tonight had been a lot of firsts for the poor Shifter Lord, and one of the few times he'd seen my magic doing something other than slamming him around or antagonizing them.

"This is amazing," Moira breathed. She ran her fingers over the trunk, magic swirling over her fingertips.

"What's it for?" Ethan said.

"I'm not sure it works yet," I said, squinting up at the sky. "But if it does, you'll know."

"When will you know?" he asked.

"Tomorrow morning." I could feel Danu's lurking presence. She was waiting to catch me off guard, but it wouldn't quite work out that way.

Tomorrow, I'd deliver myself to her like a Christmas gift.

Thirty~Two

I awoke to a ruckus. Grunting, I groped for the pillow and shoved it over my head, hoping to drown out the noise.

I scooted closer to Rowan, only to find his side of the bed cold. Normally, I'd feel him getting out of bed, but I'd used a ton of power yesterday and must have slept like the dead.

The bedroom door opened. "Go away," I muttered.

Rowan's soft chuckle sounded by the door. "You have guests. Want to greet them?"

"Not even a little bit." I needed to eat, shower, and go kick some Danu ass. Definitely in that order.

"Well, they aren't going anywhere, so why don't you shower first, and I'll throw on a pancake for you."

I yawned. "I want a lot."

"A lot you shall have." His scent swept over me as he bent to yank the covers up.

I shrieked and tried to tackle him, but Rowan, damn him, danced out of the way. "Come on, sleepy head. Get up."

I curled into the fetal position and gave him the finger. Undeterred, Rowan grinned and headed toward the door. "Fifteen minutes and I'm shutting off the hot water."

"I will stab you in your sleep if you do."

Rowan grinned. "You say such lovely things to me, wife."

I tossed a pillow at the door, but he was gone.

SOMETIME LATER, I had a text from Rowan telling me to meet him on the patio. I was dressed in yoga pants, tennis shoes, and a loose sweater, all clothes designed to fight and run in, and nothing I would be too upset about losing. Danu would fight dirty, no doubt about it. With Titania wiped out, she'd be at a slight disadvantage, but I had no doubt she had an ace up her sleeve.

But so did we. Mom had given me some intel last night that I planned to use if forced to. I wasn't keen on doing so, but I also wanted this to finally be over. I'd made mistakes, but none of them were on purpose. We couldn't hold an entire people responsible for the actions of one.

I didn't start this conflict, but I planned to finish it. Dad was currently fishing out some potential leadership for new territories, and Mom and Tess were scoping out properties by using their network of ghosts and other banshees. Who knew the dead would be so knowledgeable about real estate?

Guess it made sense if you couldn't move very far from where you were buried, and land constantly changed hands. They'd know all the details. After all, what else was there to pay attention to?

By tomorrow, if we were all still alive, we planned to present the idea at court.

Officially, with Rowan beside me as king.

So weird to think about where I'd started versus where I was now. Married. Mated on both sides of my nature. I had my parents and people who loved me backing me up. A decade ago, I would have laughed had someone told me I'd be standing here today.

I poured myself a giant mug of coffee and followed the smell of pancakes.

An overwhelming array of scents hit me the second I stepped

onto the patio. I looked up and stopped in my tracks. Hundreds, no *thousands*, of shifters stood on our lands.

Even more surprising was the Lords sitting around the patio table.

Caelan was there. He lifted his coffee mug to me in greeting. Soren sat beside him, a twinkle of amusement in his eyes. Ben was next to Soren staring at Pax wearing a slightly befuddled expression. Even Thorvin had shown up, though he was wearing a Mr. Rogers cardigan and holding a book.

Appearances with the Lords could be deceiving. There were four of us here who knew Thorvin was a crack shot with a rifle.

Ethan sat beside Thorvin, watching me with an amused expression. Rowan sat beside him, holding up an enormous plate of pancakes. I moved toward him like a robot and took the plate.

"What's going on?" I asked, knowing everyone could hear me even if I whispered.

"They're here to help with Danu," Rowan said cheerily. "I believe this is the first time all the Lords have agreed on something since the creation of the Council."

Ethan rolled his eyes. "Careful, bear."

"How did you all get here?"

A golden hand rose in the air from the lawn. Mom and Dad appeared through the crowd. Neit walked beside my Mom, and I realized what a striking couple they made. My dad, wearing a pissed off expression, seemed to think the same as he kept glancing their way. "That would be us," Dad grumbled.

I sank onto the seat Rowan pulled over but didn't start eating. Overwhelmed, I let my gaze wander through the crowd and realized there were so many shifters I couldn't see the back.

"Thank you," I whispered.

Mom dropped a kiss on top of my head and reached for the coffee. Dad leaned against one of the supports and watched everyone like a hawk. All these shifters around his daughter must be making him twitchy.

Ethan let out a heavy exhale. "Please accept our apologies.

We've been just as guilty as the fae at judging someone based on the markers of their blood rather than the content of their character. You've done many positive things for us over the past year, but what you did for Caelan cemented our decision."

Rowan cleared his throat. "Caelan is actually the one responsible for this."

Tears clogged the back of my throat. "Truly?"

Caelan's smile was edged with sadness. "Figured it was the least I could do."

"You bet it is," Rowan said under his breath.

Caelan laughed this time. "I'm well aware of the current state of my amends and know I'll be making them forever." He rolled his eyes. "At least to you."

"Children," Ethan said. "Can we focus?"

Rowan picked up my fork and handed it to me. "Eat. You'll need the energy."

The first bite was full of maple syrup and real butter. He knew exactly how I liked my pancakes. I ate like a maniac while the other Lords spoke amongst themselves; Rowan occasionally adding more bacon to my plate.

When I finished and set my plate down, Ethan caught my attention. "What exactly is your plan this morning?"

I shrugged and sipped my coffee. "She's been waiting at the edges of our property for days now hoping for a confrontation. I plan to step outside the wards and give her what she wants."

No one said a word.

"Right. As soon as I finish this coffee."

HALF AN HOUR LATER, we stood toward the edge of the property boundary. Danu lurked close, her oily presence a heavy cloak against our wards.

"Ready?" I murmured to Rowan.

"You sure you want to do this?"

"If I don't do it now, then when? I'm sure the Lords want their lands completely in their control again, and Danu is a blight upon our people. I don't want to wait anymore."

Rowan tugged me close and planted a searing kiss upon my lips. Wolf whistles and catcalls rang out.

I laughed and clutched my husband to me. One last kiss to remember him, no matter what may come.

When we pulled apart, I glanced at Dad. "Drop the wards."

As soon as the shimmering veil dropped, I stepped over the boundary.

Seconds later, Danu rose from the ground.

She wore her crone guise today, tangled grey hair lying in a shapeless lump down her back. Her nose was humped and crooked, and her face lined with heavy wrinkles. She wore a gown of forest green dotted with glowing mushrooms and flora. Danu looked ancient, ageless, and powerful.

I was in yoga pants with clean tennis shoes and wet hair tied into a messy bun on top of my head. We were not the same.

"You've been hanging around for a while. Seems like you want to have a conversation." I spread my hands out. "I'm here. Let's chat."

Danu looked out at the shifters spread out behind me, a flicker of surprise in the depths of her eyes. "You've brought an army for a simple conversation?"

I shrugged. "Seemed appropriate."

Danu waved her fingers. Thousands of fae appeared behind her, some on the ground, some floating in the air.

Not unexpected, but I was hoping word had spread about my ability to send them home. The fae and Lords had done nothing but make my job harder from the day I got involved with them. Stifling a sigh, I addressed the unfamiliar fae standing before me.

"We can send you home if you'd like. If you stand against us, we will remember. I am not my father. If you fight, you are no longer my people. You are my enemy. As such, once this is over, I will track you down and banish you from our lands."

A few exchanged looks. Some blipped out right away. Too many held firm. The shifters would have difficulty with this many fae. We had mages on our side, but human and witch magic followed rules. Fae magic, as we'd found out, doesn't have to.

"Right. What do you want, Danu?"

A smile showcased crooked brown teeth. "You know what I want."

"And we've established that's not happening. There is such a thing called compromise if you want to try it."

"You are no queen, Evie. No matter how much you pretend."

"And you could go quietly into that good earth and stay there and yet, here we are."

"Is this your final answer?" Danu's eyes glittered with the thrill of taking me down.

"Didn't realize we were on Jeopardy, but yes. That's my final answer. You and everyone still standing here can fuck right off."

Rowan huffed a laugh.

"Then let us dance, Pretender Queen."

The earth bucked underneath our feet, tossing us into the air like chess pieces during an earthquake. Beside me, Neit curse and rose through the air, his ability to fly a distinct advantage on this playing field.

There was so much magic mingling in the air I had no idea who held what kind of power level. Shifters and mages behind me swelled with power seconds before leaping over me and straight into the fray. Magical attacks came from every direction. Mom and Dad were somewhere around. I knew so because a gentle gust of wind caught me and set me back onto my feet when the ground started moving.

Danu, that sneaky bitch, had sunk back into the ground. I'd managed to repel her from beneath the earth before, but I felt like I did my best work aboveground. Getting her to resurface might be tricky, since she was right at home in the dark, creepy crawly nethers of the world.

I spotted Rowan's chestnut colored hair, along with Ethan's silver streaked temples. Caelan's familiar roar sounded somewhere to my right. A hand at my elbow made me spin. Pax stood at my side. "I will protect you."

His words made me chuckle. "Thanks, but I don't think you fully understand what I am. Look for our court. Moira is out there somewhere. Help her or any of the others. I'm fine on my own."

Pax didn't love that answer, but he nodded instead and leapt away. With one final look at the raging battle, I allowed myself to sink deep into the heart of the earth as I sought to drain the being poisoning it.

With everything happening above, I couldn't afford to send only my consciousness below. My body was too vulnerable to be left unattended. The feeling was strange. Thousands of pounds of dirt and rock pushed against me on all sides, and I had to remember to keep a small pocket of fresh air surrounding me. If I lost it, I wouldn't die, but it might be a distraction I couldn't afford.

I followed Danu's presence through the earth. She laughed as I chased her, and after a while, I realized the old bitch was trying to lure me away from the others. Unwilling to allow her to do so, I rose, my focus on the people who chose to stand with Danu.

At my command, vines tore through the surface spearing any fae unlucky enough to be in their path. Careful to avoid any of the shifters, I coaxed and wove poison tipped barbs through those fae —a touch of poison here, a cut there, a drop there—and ever so slowly, the fae began to succumb, allowing our side to go in and finish them off.

I noted every fae who saw the tide turning and disappeared, and from my father's glowing eyed scrutiny, so did he.

The other Lords were a whirlwind on the battlefield, teeth and claws and fury. I did my best to help them when I saw fae coming for their vulnerable spots, and even when her people were dying, Danu still did not come.

I had two last resort weapons in my arsenal—one far crueler than the other. The bond between me and Rowan stayed strong and steady. He was here somewhere in the fray, fighting for me and our people. But we weren't completely victorious. Fallen shifters lay on the ground, some too late to save.

Tears of fury burned at the backs of my eyes, and once I saw the fae's numbers dwindling enough to where they became easy pickings for the shifters, I closed my eyes and focused on Danu, finding her watching like a spider. I sent magic underneath her, ensuring she was distracted, and punched power underneath her, so ferocious it sent her physical form erupting from the ground like a geyser.

I yanked her from the air with a poison-tipped vine, delighting in the choked *uuurk* sound she made as I pulled her to me. When she was inches away, wrapped in vines and unable to move her limbs, I smiled.

"And so the spider becomes the prey."

Blood slipped from Danu's lips, her teeth pulling back from her lips in a grimace. She tried to speak but couldn't. I loosened the vines just a hair, hoping she'd cry uncle. But the bitch spat, "Everyone you love will die."

I was officially over it. I was over the fae, over the people who continually pressed me because they weren't worried about the consequences, and over looking over my shoulder every time I stepped foot off my land. As much as I hated to do it, there was only one way to get Danu to stop.

Flinging away my doubts, I reached for the heart of her power, her connection to each of the realms, enabling her to freely traverse through them.

Her eyes widened as she realized what I was about to do. Power ripped from her. She flung herself away from my barbed vines, blood spraying as she ripped herself free. Danu fell to the ground, slamming her hands against the earth.

Terrible twisted thorned limbs burst from the ground, viscous poison worse than anything I'd ever created dripping from their barbed edges and headed straight for each of the Lords.

No.

Everything you love will die.

A roar erupted from my throat as I went for Danu, my hands extended to reach for her throat as I ripped her power from the world. Just as the magic dimmed from her eyes, a searing, rending pain tore my chest wide open, my bond with Rowan fading away as if it had never been.

CHAPTER

Thirty~Four

MOIRA

Caelan fell first. Then Thorvin, Soren, Ben, and Ethan. They stood no chance against the unholy power tearing straight for them. Rowan, still fighting in the fray, only had a moment of confusion, followed by horrifying realization, when that same power came for him, tearing into his chest.

He was the last to fall, the spark that made him who he was fading as his life's blood spilled onto the ground. I felt the moment their bond sundered, a ripping sensation tearing through my chest that left me breathless.

A keening, heartbreaking wail shattered the air, and as one, everyone stopped fighting, the loss too monumental, too horrific for anyone with even a small piece of heart left to comprehend.

I staggered to a stop, my hand over my heart as grief exploded within me. Six Lords, six rulers, one of those a mate to my best friend, had fallen, their lives snuffed out in an instant.

They were never a match for a goddess, not being taken completely by surprise as they were. Danu and Evie had been focused on each other. They had no reason to worry.

And so they'd pressed on.

Evie screamed and screamed and screamed. She scrambled to

her feet and ran, tripping over broken bodies, fae and shifter alike, as she found Rowan on the battlefield. Dropping to her knees, she gripped him by the lapels and shook him.

"Rowan!"

His head lolled, the shell of his body empty.

"ROWAN!"

Nothing.

"No. No no no no no no." Evie gagged and pressed Rowan to her chest, glowing with the earth's power, but raising the dead was beyond her. It was beyond me and everyone else here. Death was a force few understood and even fewer tried to reckon with.

Tears spilled down my eyes as I sought Ethan out. He lay on his back, eyes wide and sightless, his chest a smoking, poisoned ruin. I crouched beside him and closed his eyes with my fingers, mourning the potential of what could have been, and rose to go to Evie.

She gently set her mate down and rose, a terrible expression on her face. My best friend turned to those fae, eyes glowing with the power of a furious goddess, and spoke.

"DIE." She lifted her palm to the air and squeezed. Nothing happened for a moment until the first fae sucked in a shocked gasp, her face going dry and cavernous.

"TO DUST YOU WILL RETURN," Evie boomed, her voice carrying like a bomb through the land.

Every single fae left on the battlefield collapsed into a pile of dust the earth opened to contain and recycle, their immortality gone in an instant, just as Danu had done to Evie's mate.

A terrible vengeance and one Evie might mourn later. But right now, my friend was a terrible power to behold. Gone was the woman I shared pasta and wine with on the weekends. Gone was my best friend who lent her shoulder to cry on when I needed it.

Before me stood the fae queen hellbent on vengeance. She raised both hands into the air, palms up, and spoke once more.

"RETURN."

Cernunnos, Cliona, and Neit sucked in shocked gasps as they blipped from existence.

I had a terrible feeling I knew what she'd done, that hybrid tree a conduit for her bridge power and one she'd planned to use for good until she had no choice.

There would be consequences for this day. For Evie and everyone else.

When the battlefield was quiet, the only sound the soft *shhhh* of ash as it continued raining down, Evie sank to her knees and sobbed, cradling Rowan's lifeless body in her arms.

I didn't try to touch her or console her. Nothing I could say or do would make this any better. There was no comfort here today, nor would there be in the coming weeks.

All I could do was be with her.

Pax came and sat down beside me, his eyes glowing with power. His face was stark and his eyes filled with grief. He'd felt that bond rip the same way I had through our bond with her.

Garrett and Simone were next. They simply sat down too, enclosing Evie in a half circle. Her face was turned away, her bun long gone and her hair obscuring her face as she rocked Rowan, murmuring something none of us could make out.

Evie lifted her hand once more and flicked her wrist. Every shifter who did not belong to us was gone in an instant. Dead or returned, there was no way to know, not with Evie's current state of mind.

One by one, the shifters still standing from Rowan's lands came and sat beside us, forming a circle of grief as their lady mourned the only one she'd ever love again.

I don't know how long we sat there. The sun had long dipped behind the clouds, and still Evie rocked Rowan, holding him tight in her grip. She'd enclosed our circle in a cage of thorns, all but daring anyone to interfere.

A soft trickle of orange came up over the mountains, followed by a vivid shade of purple as Fee sailed overhead. The enormous phoenix encircled us, her crystalline gaze taking in everything.

Poe came next, his loud cry a screech shattering the quiet. He landed on Evie's shoulder, one wing out over her neck, as if he was trying to hug her in the only way he knew how.

Fee kept circling, unable to find a spot to land inside our circle. The bird had always been wary of people, Poe and Evie's influence no doubt. Instead, she soared over to where Caelan had fallen. She nudged him with her bright beak, but Caelan would never rise again.

A soft trilling noise came from her throat.

And as she began to glow, a terrible hope rose within me. I said nothing, did nothing, not until I was sure. In her grief, Evie was too distracted to notice Fee's presence.

Fee's glow began to take on an almost painful brightness. I nudged Pax and gestured for him to quietly rise. As the other shifters realized what was happening, everyone rose and moved away from Evie.

Caelan began to glow with a soft violet light. Fee moved to Ben, then Soren, Thorvin, then Ethan, encasing every Lord in her light. And when she came to Evie, her flight slightly off due to exhaustion, Fee nudged the Lady's hands and encompassed them both in her magic.

I stood there staring in awe, tears falling down my cheeks at the miracle occurring. Fee leapt from the ground and let out a shattering, musical cry, her wings spread out several feet wide as she soared.

As she sang, magic hummed around us, until even Evie had to take notice. She lifted her tear-stained face up to the phoenix in the sky and watched, her lips parted with awe.

And as Fee revived every single Lord on that field, she gave her life force, every single drop of herself to save the Lady who had once saved her. Her magic began to dim, and as I watched, Fee turned, our eyes locking.

An ancient knowledge burned in the phoenix's eyes as she sailed right toward me.

I took a step back but could not avoid the collision. Right

before she hit me, Fee turned into a swirling ball of powerful magic and sailed right into my heart, her physical form gone as she died.

Staggering power sent me crashing to my knees, the spot Fee hit burning like fire. I cried out as everything within me reformed, magic sparkling like champagne through my blood, short circuiting all my senses.

And just as I crashed to the ground, I heard a soft murmur come from one of the Lords.

"Evie?"

The bond slowly re-knitted, restoring Rowan as the fae king.

Epilogue

SIX MONTHS LATER

I ruled the fae with an iron fist at first, hunting everyone down who stood with Danu and banishing them to inhospitable realms as punishment. Some I outright killed.

Keeping my promise to disperse more land became a little complicated, as things did when the human government got involved. But we were working through it, and we'd managed to grant two territories to two new fae leaders who proved themselves worthy. Though I'd be watching them closely for a long time.

I'd dropped all my claims on everyone's territories, Danu's poison purged with her death. I'd kill the bitch a hundred times over if I could but turning her to ash and scattering those remains through different realms had reassured me she was really dead.

The Lords were...different.

Not personality wise, though they'd all come back shaken up. Every single Lord had new magic, and no one was fessing up. I smelled it on them every time I saw them, which was more often than usual after Fee had saved everyone's bacon.

I missed the bird with a vengeance. Poe had left my side and hadn't returned. I assumed he'd gone somewhere private to grieve.

And Moira…my best friend was forever changed. Only me, Moira, and my father knew her secret. I had him wipe everyone's memory of what Fee had done, once I allowed him back into this realm. Dad hadn't even been angry about it. I suspected he and Mom could have come back at any time, but they'd chosen to respect my wishes not to see a single fae until I was ready.

Moira had gone back with Ethan, and I hadn't heard much from her since. A phone call here and there, but like me, Moira had her own shit to deal with.

I sat cradled against Rowan's chest, his steady breath a balm to my wounded soul. All these months later, I still woke screaming in the middle of the night, reliving the tearing of that bond over and over again.

"I'm here," he would whisper when he felt my distress. "I promise."

Rowan never spoke much about that day, but I caught his haunted look when he thought I wasn't paying attention.

Things were slowly getting better. The Lords were closer than ever, though everyone was getting used to a new normal with the gifts Fee left behind. Even Rowan hadn't told me what she'd done, shaking his head every time I asked.

I'd find out one day. We all would. She'd even left something behind for me—something I couldn't quite figure out.

I entwined our fingers and lifted his hand to kiss the back of his palm.

"I love you," I whispered.

Rowan smiled against my hair. "Love you, too."

He paused. "Evie?"

"Hmm?"

"When are you going to build that garden Pax has been drawing when he thinks I'm not looking?"

I grinned, knowing he couldn't see my face. The bond sparked between us. "I have no idea what you're talking about."

His chest rumbled with a chuckle. "Mmm hmm. Build it, Evie.

Make this place into your dream, and I will walk beside you every single day for the rest of our lives."

I exhaled and turned my face up, smiling when he kissed me.

The only dream I had was Rowan, and every single day I had with him was a blessing. No matter what may come, as long as we had each other, I knew we would be alright.

———

Keep reading for a look at Book Ten
Shift Happens

BOOK 10, SHIFTER LORDS

Moira is a new power player in a world of hungry paranormals, but she'd rather be curled up with a blanket, ignoring the world.

Unfortunately, the Shifter Lords have other plans for her. Moira still works at her best friend's flower shop but also serves part-time as a magical consultant for both the fae and the Lords. Her cases run the gamut from investigating petty crimes all the way to working in close proximity to the Lords as they track down rogue shifters.

But when she's asked to take a case working with Soren, an infuriating Lord she has history with, Moira refuses, only to find out the case they're investigating involves someone from her past. Reluctantly, she accepts the gig, only to start sabotaging Soren around every corner.

She holds no loyalty to anyone these days, and certainly not to someone who'd stab her in the back with the least provocation. But when the case proves more difficult than she anticipated, and she and Soren get in way over their heads, they must find a way to work together or die.

When it turns out Soren is hiding a very unique talent—one that ensures they could survive what's coming after them—Moira must learn to trust her enemy and hope he's not still mad about that teeny tiny time she stabbed him in the back...

Trailer Park Transylvania

Psychic Cleaner

The Magical Soapmaker Mysteries

The Goddess Chronicles

Vikings of Virginia

The Deadicated Matchmaker

Sheryl likes cake too much and can be found hoarding it while hiding from her children in the pantry closet.

Follow her on Amazon at: https://www.amazon.com/S-E-Babin/e/B00J1J236A

A small press bound by the belief that every voice matters.

Sign up for our newsletter to learn about new releases and more.

Buy directly from us to save on ebooks, book bundles, and special editions.

Follow us on social media:

facebook.com/oliverheberbooks
instagram.com/oliverheberbooks
tiktok.com/@oliverheberbooks
bsky.app/profile/oliverheberbooks.bsky.social
youtube.com/@OliverHeberBooksPublisher
oliverheberbooks.substack.com
amazon.com/oliverheberbooks